It was a very small scrap of paper, and th.
been written in haste. Creasy looked up into the old man's worn
face. He said gently, 'Mr Bentsen, this is probably a dirty kind
of joke. It's happened before. Jake was killed on the Vietnam-
Cambodian border twenty-six years ago . . . '

The old man said: 'He used to write about you. Jake never really had
heroes. In a way he was his own hero. He lived in his own image. But
he looked up to you like no other man. He was twenty-one years
old on that day, Mr Creasy, when he was cut down. They never
found the body. Nobody went back to look for him, Mr Creasy.'

Slowly, Creasy lifted his scarred face. He reached out and touched
the dogtag and then picked it up. His fist closed around it. He
said: 'And you think that now somebody should.'

A. J. Quinnell is the pseudonym of the author of ten novels including *Man on Fire* which was made twice into Hollywood Films - most recently directed by Tony Scott for Twentieth Century Fox in 2004, starring Denzel Washington, Christopher Walken and Dakota Fanning. The book sold more than eight million copies in paperback and was translated around the world.

Full list of titles:
Man on Fire
The Mahdi
Snap Shot
Blood Ties
Siege of Silence
In the Name of the Father
The Perfect Kill
The Blue Ring
Message from Hell
Black Horn

MESSAGE FROM HELL

MESSAGE FROM HELL

A. J. QUINNELL

For

Mormor

In

Memoriam

AUTHOR'S NOTE

My thanks to Sgt. Mik Allen for leading me
through dangerous places.

CONTENTS

PROLOGUE

The man was old, and the fingers of his right hand were thin and bony. More of a talon than a hand. The metal glinted as it nestled in his palm.

'It's a dogtag.'

'I know what it is.'

'It's a US Army dogtag.'

'I know that. Let me see it.'

The talon closed around the metal as though protecting a precious jewel.

'It's my son's dogtag.'

'Your son is dead. I saw him gunned down.'

'Did you see him die?'

'No, it was a firefight. We'd been ambushed and were getting the hell out; but I saw Jake get hit. He was cut down by machine-gun fire. He was about a hundred metres away and there was no chance to get back to him. I got hit myself and was lucky to get out.'

'I know. But did you see him actually die?'

Creasy shook his head.

'No, Mr Bentsen. If anyone did, it was the guys who shot him.'

They were sitting at a corner table in a bar in Brussels. Creasy had dropped in to have a drink with the bartender, who was an old friend. Before he had a chance to take the first sip, the old man had appeared at his shoulder and asked to speak to him. It was a bar much frequented by mercenaries, ex-mercenaries, pretend mercenaries and would-be mercenaries.

The old man had a stiff urgency. He had said: 'Can I talk to you Mr Creasy; privately?'

Creasy had studied his face. He had a memory for faces, but this one stirred no memory. There was something in the old man's eyes which made Creasy cross the room and sit down at the table. The old man sat opposite, and said: 'I'm Jake Bentsen's father.'

With that he had reached into his pocket and pulled out the dogtag.

'How did you find me?' Creasy asked.

The old man sighed. 'It was not easy. But my neighbour has a cousin who's an analyst with the CIA at Langley. He did some research and told me that if you were still operative you could be located via this bar. I've been here a week, Mr Creasy, and I've been in this bar every day. Of course I asked the bartender, but he told me nothing. I was going home to San Diego on Monday.'

'Well, I'm not operative,' Creasy said. 'I happen to be in town visiting an old friend. I'm leaving tomorrow. How did you recognise me?'

'From the description in one of Jake's letters. He described every scar on your face.'

Creasy looked at the old man thoughtfully, and then said: 'Show me the dogtag, Mr Bentsen.'

Slowly the fingers uncurled and turned, and the small metal disc dropped onto the table. Creasy reached forward, pulled it towards him and looked at the name and the number embossed on it. He looked at it for a long time, then took another sip of his drink and asked: 'Where did you get it, Mr Bentsen?'

'It was delivered to me two weeks ago at my home in San Diego.'

'Who by?'

'I don't know, Mr Creasy. At least I don't know his name or where he came from. My doorbell rang. My wife answered it. There was a short man, an Oriental. He handed her a small package and went away.'

'And this was in the package?'

'Yes.'

'Was there anything else?'

Again the bony fingers reached into the jacket pocket, and came out with a crumpled piece of brown wrapping paper. He pushed it across the table. Creasy smoothed it out and read the scrawled words. There were just three of them, spelled out vertically.

CREASY

'NAM

'BODIA

It was a very small scrap of paper, and the words had obviously been written in haste. Creasy looked up into the old man's worn face. He said gently, 'Mr Bentsen, this is probably a dirty kind of joke. It's happened before. Jake was killed on the Vietnam-Cambodian border twenty-six years ago.'

The old man's eyes were fixed on the dogtag and the scrap of paper. Without looking up he said, 'I took it to the MIA in Washington. They told me that as far as they could tell it's authentic. Jake's body was never found; or the dogtag. It's not possible to tell if the writing on the paper is Jake's. I took it to a handwriting specialist who compared it with some of Jake's letters home. He said he thought it might be.'

Now he looked up, but could not see into Creasy's eyes. Creasy had leaned forward and was looking down intently at the metal disc and the scrap of paper.

The old man said: 'He used to write about you. Jake never really had heroes. In a way he was his own hero. He lived in his own image. But he looked up to you like no other man. He was twenty-one years old on that day, Mr Creasy, when he was cut down. They never found the body. Nobody went back to look for him, Mr Creasy.'

Slowly, Creasy lifted his scarred face. He reached out and touched the dogtag and then picked it up. His fist closed around it. He said: 'And you think that now somebody should?'

CHAPTER ONE

'You feel guilty!'

Creasy sighed, and answered: 'It's not guilt.

'Then what is it?'

Creasy looked at his friend across the table. He had known Maxie for more years than he liked to remember. As mercenaries, they had fought together at different times over a score of years until Maxie had married and bought his bistro in Brussels and settled down in a sporadic sort of way.

They were sitting in that bistro now, together with a Dane called Jens Jensen and a small, round-faced, bespectacled Frenchman known always by his nickname 'The Owl'.

Jensen was the ex-head of the Copenhagen Police's missing persons department. The Owl was an ex-gangster and bodyguard from the Marseille underworld. Some years ago, in a surrealistic series of events, Creasy had matched them together and they now formed an unlikely partnership as a private detective agency which specialized in looking for anything that was missing, be it a husband or wife, a lost dog or a diamond. The Dane was in his late thirties, slightly overweight with thinning blond hair and with a school-teacher wife and a young daughter. Apart from his family and The Owl, his only other attachment was a portable IBM computer which never strayed more than a few metres from his side. In an era when people were talking about the Information Superhighway and the Internet, Jens Jensen was already locked into them.

1

The Frenchman was in his mid-forties, and hid his character behind the thick round spectacles which gave him his nickname. The four people who mattered in his life were Creasy and the Jensen family. He had two other attachments. One was the Sony Walkman which was permanently fixed to his belt and which gave him the only relaxation he ever needed: the sounds of the great classical composers. He was a walking encyclopaedia of their works and their lives, and for him God was called Mozart. His other attachment was a MAB PA 15 pistol with the rotating barrel. It nestled in a soft leather holster under his left armpit and, when necessary, he used it with a speed and accuracy that would have turned Wyatt Earp green with envy.

It was a good partnership. Jens Jensen had a gift for getting into trouble; and The Owl had a gift for getting him out of it. Jens was the brain and The Owl was the gun.

Jensen and The Owl had been in Brussels looking for the runaway wife of a Danish industrialist. They had located her the previous night, in the bed of a black saxophonist. Since she was clearly content to be there, Jens had merely retrieved the five-carat engagement ring and the heavy gold wedding ring for his client, and phoned through the news that he may as well begin divorce proceedings. He and The Owl had worked with both Maxie and Creasy on previous jobs some years earlier and so they had naturally gravitated to Maxie's bistro for their last supper in Brussels. They had been surprised and pleased to find Creasy in attendance, and together with Maxie had listened to the story of the supposedly dead GI and the mysterious return of the dogtag with the scrap of paper.

Maxie repeated his statement. 'You feel guilty!'

Creasy shook his head. 'Maxie, you know how it is. You've been there dozens of times. You see a guy get hit and you have an instinct which tells you whether the hit was fatal or not. Nine times out of ten your instinct is right. I was running for cover but I saw the kid get hit. He went down like a spinning top. I was also hit, but not badly. I managed to get away.'

'So what are you feeling guilty about?'

Creasy sighed again with irritation. 'I'm not feeling guilty. It's just that, maybe, we should have gone back to make sure. I wasn't hurt bad. I just needed a few stitches and a day at the MASH. Of course we couldn't go back right away, but we could have returned a couple of days later, in force.'

The Dane sipped at his wine and asked: 'Were you in command of the unit?'

Creasy shook his head. 'No. It was a US Special Forces patrol. I was attached to it as a very unofficial "irregular".'

'So it wasn't your responsibility?'

'No, but the guy in command was an asshole. Maybe I could have got a few of the other irregulars together and gone back to take a look.'

Maxie was looking at his friend with curiosity. He said: 'For God's sake, Creasy. In a situation like that, you don't go back looking for a guy you're almost sure is dead.' He gestured at the dogtag lying on the centre of the table. 'Twenty-six years later, that turns up with a piece of paper with your name on it. Probably some bent mind, or maybe the guy who delivered them was setting up the kid's father for a con. It's happened before.'

'Maybe.'

Maxie picked up the disc and rolled it through his fingers, and asked: 'What was the kid like?'

Creasy thought about that, and then said: 'He was a good kid. A bit different. He was always frightened.'

Maxie laughed in surprise. 'Frightened. He'd graduated to the US Special Forces and had been in 'Nam for over a year; and he was always frightened?'

'Yes. He thought he never showed it. He was the macho type on the outside. I guess he was born frightened, and had spent the twenty-one years of his life trying to prove to himself that he was a hero. He used to follow me around, a bit like a puppy. Always talking tough, but always just a frightened kid underneath. I sort of came to like him. I guess, in a way, like you get attached to a puppy. When things got rough, I tried to keep him a little close, but on that day the asshole platoon commander had put him out on point. He was the first one to get cut down.'

Maxie studied his friend's scarred face. He had been present when some of those scars were inflicted. Quietly he said: 'Creasy, there's no way you should feel responsible. You were not even in the fucking US Army. You were a hired irregular whom nobody was even supposed to talk about. You were not in command. You had no responsibility. So they paid you good, but not good enough to risk going back to look for a guy you assumed was dead. Now why don't you go home to Gozo: soak up the sun and put it out of your mind.'

Creasy reached out and picked up the scrap of paper. He said: 'Thanks for the advice, Maxie. But 'Nam has opened up again and so has Cambodia.' He smiled wryly. 'I guess I'll go and look for the puppy.'

In astonishment, Maxie glanced at Jens and The Owl. It was as though he had just heard the Pope announce that he was off to get married.

The Dane said: It sounds like a wild goose looking for a needle in a thousand hectares of wheat. Where will you start to look?'

Creasy was holding his wine glass and slowly swirling the contents. He looked up at the Dane and then at The Owl and asked: 'Are you guys busy at the moment?'

'Not very,' Jens answered. 'We just wrapped up a job. We figured to take some time off.'

Creasy put down his glass and said: 'How would you feel about working with me on this?'

The Dane and the Frenchman glanced at each other. Then The Owl asked: 'Does this kid's father have plenty of money?'

'I doubt it. He's a retired clerk. I guess he has his pension and no more. If you joined me, I would be the client.'

Again, glances of surprise passed around the table, and Maxie asked: 'You'll do this for nothing?'

Creasy shrugged. 'You talked about guilt. The fact is, I'm not feeling guilty, but I am curious. I want to know where that dogtag came from, and why.' He looked at the Dane. 'I want to hire you and The Owl for at least a couple of weeks. How much do you guys charge per diem?'

Suddenly, there was a strange noise. It emanated from The Owl. The other three looked at him with concern; then they realized that he was laughing. He controlled himself and said: 'Creasy, I never expected to hear such a question from you. Three years ago you came into what I thought was a life and turned it upside down . . . Gave it a purpose.' He gestured at the Dane. 'You matched me up with Jens and, in a sense, gave me a family for the first time. Now you have the balls to sit there and ask how much I charge you for what is nothing more than a favour.'

The Dane was nodding thoughtfully. He said: if it wasn't for you, Creasy, I'd still be sitting in a small office at Copenhagen Police Headquarters pushing papers around. So shut up about money and just tell us what you want done.'

Creasy looked at Maxie, who stated: 'It's not a good thing to insult old friends.'

There was a brief flash of anger in Creasy's eyes. Then he relaxed and sat back in his seat. He said to Jens: 'You have my thanks. Of course, I'll cover your expenses. And who knows, maybe some money will come out of all this. It often does. If so, we split it three ways.'

'It's a deal,' Jens said. 'Now what do you need?'

Creasy thought for half a minute and then said: 'The US Army has a permanent Missing-in-Action section based in Washington. It's a big section. The American people are highly sensitive about their Armed Forces personnel who go missing in foreign wars. It's a very emotive issue, so the politicians make a lot of noise about it. They're still trying to find GIs, or their remains, who went missing in Korea forty-five years ago. They still refuse to recognize Vietnam until they've used up every effort to locate their missing persons.' He glanced at the Dane. 'In a way, Jens, it's the same thing that you and The Owl specialize in, which is why I can use your help. I'd like you to go to Washington and talk to the people at the Missing-in-Action section. Of course Bentsen has been in contact with them about that dogtag, and they think it's authentic. I want you to get as much background as possible. Ask questions; snoop around. Try to get a general impression of the case. Those guys must get all kinds of information, a lot of it purely speculative. The kind of information they cannot pass on to the families of the missing because it may raise false hopes. But that information could be useful to me. Meanwhile I'll head for San Diego. We take it one step at a time. I made some inquiries. The guy who heads up the US Army Missing-in-Action section is a Colonel called Elliot Friedman. Please go talk to him.'

The Dane did something that he always did at such moments. He reached down to his feet and pulled up the small case containing his computer. He laid it reverently on the table and a few seconds later was tapping in a file entitled, 'Puppy'.

CHAPTER TWO

Of course it was logical: first find the messenger, and through him find the sender.

Where to start looking? Obviously, at the place where the message was delivered.

Creasy sat in the overfurnished living room in the house in San Diego, sipping a Budweiser. The old couple sat opposite drinking coffee, their faces showing anxiety and a little embarrassment.

The woman said: 'We have our savings, Mr Creasy . . . and we both have pensions. We can afford to pay you something.'

Creasy was deliberately blunt. 'Mrs Bentsen, for a job like this I'd normally ask for a hundred thousand up front . . . and a whole lot more for expenses. But this is not normal. I'm going to spend a couple of weeks to satisfy my own curiosity. Right now I'm flush with money from the last couple of jobs. What I need is not money but your memory. Think carefully, and describe the man who delivered the dogtag.'

Marina Bentsen was old, with a pinched, narrow face, but her eyes were bright and sparkled with intelligence. Those eyes narrowed in concentration as she spoke.

'He was definitely Asiatic. We have quite a big Asian community here in San Diego. Japanese, Chinese, Korean and of course Vietnamese. For us, it's always hard to distinguish. Not only their nationalities, but their ages. He was not young, I would guess between fifty and sixty . . . His face was unlined. His hair, of course, was black and quite short . . . parted in the middle. His eyes were small and very dark. His nose was slightly hooked and his chin was uncommonly narrow. He was wearing dark blue trousers, and a light blue windbreaker. Also, sneakers. When he walked away I noticed that he had a slight limp.'

'Which side?'

'He favoured his left leg.'

'You're very observant, Mrs Bentsen.'

For the first time, the thin lips on the narrow face smiled. She said: 'I guess it comes from being an artist.'

'You're an artist?'

She gestured at the walls of the room. Creasy silently studied the half-dozen paintings. They were all landscapes apart from one portrait of a young man. Creasy recognized the face of Jake Bentsen. With sincerity he said: 'They're very good; and the likeness of your son is excellent.'

Her query was wistful. 'So you recognized him, Mr Creasy?'

'Yes, but I'm going to need several photographs, which I'll get enlarged.'

The old man pushed himself to his feet, saying: 'We have plenty. We had them enlarged and printed for the MIA.' He walked over to a bureau, opened a drawer, and took out a large envelope.

Creasy studied the score or so eight-by-ten prints and nodded with satisfaction, then looked up at the old woman and asked: 'Can you make a drawing from your memory, of the messenger?'

She leaned forward. 'I did that the same night that he came here.'

Her husband had not sat down. He went again to the bureau and came back with a tube of paper bound by an elastic band.

Creasy slipped off the band and unrolled the thick paper. The portrait was drawn with broad strokes of charcoal. The face seemed to be alive, especially the small black eyes between the high cheekbones. For a long time the old couple watched him study the drawing. Then he turned back to the woman and asked in a very quiet voice: 'Are you satisfied that this is a good likeness?'

She was emphatic. 'Yes. The face was stamped into my mind. I worked on the drawing late into the night. Mr Creasy, that's the face of the messenger.'

Creasy turned the portrait around and looked at it again. The old man asked: 'Will it help?' Creasy looked at him and said: 'Mr Bentsen, I knew this man.' Silence hung in the air, finally broken by the excited voice of Marina Bentsen. 'So it does help!'

Creasy was looking at the charcoal face. He said: 'Yes and no.' 'What does that mean?'

Creasy tapped the portrait. 'Like your son, this guy should be dead.'

The old man was the first to find his voice. 'Are you sure?' 'Yes . . . I killed him.'

CHAPTER THREE

After he had left, the old couple sat silently for several minutes. Then the woman stood up and went to the bureau in the corner. She returned with a shoebox, laid it on the table and took from it a bunch of envelopes tied with a yellow ribbon. She knew exactly which letter she wanted. She flicked through the bundle and pulled it out. The pages crackled in her hands. Her husband watched patiently as she looked for the paragraphs. Then she started to read out loud.

'My outfit is doing long-range patrols (LRPs) into VC territory. We go in for days, and sometimes weeks, at a time. Not like the units who go on a forty-eight-hour hike and have their hot breakfasts flown in by the choppers. Sure it's dangerous work; but don't worry overmuch. Ours is an elite unit. We know what we're doing. It's mainly recce work but occasionally we make contact. The firefight is always short and sharp. Over the weeks we've come out on top, although we've suffered some wounded. We have a few "unofficials" with us. I'm not allowed to tell you where they're from. Let's just say these guys have been around in a lot of wars and compared to them we're kinda green; but we learn fast.

'One of those guys is sort of a friend. Well, maybe not a friend. I don't think he has any friends. He doesn't talk much. Fact is he hardly talks at all. There are all kinds of rumours about the guy, that he was in the French Foreign Legion and fought all over the place. He's got scars just about everywhere. They say he also fought in the Congo and Biafra. Thing is, when you ask him, he just shrugs and says he can't remember.

'I'm the youngest in the outfit and some of the guys kinda trash me. But not this guy. He takes me seriously. Sometimes he gives me pointers on weapons and things. For sure, he knows a hell of a lot more than the NCOs and the lieutenant. When he occasionally says something you'd better believe they listen.

'When there's a firefight I always look for him. I guess it's natural. Also I get the feeling that maybe he keeps an eye on me. Nothing obvious but just a feeling. I can't explain, but I want to be his friend. His name is Creasy.'

She folded the sheets of paper and slid them back into the envelope. She pulled out another letter from the bundle and read: 'We just got back from another LRP way up north. I never thought a man could get so tired as I did. I guess I only kept going because the others did. Maybe that's the way it works. Everybody watches the others, waiting for the first one to crack, waiting for an excuse to give up yourself. We made no contact with "Charlie" but something interesting happened. Our orders were to check out a valley and a small Vietnamese village in it. We entered the place at dawn and picked up the headman and took him away for questioning. This is a dirty war and you won't be shocked to know that the questioning can get rough. Of course, we good guys don't get involved like that. We always have a couple of NVA guys along to do the translating and the dirty work if necessary. But it turned out that the headman was educated and spoke French. Our lieutenant is supposed to speak French but I guess it was third-grade stuff because the guy couldn't understand more than a word or two. The lieutenant got mad and told the NVA guys to work him over. But Creasy told them to wait. Then he had a long conversation with the headman in French. I guess he must have been in the Legion. They seemed to get on fine, the headman was smiling and laughing. Creasy told the lieutenant that he had learned all they needed to know. Then he spoke a few more words with the headman and then he beat the guy up. Beat him up bad. He didn't break any bones but the old guy was bleeding all over. None of us could figure it out. Not even the lieutenant. I mean, the headman had co-operated. Most of the guys figured that Creasy was just a sadist getting his kicks. I didn't believe it. Over chow that night I went over and asked him about it. He just told me to use my brains and think it out. A couple of days passed. Then I worked it out. We had been deep into VC territory. For sure the next time the VC visited that village, they would find out that we had been there and questioned the headman. If he was unmarked, he would face their suspicions. If he was only roughed up, the suspicions would be deeper.

'The point is that Creasy never bothered to explain this to me or the other guys. He's different. He just lives inside himself.'

She folded that letter too, and slid it back into the envelope. Then she read the final letter, which was full of enthusiasm. He had just completed an intense final six weeks' course in mine laying and clearance. Together with his qualifications from earlier courses, this meant he was now promoted 'specialist first class'. She remembered their pride when they had received the letter; it was as though their son had graduated with honours from Harvard University.

And then, three weeks later, the letter from the Pentagon. Missing in action. The weeks and months of waiting and praying and hoping to hear that he had been taken prisoner. The twenty-six years of waiting to hear anything at all.

Her husband stood up, gently took the box from her hand, and locked it away in the bureau.

CHAPTER FOUR

'Fucking computers!'

Colonel Elliot Friedman looked around the spacious office, and then said to the Dane: 'I've been working in this department for thirty years now. I remember when the whizz-kids first came in with the computers. They told us all the paperwork was going to be eliminated. Bullshit! We generate more paper now, in spite of the fancy machines. Do you know why?'

Jens Jensen shook his head. 'I don't know why, but I guess it comes down to bureaucracy. I used to work in the Missing Persons Department in the Danish Police. Of course we had computers, and of course we had giant printers that spewed out paper all day long. It reminds me of a story back in the last century, when Bismarck discovered that the German bureaucracy had two great warehouses full of documents that were completely useless. He gave an order to burn all that useless paper. Two years later he remembered the order and asked his chief of staff to check whether it had been carried out. The chief of staff returned and reported that after two years only ten per cent of it was burned. "Why?" asked Bismarck. The chief of staff replied: "Because the bureaucrats told me that it would take many more years to make copies of the documents before they were burned."'

For the first time the Colonel smiled. It changed his tired, lined face. His was not a job to envy. The building contained tens of thousands of files which held the details of American servicemen missing in action, going all the way back to World War I. Of course by now it was only those missing since the Korean War in the early fifties, and through the Vietnam War, which caused the heartache of so many thousands of relatives and loved ones. No other country in world history had spent so much time and money trying to trace their missing servicemen. It was emotive and it was political. And it was why in the modern age American presidents were so reluctant to commit their servicemen to wars; and why they so often used a hammer to crack a walnut.

Jens knew all about that. He had been in Washington only one week, but had burrowed like a beaver, and he now knew a great deal about the Missing-in-Action department. He knew that the colonel was efficient and conscientious. He knew that in spite of his rank he had never fired a gun in anger. He had a staff of over three hundred which included experts at identifying human remains.

The Dane passed across the dogtag, saying: 'I know your people have seen this before. As far as they know, it's authentic.'

The colonel studied the dogtag and nodded his grey-haired head.

'It looks authentic,' he said. 'Vietnam era. What's your interest?'

'Concerns a friend of mine. A very close friend. That dogtag belonged to a special forces GI. He was with my friend when he went missing in action near the Cambodian border back in nineteen sixty-eight.'

The colonel was still looking at the dogtag in the palm of his hand. He said: 'That was a bad year. Was Jake his given name or a nickname?'

'His given name.'

The colonel was looking at his computer console. He shrugged, smiled wanly and said: 'Of course I could press the little buttons on this thing and the file should come up on the screen. But like Bismarck's boys, I'm kinda old-fashioned.'

He reached forward, pressed a button on his desk console and said: 'Susanna, I want the file on SFC Jake Bentsen missing in 'Nam . . . sixty-eight.'

During the ten minutes' wait for the file to arrive, the colonel poured three mugs of coffee from a machine in the corner of his office; then, with a wink, he opened the desk drawer and pulled out a bottle of Martell brandy.

'It improves the taste,' he said. 'Believe me, army coffee needs all the help it can get.'

He poured a generous slug into each mug, pushed one across the desk to the Dane and passed another to The Owl, sitting silently to the side. 'Skål!'

'Skål!' said Jens. 'Have you been in my country?'

'Yes, back in the seventies I spent a lot of time in Sweden. We had quite a few guys who deserted during the 'Nam war, and others who ducked the draft. Many of them ended up in Canada and quite a few in Sweden, especially the black ones. There were several cases where they pretended to go MIA and then found their way to Sweden. My job then was to liaise with the Swedish government.' He shrugged. 'I have to say that I found Stockholm and the Swedish pretty boring. So on weekends I used to catch the ferry and take a little R and R in Copenhagen. Danes have a better sense of humour, the booze was cheaper and the girls were great.'

Jens asked, 'Where did you hang out?'

'Kakadu . . . Is it still going?'

'Yes, it is. The girls are still there but these days the customers are mostly Japanese.'

There was a tap on the door. A woman wearing a captain's uniform brought in a thick file. She glanced at the Dane and then at The Owl before she quietly left the room.

The file had a red cover closed with black elastic. On the top right-hand corner were stamped the letters MIA (EXL). The colonel pushed the file across the desk, saying: 'This is against regulations. But since I had some good times in your city, you can look through it. I am not allowed to give you copies of any parts except by written permission from the Secretary of Defence.'

The Dane nodded his thanks, then tapped the letters on the file and asked: 'What do these signify?'

'It's part of a grading we use. The letters EXL signify that it's low grade. We have very little expectations either that your man is alive or that his remains will ever be found.' He looked again at the dogtag on his desk. 'But maybe, since this was hand-delivered to his parents' home, we should upgrade the file.'

Jens had opened the file and was reading through the papers. They consisted of dozens of reports, starting with the action report of the lieutenant in command of the unit. It was followed by a report from the Divisional Combat Intelligence Office and then reports concerning prisoner interrogations, returned POW debriefings, Red Cross reports and finally analyses of information given by the unified Vietnamese government after they began co-operating with the US government in an effort to get sanctions lifted. Every single report was totally negative.

It took the Dane half an hour to speed-read it. Meanwhile, the colonel recharged the mugs from the bottle of Martell until Jens realized he was drinking almost pure Cognac.

He closed the file and said, 'I can understand why you gave it a low grading. But still, the work that went into this file was very extensive. I congratulate you.'

The colonel's face had turned sombre. He was looking at a framed photograph on his desk. He said: 'I lost my own son in Vietnam in sixty-seven. They shipped his body back and he's buried in Arlington. Sometimes it's difficult to understand what it means to a parent to know that his child is at rest, even if it is below the earth. A lot of the officers working in this depart-ment, men and women, are in similar situations. We take our work seriously. We see a lot of prolonged grief. That grief is our motivation.' He was now looking out of the window, across the Potomac River. His tone was reflective. 'As I look back over the past few years, I notice the changes here in America. Up until the sixties the family units were very strong, and of course our soldiers went to fight in Europe and Korea knowing they had a mission. They understood what they were risking their lives for. I guess 'Nam changed all that, and the sixties changed the family ties too. But the parents of the ones who went missing did not change. They still like to think that their loss had a meaning. They still hope that the sacrifices were not in vain.' He turned back to the file. 'The parents of Jake Bentsen must be in their seventies now. Suddenly getting that dogtag after all those years must have been a combination of hell and hope.'

Abruptly, he changed the subject. 'This friend of yours. Was he regular army?'

The Dane shook his head. 'He was a Marine. But that was before he was a French Foreign Legionnaire and a mercenary. He was in Vietnam in the latter capacity.'

The colonel nodded thoughtfully and said, 'Yeah, we had quite a few of those. But I have to admit they weren't the kind of guys who would go on a wild-goose chase twenty-six years later looking for a soldier who is almost certainly dead. They must have been very good friends.'

Jens Jensen shook his head and stood up, saying, 'They were not close friends, Colonel. The truth is I don't really understand why my friend is going back . . . Then again, he is not like the others, who just fought for money over there.'

He picked up his briefcase and from his top pocket pulled out a card and placed it on the desk. 'A thousand thanks. If you ever find yourself in Copenhagen again, please call me and we'll go and have a Schnapps together.'

As he reached the door the colonel's voice stopped him.

'If your friend travels under a US passport, he might have trouble getting into Vietnam. And if he does get in, he'll have more trouble if he starts asking unofficial questions about US MIA's.'

Jens answered: 'You might be right, Colonel. But then I'm just a detective. When it comes to trouble, my friend has a history of taking care of himself. Again, a thousand thanks! Or as you may have heard the expression on one of your nights in Copenhagen and the Kakadu, "Tusind tak".'

CHAPTER FIVE

'It's a set-up. That's the only answer.'

They were in a hotel room in downtown San Diego. Creasy was standing at the window looking out on sheets of heavy rain. The Dane was sitting on the bed with the open briefcase beside him and the computer on his lap. The Owl was sitting on a chair in the corner.

'Set up for whom?' Creasy asked over his shoulder.

'For you, of course,' Jens answered. 'First the dogtag and the scrap of paper with your name on it. Then you find out that it was delivered here to the Bentsens' by a man you know but who you thought was dead.'

Creasy turned and said: 'Of course it's not certain that I know the man. All I saw was a sketch of his face, added to the description that he limped on his left leg.'

The Owl entered the conversation. 'I don't believe in coincidence. Who is the man you thought was dead?'

'It was a guy who worked for the South Vietnamese police. His name was Van Luk Wan. He was a senior officer in the Intelligence Department, which meant that he tortured a lot of people. One of them happened to be a friend of mine. She was just a girl who worked in a bar in Saigon. Van had the idea, without any basis, that she might be a VC informer. I don't think he cared one way or the other. He was that kind of man. She died slowly and badly.'

'So you killed him?' Jens asked.

'I thought I did. It was at night and the light was not great but he was only five metres away. I don't usually miss at that range.'

'You didn't double-check?' The Owl asked.

'There was no time. It was that kind of situation. One shot, and I was gone.'

Jens leaned forward and asked: 'You heard nothing about it later?'

'No. That night I flew out from Than Son Nut airport for Bangkok. I never returned to Vietnam. By that time I was sick of it. Sick of the whole damned charade!'

The Dane was pecking away at his computer console. He glanced up and asked: 'This policeman, Van, did he know you well?'

'Yes, very well. A week earlier he had picked me up for interrogation. There was no rough stuff. They didn't do that to Americans: only to their own benighted people.'

The Owl intervened again. 'So why did he pick you up?'

Creasy had turned back and looked down again at the rain as he said: 'You have to understand the time and the place. The war was at its apex. There were all sorts of people running around Saigon. It seemed like every crook and conman had made it their home. I worked for the American military as what they called an "irregular". They had their Green Berets and their Rangers and other special forces. But when there was a very high-risk job to be done, they hired guys like me. In their jargon we were called "expendables". We had no mothers or fathers to cry over the body bags when they were shipped home. Sometimes they used us to beef up their regular forces. The money was good and so it attracted all kinds of assholes. A sort of refuse that came out of the Congo and Biafra. There were some good guys among them, even a couple of ex-legionnaires. But most of them were the worst kind of dogs. And when they weren't out in the field, they were into every racket you can think of, from drugs to prostitution, gun-running to extortion. This guy, Van, was supposed to be in charge of the Saigon police department which was set up to combat those rackets.' Creasy laughed without mirth. 'But he, and most of his team, were part of those rackets. The corruption in that city was incredible. Of course he had to make a show to his superiors, so every once in a while he would pull one of us "irregulars" in for questioning.'

Jens asked: 'Did he know it was you who shot him?'

'Yes. I didn't shoot him in the back. Before I pulled the trigger I said: "This is for Ming". He knew she was a friend of mine. He knew why he got the bullet.'

The Dane was again tapping at his computer. He said: 'Can you remember the date that you shot him?'

'Is that relevant?'

'Yes. It's possible I can find a way to check the hospital records and find out if he died or lived.' He looked up with a smile that was almost smug. 'That's what detectives do. Common soldiers like you wouldn't know about things like that.'

Creasy glanced at The Owl and remarked: 'Sometimes this prick forgets that I'm paying his expenses.'

The Owl replied: 'You're quite right. But the problem is that his brains are bigger than his balls.'

'Enough levity,' Jens said. 'Try to remember the date, or at least the week.'

Creasy dropped his chin onto his chest and thought. After half a minute he said: it was sixty-eight, the week before Christmas. It was a Thursday evening.'

The Dane's fingers tapped the keys of the computer. 'I'll get a calendar and check the dates for sixty-eight.'

The Owl did something surprising. He stood up and started pacing the floor. He was normally a sedentary man. He began to talk to Jens as though Creasy were not in the room.

'If this guy, Van, did survive, and had a motive of revenge against Creasy, why would he wait all those years? If that dogtag was the bait on a hook, he would know that Jake Bentsen's father would find Creasy. Which means that he would know where to find Creasy himself; in which case he could have gone to Brussels and bushwhacked him.'

'That's true,' Jens answered. 'He obviously wants to lure Creasy back to South East Asia. My guess is that Jake Bentsen is dead long ago. The dogtag and the scrap of paper are just bait. There's got to be somebody else behind Van Luk Wan.'

Creasy pushed himself back into the conversation. 'And how do the brilliant detectives deduce that?'

The Dane lifted the computer from his lap, closed it, and laid it reverently on the bed. He stood up and stretched his portly frame, then gave one of his ultra-intelligent looks to Creasy and said: 'Sometimes even geniuses rely on intuition. To use an Americanism: some big shot in South East Asia wants your ass. How many big-shot enemies have you got over there?'

Creasy thought about that for a moment, then looked at his watch and said: 'Let's go get something to eat and I'll think about it. Then I'll write you a list.'

CHAPTER SIX

She had a curved face and at first glance it appeared beautiful. A second glance changed that perception. The cheekbones were just a bit too high and the nose slightly too hooked: but it was the eyes that dispelled any thoughts of real beauty. Behind her back she was known as 'the Cobra', and it was the latent venom in the eyes that gave her that name. Nobody would be so foolish as to say it to her face.

Her real name was Connie Lon Crum, and she combined cruelty with sophistication; designer jeans with a black heart. The well-dressed Thai businessman seated opposite her knew something of her history. Her father was the notorious Bill Crum, a half-Chinese, half-American rogue. During the Vietnam War he had amassed a fortune selling whisky and other merchandise to the US Army PX's. In order to do so, he had bribed scores of American soldiers, from two-star generals down to supply staff. He had met his death in 1977 in a mysterious fire in the New Territories of Hong Kong.

Her mother had been a Cambodian prostitute. Connie Lon Crum had contrasted a French education with marriage to a senior Khmer Rouge officer, whom she had later killed in a fit of jealous rage. She had inherited her father's gift for shady business and her mother's wiles for manipulating men.

As he looked at her, the Thai businessman felt a surge of sexuality, tainted by the tinge of fear.

Standing behind her to each side were two short, wide, young Cambodian women. They were dressed in black tunics and trousers and had holstered pistols strapped to their waists. Their faces were flat and expressionless but their eyes never wavered from the man.

He was incongruously dressed in an Italian suit, a silk cream shirt and a silk striped tie. His shoes were by Gucci. It was not the normal attire for a meeting in a hot jungle on the Thai-Cambodian border; but then, it was not a normal business meeting.

She pushed the flat wooden box across the table towards him and said: 'I'm in a hurry. You have fifteen minutes to make an offer. Payment will be in US dollars, Swiss francs or gold.'

He opened the box and looked down at the gemstones. They were sapphires and pieces of uncut jade. He picked up a piece of jade weighing about fifty grams. A tiny 'window' had been sliced open on one side. The colour was pale green, almost translucent. He looked up and saw the mirthless smile on her lips. She said: 'Of course, under normal circumstances, you would like to take it back to Bangkok and have an even greater expert than yourself look at it: but you have no time, Mr Ponnosan. In this place, life is always a gamble.'

The hut was not air-conditioned. He could feel the sweat running down his chest under his shirt. He had an urge to loosen his tie, but he resisted it. It was the first time that he had done business with the woman. Others from Bangkok had traded with her for many months. Some had made a lot of money and others had not. He realized that he was in a sort of jungle casino. She glanced at her gold Rolex and he concentrated on the stones. There were about two dozen. He separated them within the box. She watched and said: 'You take all or nothing.'

He knew the procedure. He said: 'Fifty thousand US dollars.'

She gave him a cynical smile. 'Calm down, Mr Ponnosan. You are buying jewels, not glass.'

The trading lasted for less than five minutes, after which they agreed to $85,000. She reached forward, closed the box and pulled it back to her side of the table, saying: 'Hold out your left hand, palm upwards.'

He complied, knowing what was coming. One of the two young women behind her came round the table, took his hand in hers and studied the palm intensely. She then turned to Connie Crum and nodded. Connie pushed the box into the centre of the table. He had passed the test. He stood up, unbuttoned his jacket and shirt and pulled out the canvas money belt from around his waist. He first extracted a single thousand-dollar bill and passed it to her. She held it up to the light, examined it closely and then nodded. He counted out eighty-four more bills, and then departed with the box.

As his Mercedes drove off down the dirt track towards Thailand, a battered Willys jeep pulled up at the hut. A middle-aged man jumped down. He wore thick spectacles and faded denims. As he walked into the hut the two Cambodian women looked at him alertly, then they relaxed. Connie Crum was putting a thick elastic band around the dollar bills. She gave him a genuine smile.

'Welcome back!'

He sat down, glancing at the big wad of money. He spoke in French: 'A good trade?'

Her smiled widened. 'No, Van. A very bad one. He paid eighty-five thousand dollars for stones worth twice that much.'

'Have you become a philanthropist?'

'Not at all. He was a virgin. It was his first time. When he gets back to Bangkok he will make a big profit and believe that I'm not as clever as he had heard. He'll come back for more, and again he'll make a very good profit. That will happen three or four times, and then he will be both confident and very greedy. That's when I'll castrate him.'

The Vietnamese grinned at her with affection.

She asked: 'What news do you bring from America?'

'It moves along,' he answered. 'I delivered the dogtag and the piece of paper on the third of last month. The old man left for Europe two days later and returned to San Diego after a week. Our people saw Creasy entering his house on the evening of the thirteenth. He stayed for one hour. As instructed, our people did not try to follow him.'

She had sat back in the rough wooden chair. Her eyes were fixed at a spot on the wall above and behind Van's head. 'Can you trust those people?' she asked.

He shrugged. 'They are American and they love money. The detective agency has a good reputation. They did not know Creasy's name; they only had his description. They described the man who entered the Bentsens' house exactly. There is no doubt it was Creasy.'

She reached for the dollars, stood up and stretched her lithe body. She did not look feline. It was the body of a racing snake: but her smile was as contented as that of any cat that had just spied a sleepy mouse.

CHAPTER SEVEN

It has been said that if you want to make contact with any individual in any city anywhere in the world, it should not take more than three phone calls.

Jens Jensen believed in that saying. In this case, he needed a reliable Danish contact in Ho Chi Minh City. During his years as a policeman he had done a few favours for journalists but never asked for anything in return. But now he was no longer a policeman. He picked up the phone and called the foreign editor of the *Morgenavisen Jyllandsposten*. After an exchange of pleasantries and the promise to meet for a drink or a lunch next time he was in Århus, he raised the subject.

'Do you have a correspondent in South East Asia?'

'We have two. One in Hong Kong and one in Bangkok. They cover the whole area, so they travel quite a lot. What do you need . . . ?'

'I need to make contact with somebody in Ho Chi Min City . . . That's the new name for the old Saigon.'

He heard the snort of disgust down the phone. 'I happen to know that. I happen to be the foreign editor of the Danish newspaper that has the most foreign correspondents around the world.'

Jens laughed. 'OK, relax. I know you're a genius . . . Can you help?'

'Are you at home?'

'Yes.'

'I'll call you back.'

Jens' wife Birgitte had prepared lunch of *skipperlabskovs*, which translates as 'the ship's captain's favourite dish'. It was a sort of stew with potatoes, meat and vegetables with a topping of ham. It was also Jens' favourite dish, and he had just sat down to a piping hot plate of it when the phone rang. Birgitte answered it, then held it out, saying: 'it's Henrik from Århus.'

Jens cursed, but went to the phone. He said: 'You always did pick the worst time to return a call.'

Henrik laughed. 'Were you having sex with your lovely wife?'

'No. Something better than that. I just sat down to a plate of *skipperlabskovs*.'

'My sympathy. But when you ask a favour you can't stipulate the time . . . Do you have a pen and paper?'

'Yes. Go ahead.'

'I talked to my guy in Bangkok. He's got a drinking friend who has just been transferred from A. P. Møller's office there to their new liaison office in Ho Chi Minh city; which by the way used to be called Saigon.'

'Good. So forget the sarcasm and give me the details.'

After his meal and lavish compliments to Birgitte, he roughly calculated the time difference between Copenhagen and South East Asia. It would be late evening in Ho Chi Minh City. He looked up the international code and then dialled the number. His contact was at home, and obviously very happy to hear a Danish voice. After establishing his credentials, Jens made his request. He gave the name of the Vietnamese policeman and the date when he was shot. Then he hung up, put on his overcoat and went to watch the football match between Brandby and OB, reflecting that it was nice to have other people doing the legwork for a change.

CHAPTER EIGHT

'He lived.'

'Who did?'

'Your friend Van Luk Wan. He entered the hospital on December 19 1968 with a severe gunshot wound. They operated immediately and he survived. He was discharged on January 27 1969.'

Creasy was in Guido's penzione in Naples, with the phone in one hand and a glass of wine in the other. He was impressed.

'How did you find out?'

In Copenhagen, Jens chuckled down the line. 'For a man like me it was very simple. I chartered a plane to Saigon, managed an introduction to the head nurse, took her to dinner at the Continental Hotel and plied her with champagne; seduced her and persuaded her to break into the records of the hospital that night and, using the Minox camera I supplied, she photographed all the records during that period . . . I can tell you, Creasy, my expenses bill is going to be spectacular.'

Creasy chuckled. 'I don't mind as long as it's less than ten bucks.' He thought for a moment, and then said: 'The next thing is to find out whether he's still in the city; and if so, what happened to him after the communists took over.'

'You want me to get on with that and sniff around?'

Again Creasy paused for thought, then said: 'Give me a couple of days. I know he was in San Diego recently. Maybe he got to the US as a refugee. I can probably check that out. I'll get back to you . . . Thanks, Jens. It was good work.'

He put down the phone and walked out of the kitchen onto the broad terrace. It was one of his favourite spots on earth, high on the hills above the city with the wide sweep of the bay below. Sitting at the solitary table was his closest friend. He and Guido Arrellio had first met in the French Foreign Legion during the Algerian war of independence in the early sixties. They were in the second R.E.P., and had been kicked out after their battalion had joined the Generals' Putsch. Fighting was all they knew, so they had teamed up as mercenaries and fought in a series of wars in Africa and the Far East. Finally Guido had met a Maltese girl, married her and bought the Pensione Splendide in Naples. He and Creasy had gone their separate ways until Guido's wife died in a car crash. In his turn Creasy had married her younger sister, who had also died tragically. That shared bond drew them even closer. Neither of them made friends easily, and the casual observer would have found it impossible to see their closeness. They were not men who showed affection or emotion; but they had served together for many years, and Creasy had come to Naples to discuss the mysterious dogtag and the man who had delivered it in San Diego.

He sat down, saying: 'That was Jens from Copenhagen. He discovered that the man, Van Luk Wan, survived the shooting.'

'What was the range?' Guido asked.

'About five metres.'

Guido glanced at his friend and raised an eyebrow. 'You missed him at five metres?'

'I didn't miss. He went down like he was poleaxed. I had no time to make sure.'

Guido looked out across the bay. An American frigate was swinging slowly at anchor. That night the sailors would be drunk and brawling in Naples' red light district. Some would be robbed and some would take home a communicable disease. He turned back to Creasy.

'I agree with Jens and The Owl. You're being set up. This guy Van is just the bait. Why don't you go home to Gozo and enjoy your retirement?'

Creasy took a sip of wine and answered: 'That's the sensible thing to do . . . But then, I was never famous for doing sensible things. This is nagging away at my head. It won't go away whether I'm sitting here or in Gozo.'

'So you'll go to 'Nam?'

'Yes; but first I'll phone Jim Grainger in the States. He has the connections to find out through immigration whether Van Luk Wan entered the US as a tourist or a refugee. If he was given refugee status they'll have his address. In that case I'll go and pay him a visit.'

Guido poured more wine. 'The season is over here and I'm getting a little bored. If you go to Saigon I'll go with you.' He smiled briefly. 'It'll be like old times.'

'I hope not,' Creasy answered, in the old times a lot of guys were trying to shoot our asses off.'

CHAPTER NINE

The Dutchman lost his temper.

Piet de Witt had fought in many wars and many places and on the whole had been well-paid; but he decided that if God ever wanted to give planet Earth an enema, he would put the tube into Cambodia. It was not the countryside, which was beautiful, or even the average Cambodian who, on the whole, were gentle people. It was just that his present employers had sunk below even de Witt's bottom line.

He turned to the small, brown-clad figure of the Khmer Rouge officer beside him. 'Fuck you! It's impossible to clear that minefield before sunset. Not without risking the lives of my men.'

'They risk their lives every day,' the officer replied. 'So do all our men. That's what war is all about.'

The Dutchman laughed hollowly. He looked down the green, lush valley and said: 'Most wars are stupid. This one is simply crazy.' He had a map in his left hand. He jabbed a finger at it. 'It was you people, the Khmer Rouge, who planted those mines six years ago. Two thousand of them right in that valley. You didn't even keep proper grid references or mark down the clear lanes. Now all these years later you want to send a convoy of troops through the same valley. Why don't you send them by another route?'

The Cambodian looked up at the giant Caucasian beside him. 'Because in those days we mined every valley in this area. Of course sometimes maps and grid references got lost. That's why we pay you ten thousand dollars a month to train our men to clear them when we have to.' He glanced at his watch, 'It's six hours to sunset, by which time the trucks will be ready to roll. We need a clear way through that valley by then. Those are our orders.'

The Dutchman swore under his breath. 'Maybe you'd better tell her it's impossible. I've only been here two months and I'm the only expert you've got. I've trained twelve of your people but they're still amateurs. You tell her that.'

The Khmer Rouge officer replied: 'You can tell her yourself. She'll be here two hours before sunset and will expect to ride with that convoy through the valley. I suggest you and your squad get started.'

The Dutchman worked for his money, and he worked from the front in the classic V-shaped mine-clearing procedure. The mines were mostly the Chinese K3000 antipersonnel variety, interspersed with the occasional Russian DOM K anti-tank mines. They worked at a total width of fifty metres. Two of his squad came behind at the peripheries, planting small red flags to delineate the cleared path. After two hours one of the squad made a mistake and had his right leg blown off. An hour later there was another mistake, this time fatal.

Two hours before sunset they were just halfway through the minefield. The Cambodian officer who was walking a cautious fifty metres behind shouted out: 'You have to go faster! The field has to be cleared by darkness.'

The Dutchman turned on his knees and was about to shout back an obscenity when he saw the line of trucks approaching behind the officer. The lead truck halted and the tall, slim figure of the woman jumped down from the passenger seat. She was wearing camouflaged combat gear and carrying an AK47 rifle. She spoke a few words to the officer and then walked forwards as though taking an evening stroll down the Champs Élysées. The Dutchman had heard all about her but never met her. In spite of his anger he was intrigued.

She gave him a smile, held out her hand and introduced herself. 'I am Connie Lon Crum and I'm pleased to meet you at last. I hear very good reports about your work. We're grateful.'

The Dutchman was susceptible to women, especially tough, beautiful women. He took her small hand in his big paw. His anger was forgotten, but he found himself tongue-tied.

She continued: 'Is there any way you can clear a track through before darkness?' With that technical question his military mind clicked back into place and he found his tongue.

'The only way would be to mount an intense artillery bombardment which would set off most of the mines. My squad could then clear the remainder. The only problem is we don't have the artillery to mount such a bombardment. Miss Crum, there's no other way.'

For the first time he saw the steel in her eyes; and then, a different kind of smile on her face.

'There is always another way.' She turned and shouted an order. From the front of three trucks men began to jump down or be pushed down. Most of them had their hands tied behind their backs, the others were Khmer Rouge guards holding bayoneted rifles.

'Government soldiers,' she said. 'We captured them two weeks ago near Siem Reap. They will dance a path clear for us.'

The Dutchman watched speechlessly as the prisoners were organised into three lines, each prisoner about a yard from the next, and then roped together. The guards pushed them forward to the edge of the mine field.

Then it began. First the guards had to jab them with their bayonets and then fire at their feet. They did literally dance as they moved forwards. The air was filled with the noise of their screams and then the roars of the explosions as, one after another, the mines exploded.

The Dutchman had thought he had become immune to atrocities. He had seen them in the Congo, Biafra, Angola and Mozambique; but he had never seen anything like this. The woman took his arm and urged him along behind the dying prisoners. She turned to the officer behind her and said: 'Be sure our friend here has a woman to sleep with tonight.' She smiled up at the Dutchman. 'We have a saying here in Cambodia: "a soft woman is like a soothing ointment for both body and mind".'

CHAPTER TEN

'So you are from Holland?'

'No.'

'Then why do they call you the Dutchman?'

Piet de Witt sighed, and said as though repeating a litany: 'I'm from South Africa. An Afrikaaner of Dutch descent. For some reason, everybody calls Afrikaaners Dutchmen.'

He was lying on his back looking up at the white mosquito net. She lay in the crook of his arm with her long black hair across his chest.

Connie Crum had been right. This girl had soothed both his body and his mind. It amused him slightly to think that his mind needed such treatment. He prided himself on being a hard man in every sense. During his life and his work he had committed many acts of violence, some of them mindless. He had learned that early, from his rugby coach at school who had told him 'always get your retaliation in first'. That had become his doctrine in life. If he was in a bar and someone threatened him with a fight, he always struck first; and he kept striking until the fight was over. Under such conditions he had the ability to flick a mental switch and go on to auto-pilot. That ability created fear among his peers.

But during the events of the evening he had not been able to flick that switch. Somewhere deep down he did have a bottom line. He had never tortured anybody or deliberately killed an innocent. He had seen it done many times. And although he had not intervened, he had never felt the repulsion that a normal human being should have. He reflected that he might be getting old; might even be getting soft. He felt a strange tenderness for the slim girl lying by his side. It was an alien feeling. He had used women in much the same way as he had used weapons or eaten a plate of food. He had not even loved his mother.

'What's your name?' he asked the girl.

'Tan Sotho,' she answered.

'You're Vietnamese?'

'Yes.'

'What the hell are you doing here?'

Her voice was wistful. 'My family had lived here for generations. We had our own land. When the Khmer Rouge came they killed all the men and the old women and the male children. They kept the young women and girls alive, mostly to use as forced labour. But some of us were put in this brothel.' She turned her head and looked up at him. 'We're more or less slaves.'

'You never tried to escape?'

'No. A friend of mine tried and they caught her. I won't tell you what they did to her, but it was enough that the rest of us never tried.'

There was a long silence while he looked out of the mosquito netting around the almost bare room. She said: 'I hear you clear the mines.'

'That's my job.'

'It's very dangerous.'

'They pay me well.'

She lifted her head in surprise. 'They pay you?'

He laughed. 'Of course they pay me. Otherwise, why would I risk my life?' He looked at her face and saw the disbelief in her eyes. 'Is that so strange?' he asked.

'Yes . . . they never paid the others.'

'The others?'

'Yes. The Americans.'

Now the surprise was in his eyes. 'They had Americans here?'

'Yes. There were three of them. I suppose like me they were slaves.'

'Where the hell did they come from?'

'They came from the war, of course. They were captured by the Vietnamese. In those early days they co-operated with the Khmer Rouge. I think they were sold to the Khmer Rouge.'

Full of curiosity, he pushed himself onto his elbow and looked down on her oval face. 'What happened to them?'

'They died,' she said. 'One by one, in the minefields. The last one died two years ago, on the seventeenth of November.'

'You knew them?'

'Yes. The only pleasure they had in their lives was to be allowed to come here once a month. I liked them all. I suppose it was because we were trapped in the same hell.'

He lay back against the pillow and abruptly a noise intruded into his thoughts. It was a child crying. The girl said: 'Please excuse me.' She slipped out of the bed and under the mosquito net.

He watched as she padded across the floor towards a wooden door. She went through and switched on the light, leaving the door open. He could see the child lying in a cot. She bent over it, whispered some words and stroked the child's face. The crying stopped. Ten minutes later she returned to the bed with a warm wet towel. Slowly and carefully she wiped all of his body, kneeling beside him.

'The child is yours?' he asked.

'Yes. He's my son.'

'How old?'

'He'll be three next month. They were angry when they found out I was five months pregnant. I was able to conceal it until then. But they let me keep him. He is the only thing I possess.'

She was wiping his face with the towel, gently probing into the sockets of his eyes. She asked: 'How long have you been a mercenary?'

'Too long. I guess about twenty-five years. This is going to be my last job. Then I'll buy a farm in the Transvaal and raise cattle.'

'Did you fight in many places?'

'Too many.'

'Did you ever meet a man called Creasy?'

She felt his whole body stiffen and the towel was pulled from her hand. His head lifted from the pillow and she winced as he gripped her arm.

'What did you say?!'

'I just asked if you knew a man called Creasy. He was a mercenary like you.'

His voice was like sandpaper. 'Do you know him?'

'No. It's just that I heard about him from one of the Americans.'

He relaxed. His head dropped back onto the pillow and he released her arm. She looked down at his face, curiously. His eyes were far away. She asked: 'Did you know him?'

'I knew him.'

'Is he still alive?'

'I don't know.'

She was slowly stroking his chest in a way that was almost maternal. She asked: 'What kind of a man is he?'

He lifted a hand and put it over hers to stop her movements, and answered: 'He is death.'

CHAPTER ELEVEN

She hated Vietnam; the more so, because it fascinated her. It was a land of both sadness and poignancy. It was like an axe that cut a cleft between her heart and her mind; and it constantly drew her like a moth to a flame.

The Thai Airways plane from Bangkok dipped its nose and banked for its final descent into Ton San Nut airport. She closed the lid of her IBM Notebook and reached for her briefcase under the seat. Her mind was on the report she had just read on the small screen. She had read it several times since it had been loaded into her computer two days ago.

It was the FBI report on the Danish detective Jens Jensen. It had linked him with a mercenary called Creasy. That in itself did not ring any alarm bells for either herself or her boss Elliot Friedman. What did ring a shrill alarm was a suffix at the end of the report. It stated that any inquiries made to the FBI which involved a mercenary called Creasy would be automatically referred to Senator James Grainger, the senior Senator from Nevada and the chairman of the House Ways and Means Committee, a very powerful individual. She happened to be in Friedman's office the next morning when the expected call came through. Friedman had glanced at her and then flicked the phone onto the conference speaker.

The conversation was fairly typical of that between a very powerful politician and a moderately senior army officer. The politician was at first polite in the extreme. He complimented the colonel on the fine work he was doing under such difficult circumstances. For two or three minutes they chatted about the missing-in-action problem; And then Senator Grainger said: 'It's come to my attention that yesterday you requested a report on a Dane called Jens Jensen.'

'Yes, sir.'

'I assume you have received it.'

'Yes. It's on my desk at this moment.'

'Why your request, Colonel?'

'It's routine, sir. He came to see me the day before yesterday together with his associate. He's a private eye who specializes in missing persons. A very pleasant guy, I guess we have something in common in our work.'

'What did he want, Colonel?'

'He had the dogtag of a MIA. It had been delivered to the MIA's parents' house in San Diego. We extracted the relevant file and I have to say, Senator, I broke the rules a mite and let him read it.'

Susanna heard the Senator's chuckle through the speaker. 'I guess some rules are just there to be broken, Colonel. Were you able to help Jensen?'

'No, sir. Not beyond showing him the file. I asked him to keep me informed and to come back to me if he needed any further assistance.'

There was a silence. Even the phone's speaker seemed to be thinking; then the Senator's voice came through it. 'What was the code on the FBI's report?'

Colonel Friedman pulled the papers towards him and read out loud: 'CN/D/404082A.'

Another silence. Susanna thought she could actually hear the shuffle of papers through the phone. Then the senator said: 'That report refers to a man called Creasy.'

'Yes, sir.'

'Apart from what you have read in that report, do you know anything about that man Creasy?'

'No, sir. Just that he's a mercenary.'

The tone of Senator Grainger's voice changed. He became almost musing. He said: 'Colonel Friedman, can we talk off the record and in confidence?'

Friedman glanced at Susanna as if for advice. She simply shrugged and started to walk towards the door. Friedman stabbed the hold button and told her: 'Stay where you are, Susanna. When a senator wants to talk to an officer in confidence, it's better to have a witness.'

Very intrigued, she returned to her seat. Friedman reopened the line and said: 'Of course, Senator. This conversation is between you and me.'

'Good. I'm going to ask nothing that will compromise you. It's simply a request. I would like you to keep me informed of any further contact you or your department have with this man Jensen or with the man Creasy. I would also ask that in the event of such contacts, you render all assistance possible.'

The colonel looked up at Susanna, who again simply shrugged. A few seconds passed, then Friedman said: 'I'll be happy to do that, Senator Grainger, under any circumstances. However, you will understand my curiosity. Can you explain why?'

Friedman and Susanna looked at each other through the silence. Through the speaker, she could hear the Senator's breathing. He said: 'I'll be in Washington next week. Perhaps you would join me for lunch at The Red Sage?'

Susanna saw Friedman's eyebrows rise in surprise. It was a very rare event when a senior Senator invited a colonel to the best restaurant in town.

'It will be an honour, Senator.'

'Good. I'll have my secretary phone you and fix the appointment. Thanks for your co-operation.'

The line went dead. Friedman sat back in his chair and looked thoughtfully at the ceiling. Then he lowered his gaze to Susanna.

'What the hell is all that about?'

'It's about having perhaps the best meal in your life.'

A thought struck him. 'Should I wear uniform or a suit and tie?'

'Ask the secretary when she phones. I would certainly polish my shoes.'

He was thoughtful again. 'Put your thinking cap on, Susanna. What the hell is behind all this?'

'I don't know. But my guess is that his interest lies more in the mercenary Creasy than in the Dane.' She had stood up. 'But Elliot, one thing is for sure: you had better go to that lunch fully prepared. You need to know more about this man Creasy.'

'That's true. But if I ask for a more detailed report from the FBI, they'll alert Grainger. I have to find another way.'

She nodded. 'You have to have the advantage of knowledge without the Senator being aware of it.'

'So what do I do?'

'You put a routine inquiry through to Interpol in Paris.'

'Interpol? But he's a mercenary, not necessarily a criminal.'

'Yes, but I read somewhere that for the last couple of decades Interpol have been keeping a registry of all known mercenaries. It's no problem. We often put inquiries through to Interpol, and I doubt if Senator Grainger has any influence there.'

She closed her eyes as the plane screeched onto the runway. No matter how many times she flew, she could never relax during the take-off or landing. A voice from the seat beside her drawled, 'I know how you feel, ma'am. To me it's always a miracle that these damned machines ever get off the ground.'

She opened her eyes and turned her head. From an earlier conversation she knew that he was a Texas oilman. She would have known it anyway. He was all boots and a big brass belt buckle and a friendly courtesy. He helped her off with her bag and invited her to share a taxi into town. She declined politely, not relishing the idea of conversation or an invitation to dinner.

During the half-hour journey she noticed the increased bustle of the city. There were ever more street vendors and Honda mopeds. Capitalism was returning to Vietnam with a vengeance.

Her thoughts turned back to Washington and to Elliot Friedman. Interpol had answered their query within hours. She had watched the fax come off the machine in her office. It had kept coming and coming until more than five yards of it had spilled onto the floor. She had read it in silent fascination and then taken it through to Elliot. After he finished reading it, he looked up and asked: 'You read it?'

'Yes. I'm sorry, I should have brought it through straight away, but I started reading as it came off the machine and I couldn't stop.'

Slowly and thoughtfully, he rolled the paper into a tube. He tapped it on his desk. 'You saw the connection,' he said.

'Yes. Lockerbie, Pam Am 103. Creasy's wife and child were on it. So was Senator Grainger's wife. It's known that some person or organization mounted a revenge attack against the bombers in the Middle East. That fax more or less confirms it. Creasy was involved.'

'He was involved in a lot of things,' Friedman answered grimly. 'An ex French Foreign Legionnaire, then a mercenary in the West African wars in the sixties. And then in Vietnam and Cambodia as an "unofficial" connected to our special forces.'

'The dogtag,' she said.

'The dogtag?'

'Yes, Elliot. That has to be the connection. Maybe he knew Jake Bentsen over there.'

'Let's try and track it down. I want you to scrutinize every unit that Bentsen was attached to. The records will not show if any "unofficials" were attached, but I can use my own unofficial sources to find out.' He grinned. 'Senator James L. Grainger is not the only one with connections.'

The taxi pulled up at the Hotel Continental. Every time she came to Ho Chi Minh City she always decided to stay at a modern hotel, but inevitably she changed her plans at the last minute and booked into the Continental. Her father had stayed there very often during his years in Vietnam. He had told her of its famous veranda and bar and its old colonial atmosphere. It was always a bitter-sweet feeling as she went through the door. Then, after a few minutes, it was better to have the memory and in a strange way feel his presence.

She stood under the old copper showerhead washing her hair and irreverently thinking of the line from *South Pacific*, 'I'm gonna wash that man right out of my hair'. Her boyfriend, the professor Jason, was not really in her hair. Somehow her passion seemed to be on hold. Subconsciously she was waiting for a man to come along: not to sweep her off her feet, but to light some passion that she knew must lie within her. So far it had been dormant. She enjoyed the company of the man, both mentally and physically, but the physical side had always been more or less routine. A social act rather than a blending of the body and the mind. She had watched some of her friends stumble madly into love and then usually out of it. It had never happened to her. Perhaps her mind was too logical, her life too controlled.

She rinsed the shampoo from her hair and soaped her long body. Again, her mind went back to Washington and her boss. Elliot had returned from his lunch with Senator Grainger at The Red Sage and immediately dropped by her office. She had spent the first ten minutes pumping him about the restaurant, the food and the clientele. His gossip was satisfying. He had spotted the Vice-President's wife lunching with an ageing actor, and the Attorney General with a couple of Senators. He was sure it had all been strictly business. Grainger had ordered a plain grilled steak but Elliot had been more adventurous, starting with a wild salmon mousse and going on to duck à l'orange. It had been delicious. At first Grainger had been cautious, obviously sizing up his man. But with the main course he had opened up and talked about his personal life. The conversation had slowly turned to Creasy. It appeared the two men were very close friends. It had begun with their shared tragedy over Lockerbie - indeed, Creasy had mounted a revenge attack partially funded and assisted by Grainger. A couple of years later Creasy had become involved in a sort of war against a white-slave-and-drug ring in France and Italy. Grainger had been able to pull a few strings to help the mercenary during that time. The ring had been destroyed and its leader killed. The Dane Jens Jensen, together with The Owl, had been part of that operation. A year later the daughter of one of Senator Grainger's constituents in Denver had been murdered in Zimbabwe. The local police had made no progress and the dead girl's mother had come to Grainger to ask his help in applying pressure on the State Department to get results. Instead, Grainger had introduced her to Creasy who, in his own way, had extracted justice. Jens Jensen had also been involved. So it was no surprise that the Senator's curiosity had been roused when Elliot had put in a query to the FBI about the Dane.

Elliot had been pacing up and down her small office with a coffee mug in his hand. He stopped, turned and said: 'Susanna, at this point it became obvious to me that the senator holds much affection for this man, Creasy. There and then I took a decision. I told the Senator that for the next few weeks I would routinely be basing one of my officers in Saigon. I suggested that the Senator get in touch with Creasy and inform him that if he needed any help and backup in that city, he could call on our organization in the person of that officer.'

Elliot smiled, and said: 'Who happens to be Susanna Moore.'

She was startled. She had not been due to visit Vietnam for at least three or four months.

'I want you to leave tomorrow,' he said. 'Something in my blood tells me that this could be important. I have a feeling that this man Creasy does not go charging around the world on wild-goose chases.'

She stepped out of the shower and towelled herself down. It was something of a mystery to her. Elliot Friedman was not a man to act on impulse. He had a well-trained logical mind, which is why he was so good at his job. He was also careful with his budget and not given to sending his officers on speculative trips. But then he had given her another nugget of information.

'I checked with my sources,' he said. 'Jake Bentsen went missing in action during a firefight near the Cambodian border on September 24th 1968. It was a Special Forces mission. It so happened that they were accompanied by two unofficials. Of course those guys always used false names. I tracked down the then lieutenant who led that mission. He's now a full colonel. He remembered the mission well, and the two unofficials. One was a Belgian. The other one had French papers and spoke with a slight American accent. His physical description fits that of our man Creasy. Also his actions and demeanour. The colonel remembers that young Jake Bentsen was only twenty-one years old at the time. He tended to keep close to the unofficial who fits Creasy's description.' He took a sip of his coffee and said thoughtfully: 'I see the scenario thus: Bentsen's dogtag was returned mysteriously to his parents in San Diego. They had previously drawn a blank with us. Maybe young Bentsen had mentioned Creasy in his letters from 'Nam. They managed to track him down and now he's on his way back to 'Nam to look for Bentsen or his remains. The point is, Susanna, a man like that can do things that we cannot. He can go places that we could never go. He could ask questions in a way we never could. He might turn something up. He might even throw a light on other MIAs at the same time.'

He gave her a long look and continued: 'So I want you on the scene. Keep your eyes and ears open. And if he does contact you, give him every co-operation.'

She finished drying her dark hair, went into the bathroom and slipped on a lime-green linen dress. She applied a minimum of make-up, and decided to have a pre-dinner cocktail in the bar.

As she walked down the stairs her thoughts turned to her professor back in Washington, and she tried to decide if there was any future in that situation. She tried to decide if Professor Jason Woodward was the man to spend the rest of her life with. Not that he had asked her to marry him. On the contrary, the subject had never arisen, but she knew that he would never leave her. She chuckled mentally, realizing that in a way she was like his rows of dusty books or the old, felt slippers he pulled on when he came home in the evening. She was a fixture in his comfortable, ordered life. As she tried to define her feelings, it dawned on her that she actually loved his mind. She loved the way he looked at a situation or a problem or an event: the way he analysed things without presumptions or suppositions: she loved his fairness. She enjoyed long conversations over dinner when she would act as devil's advocate, trying to probe and provoke. Of course he knew what she was doing and he would give her his gentle smile and argue with a combination of logic and humanity.

In her mind she tried to find a balance between the mental and physical. Was it enough to love a man for his mind, or was it necessary to have the juxtaposition of physical love as well? There had been many times when she wished she did not have physical desires. She had read in a biography of Gandhi how he believed that it was impossible for the mind to develop to its full potential unless the weaknesses of the body had been overcome. By weaknesses he meant sexual urges. He had deliberately cast out sexual urges in order to focus on his life's mission and destiny: but she was no Gandhi. She was a normal, healthy woman who once in a while wanted to climb into bed with a man and make love. It was that simple.

Occasionally she had cast an eye over other men intrinsically looking for a body more than a mind. There was a young lieutenant in the office. She could feel his physical interest in her. He was tall and well-built and gave off a sexual magnetism. He was also as dumb as a brick. She had often thought that she might combine someone like that with her professor; a physical release on the one side and mental stimulation on the other. So far it had been impossible. She had a bottom line in terms of morality. She knew that her professor loved her and in receiving that love, she felt she had the obligation to be faithful.

She reached the ground floor and put the professor from her mind. Tonight was tonight, and tomorrow would be tomorrow.

It was a room that intrigued her. A room full of history. She stood at the door and cast her eyes around and almost turned away. There was not a single woman in there. Most of the men were foreigners, she guessed either businessmen or journalists. The room was hazy with cigarette smoke. She decided to go out onto the veranda and order her drink from there, but as she walked across the room, a voice suddenly stopped her.

'Miss Moore, is it not?'

She turned. There were two of them sitting at a table. Jens Jensen and The Owl.

CHAPTER TWELVE

It was just before ten o'clock at night when the phone rang in the Bentsen household in San Diego. The old couple were watching *Star Trek* on the television. She turned down the sound while he picked up the phone.

She watched as he listened. About three minutes passed, then he said: 'Thank you, and good luck.'

He hung up, turned to her and said: 'That was Creasy. He was phoning from Italy. He's leaving for Vietnam tomorrow. He phoned to keep us informed. He stressed again that the chances are almost zero and that we must not be too hopeful. He will spend a minimum of two weeks in South East Asia. If anything develops, he will phone us immediately.'

She turned back to the television and put up the volume. After a few minutes she said: 'For me, the main thing is that we have now done everything possible. If Creasy cannot find him or discover what happened to him, then I'll accept that he is dead.'

She turned to her husband and gave him a smile that was almost serene. 'In two weeks' time, whatever the outcome, I will sleep a little easier.'

CHAPTER THIRTEEN

She warmed to the Dane. It took a little longer to find any mental communication with The Owl. In fact it took until halfway through dinner. The small Frenchman remained silent during the drinks in the bar and the first part of the meal in the elegant restaurant. Meanwhile she felt as though Jens Jensen was probing her mind and her competence. She was not offended, because he conducted himself and asked his questions with great charm.

He started by telling her that Creasy had phoned him that morning from Naples to tell him that he and his friend Guido would be arriving in Saigon within forty-eight hours. She told him that she would be in town for some time, and would be on hand to give whatever assistance her office could provide.

Then the questions began. The first ones concerned her private life and background. She smiled inwardly and talked about her early life in Boston: the high school years, and then university at Wellesley. She had majored in modern history. She then talked about the disappearance of her father in Vietnam and how she had taken the abrupt decision to make a career in the US Army. Jens listened with amusement as she recounted her early days in boot camp and the sudden transition from a patrician New England family to the rigours of army life.

Meanwhile, The Owl sat silently as though existing in a different world, simply eating the fine food with enthusiasm and sipping at his glass of claret.

The Dane's questions moved on to her present work. He was curious about the structure of the MIA. It was obviously a curiosity born of shared experience. They were very much on common ground. It was work of elusive frustration. A hint here; a scrap of information there; a suggestion from somewhere else. Much of the work involved instinct, guesswork and optimism. Much of the results involved disappointment. She explained that the only results had been in the form of the bones and skeletons. Recent advances in genetic fingerprinting had been a major help; but still, the success rate was less than two per cent.

'Is it worth it?' he asked.

Her answer was an unqualified 'yes'. She explained about her missing father, and what it would mean to her and her mother if one day they could lay his remains to rest at Arlington.

He seemed to understand, and suddenly, so did The Owl. He lifted his head from his rare entrecote steak, and made his first contribution to the conversation.

'Whenever I'm in Marseille, I visit my mother's grave. I clean it and put flowers on it. I was close to her and when I'm there, I still feel close to her.' For the first time he smiled. 'Do you know that in Madagascar, once every few years they dig up their ancestors' skeletons and dress them in fine cloth and take them in a parade around the towns and villages? They make a big party about it and really enjoy themselves. I like that.'

He went back to his steak. She looked up and saw Jens give her a wink. 'I can just see it,' the Dane said. 'The Owl here parading around Marseille with the bones of his parents on his shoulders. They'll lock him up and throw away the key.'

The Owl ignored him. 'Do you like music?' he asked Susanna.

'Yes.'

'What kind?'

'Mostly classical.' She saw the sudden interest in his dark brown eyes.

'Which composers?'

'Mozart, Verdi, Beethoven, and I must confess, Strauss the younger.'

He nodded slowly, and she had the absurd feeling that she had passed an important test. It also seemed that, for different reasons, she had passed the test with the Dane.

'How are your contacts with the government here?' he asked.

'Close, Mr Jensen, for two reasons. First of all they are very anxious to obtain US recognition and a lifting of all sanctions. For my government, such recognition is conditional on their full co-operation on the MIA cases. Secondly, unlike some of my colleagues, I never came here, or to Haiphong, waving a big stick. I took the trouble to get to know them, and to request their help rather than demand it.'

Jens gazed at her across the table and then made a decision. He reached for the briefcase at his feet and took from it a thin brown file. He passed it to her, saying: 'These are brief details on a Vietnamese called Van Luk Wan. In the old days he was a senior policeman in the anti-corruption branch of the Southern regime. Late in he was shot and seriously wounded. I've discovered that he was released from hospital on January 27 1969. I need to know what happened to him and if he is still in Saigon.'

She opened the file and studied the contents, then commented: 'There are three possibilities. He either escaped the country before the fall of Saigon, or he was captured and executed because of his past, or he was sent to a rehabilitation camp, in which case he might still be alive.'

She closed the file and asked: 'Can I keep this?'

The Dane nodded. She said: 'It might be of help if I know why you're looking for him and who shot him back in 1968.'

The Dane glanced at The Owl. Something telepathic may have passed between them, because the Dane answered: 'Creasy shot him and presumed he had killed him. But it turns out that he not only lived; he may have been the man who delivered Jake Bentsen's dogtag to his parents' home in San Diego.'

While she digested that, he went on: 'I doubt that Bentsen is alive.' Another glance at The Owl. 'We think that the dogtag is just a bait to lure Creasy back to South East Asia.'

'You may be right,' she answered; 'and of course Creasy knew Jake Bentsen.'

She saw the brief flicker of surprise in his eyes. 'How could you know that?' he asked.

She leaned forwards and gave him her sweetest smile. 'You're not the only detective in this room, Mr Jensen. Your friend Creasy fought here as an unofficial. I know that it's almost certain he was on that final patrol when Jake Bentsen was presumed killed. The only question I have is why, after all these years, a man like Creasy takes the risk of coming back here to look for a man who was at best, a mere acquaintance. Also why he would go to the considerable expense of sending you and your friend as a vanguard. He's certainly not doing it for payment. I checked out the Bentsens' finances. They are very moderate, certainly not enough to hire a top mercenary and his team.'

There was a heavy silence. Then Jens asked: 'How do you know that?'

'It's my job,' she answered. 'When I'm ordered by my superiors to give co-operation to a man, I like to know who I'm dealing with. There are two things that I'm sure about. One is that Creasy is a very hard human being, and the other is that he is not given to sentimentality. So Mr Jensen, if we're going to get the best out of our co-operation, I suggest that you be completely frank with me . . . What is Creasy's motivation?'

There was a pause while the waiter brought them coffee. Then the Dane said: 'First of all, please call me Jens, and allow me to call you Susanna. As for motivation, I can only guess. And it's not in my nature to share my guesses. Within a couple of days you'll meet Creasy. He may tell you. If he does, I'd be glad if you'd tell me.'

'That's fair enough.' She tapped the file. 'Meanwhile, first thing tomorrow morning, I'll start to look into the possible whereabouts of Mr Van Luk Wan.'

CHAPTER FOURTEEN

Mr Dang Hoang Long was a gentleman in every way, in spite of the fact that he was a dedicated communist. He had been educated at the Sorbonne back in the early fifties and had considered himself to be Francophile until one evening in a Montparnasse café he had found himself in conversation with a group of fellow Vietnamese. One of them had round, thick spectacles and the voice and charisma to cut through sentiment or even logic. He had been introduced as Monsieur Ho.

Later in the night, when the others had departed leaving Dang Hoang Long alone with Mr Ho, they had talked on into the early hours of the morning. Dang was due to return to Saigon and take up a post in the French colonial customs department. Mr Ho questioned him at length about his background, his political beliefs and his aspirations for a future Vietnam. Imperceptibly, Dang had found himself giving answers which surprised him. Answers which would have seriously displeased his French masters.

Finally, Mr Ho had asked for his address in Saigon and written it down in a small black notebook. As they parted outside the café in a misty rain, Dang had asked:

'What is your full name?'

The bespectacled man had turned and said into the mist: 'Ho Chi Minh.'

Four years passed before a man came to Dang's small house on the outskirts of Cholon. By that time Dang had risen through the ranks to become a senior customs officer under the newly independent government of South Vietnam. The man gave Dang a letter, waited until it was read, and then took it back and burned it. The letter had been signed by Ho Chi Minh. At that moment, as he watched the letter being burned, Dang became an agent of the then Viet Minh, and later, when the Americans arrived, an agent for the Viet Cong.

After the fall of Saigon, he was rewarded for his years of service by being promoted to the Politbureau, with special responsibilities for Ho Chi Minh City. Because of his education and his many years of experience with Americans, he found himself handling diplomatic contacts with them in the old South. His directives from Hanoi were clear: We need their recognition, we need their investments, we need their trade and their expertise. Therefore co-operate as far as you can.

The fan in Dang's office circled slowly, barely stirring the humid air. From a Thermos flask he poured a glass of chilled water for his visitor. For some reason she always made him feel paternal. It wasn't just because she was about forty years younger than him. It was her attitude. He felt that she respected him and looked up to him. She had visited his office several times over the past few years and occasionally they had dinner or lunch together. He respected the fact that she had taken the time and trouble to learn his language. He had made a particular effort to try to trace the whereabouts of her father's remains and always regretted his lack of success. He admired the fact that she treated her father's case on an equal footing with the scores of others.

He said: 'Susanna, we now have only eighteen files still open, and they are very obscure. I have to say that we are beginning to lose patience. Surely we have done everything asked of us. During the war more than two million Americans passed through our country. About fifty-two thousand of them were killed or went missing. During the same period many more of your citizens were killed in traffic accidents in America, and even more simply disappeared. What else can we do?'

She had heard such comments many times before, and she sympathized with the ageing man across the desk. 'I can only speak unofficially, Hoang Long, but the buzz around Washington is that recognition is around the corner, and all that follows. I assure you that all my recent reports have been in favour.'

He inclined his head in acknowledgement and asked: 'So what brings you to Saigon this time, and how can I help?'

She passed across a slip of paper, saying: 'I would like either to locate this man or find out what happened to him.'

He read the name and the brief details on the piece of paper, and then looked at her under raised eyebrows. 'Do your agencies now look for missing Vietnamese policeman?'

'It's tangential. He may provide a lead to one of our MIAs.'

He picked up the piece of paper and stood up, saying: 'Because you enjoy Cantonese food, I'm going to take you for lunch at one of our few remaining Chinese restaurants in Cholon. In the meantime, my best assistant will try to track down this Van Luk Wan.'

She decided he was flirting with her and she was not displeased. She knew he was close to seventy-five years old, but his charm was unfaded. With the long serving chopsticks he picked out for her the most succulent pieces of abalone.

'Why have you never married?' he asked.

She looked into his dark eyes, noting the hint of mischief. 'Because nobody ever asked me.'

'That's because you gave them no encouragement . . . I think you are too severe with men.'

'I never found a man I really wanted to encourage.'

'Then you have never cast your net wide enough.'

'Must a woman cast a net to catch a man?'

His voice turned very serious. 'Certainly. But it must be a net with big holes so that the little fish go through it. Only a big one must be caught.'

Equally seriously, she answered: 'Maybe the holes in my net were too wide even for the big fish.'

With a trace of irritation he shook his head. 'I fear, Susanna, that you have cast no net. How old are you?'

She was not surprised by his directness. Although it was unusual for a Vietnamese, she had become used to it with him. Perhaps she had encouraged it. 'I'm thirty-four,' she answered.

He reached forward and picked out another piece of abalone for her, and then gave her a long look. 'You are a captain in your army, so your career is successful. I know that you're well regarded by your superiors. You are attractive and intelligent . . . Have you had many lovers?'

She laughed. The man gave her a stern look. She asked: 'In your mind, Hoang Long, what number would be adequate or appropriate?'

He considered the question, and answered: 'Not less than five and not more than ten.'

She found herself mentally calculating and laughed again. 'You have it exactly right. There have been seven, not counting the drunken one night stand I had on my graduation night.'

'You have no lover at the moment?'

'In a way, but it's mainly cerebral.'

'Which means?'

'Which means we talk a lot and not much else.'

The waiter brought the last dish of chow fan, and again the old man served her. 'You would make a good mother,' he said. 'I know that you made a good daughter. The one follows the other.

This Vietnamese is very unhappy that your father lost his life and his presence in this country. I would like you to find happiness here. Our country has seen too much grief and blood. It is time we gave it a little happiness.'

She was disconcerted both by his words and by their sincerity. She glanced around the almost empty restaurant and saw the young woman come to the door. She watched as the woman crossed the room and handed an envelope to Dang, uttered a few words and left.

The waiter served tea while Dang opened the envelope and read from the two pages. She saw his ironic smile, then he looked up and asked her: 'Does the date 30 April 1975 mean anything to you?'

'Of course. That was the day the South Vietnamese government surrendered.'

'Yes,' he said. 'That was the day that the last Americans were helicoptered out from the roof of the US Embassy together with the ambassador and of course, his dog. There were many thousands of Vietnamese puppets pounding on the Embassy gates trying to get in. It seems that one of them was your friend, Van Luk Wan. He didn't make it. Together with many others he was arrested by the Vietnamese Patriotic Army.' He was looking down at the two pages spread in front of him. 'He claimed to be a minor functionary in the Duong Van Minh regime, and at first was sent to a detention camp in the mountains. It was then discovered that he had been a senior police officer in that same regime and he was returned to Ho Chi Minh City for interrogation.'

'And I suppose, subsequently executed,' she said.

He shook his head. 'I would have assumed that. He committed many crimes against the Vietnamese people and at that time, there was an understandable thirst for vengeance.' He looked up at her. 'Your Mr Wan was not executed. He was, in a way, ransomed.'

'Ransomed?'

'Yes. There was massive corruption in Saigon under the old regime. Regrettably, some of that corruption continued afterwards and remains to this day. A bribe was paid, a very large one. And Van Luk Wan was allowed to leave the country.'

'Where did he go?'

The old man looked down again at the paper. 'He was traded across the Cambodian border.'

She took a sip of her almost cold tea, then asked: 'Can you tell me anything more, Hoang Long?'

She could detect his air of embarrassment. He said: 'You have to understand, Susanna, they were strange times. Then as now, money talked. It appears that Van Luk Wan had a strong business connection with a man who traded in our country during the war. He was a very evil man. He bribed both Americans and Vietnamese. This report indicates that he also bribed some communist cadres after the fall of Saigon. The indication is that he was the man who paid one kilo of gold to get Van Luk Wan released.'

'What was his name?'

'His name was Bill Crum.'

She took a tri-shaw from the restaurant. It wove its way through the narrow, crowded streets of Cholon and then across the river into the equally chaotic streets of downtown Saigon. She was buzzing with excitement. Perhaps it was brought about by her competitive spirit. The detective Jens Jensen had given her a longshot of a query, and less than twenty-four hours later she had obtained the answer. She was impatient to present her accomplishment. She tapped her fingers on the armrest as the tri-shaw squeezed its way through the traffic to the hotel.

At the hotel reception desk, she glanced at the rows of keyboxes. Jensen was in room 36. The key was not there. She did not wait for the lift but ran up the two flights of stairs and rapped sharply on the door. She had composed a little speech in her mind. She would be nonchalant and simply give her information as though it were the slightest of gifts.

The door opened. She looked up, and then looked up a little higher. She was staring into a face that reflected a miasma of mystery and menace. Then, somehow, the menace was dissipated. She saw the deep-set eyes and the scars, and she found her voice.

'Mr Creasy, I presume?'

His voice was low and strangely reassuring. 'Yes. You must be Susanna Moore.'

CHAPTER FIFTEEN

She felt like an outsider. She also had the absurd feeling of being a schoolgirl reading out a report to a bunch of teachers.

They had all gone down to the bar and sat at a circular table in the corner. Creasy was directly opposite her, with his Italian friend Guido to his right. Jens and The Owl sat on either side of them. They drank beer and she drank coffee.

She felt an outsider because there was a palpable bond between the four men. They were easy with each other as though they were among family. As they waited for the drinks she listened to their conversation. They talked and joked about old friends and past times. It was not as though she was deliberately excluded; she just felt there was an invisible sheet of plate glass between her world and theirs. She felt a sudden loneliness and to get away from it, she studied the four men.

Creasy and Guido were alike, though at first sight the Italian had appeared to be simply, lazily handsome. His thick black hair was greying at the temples. His tanned face was lined in exactly the right places. His smile was easy. He wore a black, silk polo neck shirt and black slacks. He could have stepped right out of Giorgio Armani's show room. When he looked at her, he was seeing a face and a body. When Creasy looked at her, she had the feeling that he was watching only her mind.

The Owl was his usual silent self, observing and listening. The Dane had set up his computer and was studying the green screen.

He glanced up at her and said in an informal voice: 'Please proceed, Susanna.'

She started to recount the conversation with Dang Hoang Long and Creasy asked: 'What language were you using?'

'Vietnamese,' she answered.

'Do you speak it well?'

'Fluently.'

'What other languages do you have?'

'Good French and passable Cambodian.'

His face remained impassive, but she noticed his glance at Guido. She continued her report, still feeling a bit like a schoolgirl. In some ways, she was junior to these men; obviously in age, and certainly in experience. She was well informed about their backgrounds and although she was a confident woman, she could not dispel the feeling of nervousness.

They listened for a few minutes in silence, and then Guido interrupted to ask about the background of Dang Hoang Long. She gave a thumbnail sketch including his watershed meeting with Ho Chi Minh in Paris. As she spoke, Jens was tapping the information into his computer.

'Why does he trust you?' Creasy asked.

'Because I've always been honest with him, and unlike many Americans, I do not treat him, or other Asians, with condescension.'

'It's a good attitude,' he said. 'I can't think why any American should treat a Vietnamese with anything less than full respect. After all, they took on the mightiest military machine in the world and defeated it.'

She could not help herself. She said: 'You were part of that machine.'

He smiled. It was only a brief movement of his lips. He said: 'Yes, for a short time I was. And I have to say that it was an education. I came here from the wars in West Africa and even though the Viet Minh had beaten the French, I still tended to look on the Vietnamese as inferior soldiers. I was quickly disabused of that notion. When it comes to jungle warfare, only the Japanese or the Ghurkas are their equals . . . Please continue.'

She explained how Van Luk Wan had first been detained by the victorious North Vietnamese and later ransomed for a kilo of gold. Creasy leaned forward and asked: 'Do you know who provided the gold?'

'Yes, a Chinese-American called Bill Crum.'

Creasy had a poker face, but she saw the flicker in his eyes as he sat back in his chair. She asked: 'Do you know him?'

Creasy was looking over her shoulder far into the distance. His mind was obviously back into history.

She repeated the question, and he slowly nodded.

'Yes. Bill Crum is probably the most evil man I ever met - and I've met many . . .' He glanced again at Guido, who was watching him with interest. 'I've done a few things in my life which I regret. I guess we all have. But on a cold night in early 1977 I did something of which I'm proud . . . I killed a monster called Bill Crum. I killed him in a converted temple in the New Territories of Hong Kong and I burned him and the temple until nothing was left.'

Jens stopped tapping the keys of his computer. He was looking at Creasy in fascination. He said: 'You had left Vietnam ten years earlier. Why did you kill him?"

'It was a job,' Creasy answered. 'I was hired to do it. I don't normally do jobs like that, I'm not a hit-man, but on this occasion, it was a pleasure.'

'Who hired you?' Susanna asked.

He studied her across the table and then answered: 'An American group.'

The reaction was automatic. 'My government does not hire assassins!'

Both Creasy and Guido laughed and she felt her anger rising. 'That kind of thing may have happened back in the sixties, but since the early seventies our policy has been strictly against it.'

Again the two mercenaries laughed, and Guido commented: 'Since John F. Kennedy, the policy of every US President has been not to issue executive orders for assassinations under any circumstance; but Miss Moore, sometimes they use what we call in the business "Becket approval".'

'What do you mean?'

The Italian leaned forward. 'Do you know who Thomas à Becket was and how he died?'

She felt he was being condescending, and the level of her anger rose further. 'Yes, Mr Arrellio, I do have an education.'

Guido inclined his head in acknowledgement. He said: 'Then you'll know that when Thomas à Becket was being a nuisance to his king, the king commented to his knights: "Who will rid me of this turbulent priest?" Four knights promptly rode off to Canterbury Cathedral and ran their swords through Thomas à Becket. The king claimed to be dismayed. In present times, when a US President is having problems with a foreign leader, it has often been the case that he might mumble to his Chief of Staff or National Security Adviser or the Director of the CIA something like: "I wish to God that bastard would go away!" Of course it's not an executive order and of course the President would be horrified to think that he had given any encouragement.' The Italian smiled. 'But in the business it's called a "Becket decision" ... Console yourself with the fact that it's not only US Presidents who have, and will use, such moral armour.'

Looking at Creasy, she asked: 'How much did the CIA pay you to kill Bill Crum?'

His answer was direct. 'It was not the CIA. It was a group of senior American officers who were being blackmailed by that gentleman. They paid me two hundred thousand Swiss francs, which in those days was a lot of money. But then, part of the job was to destroy all the documents in that temple. I read those documents before I burned them. It was not edifying reading.'

Her anger had been replaced by massive curiosity. 'Are you saying that there was a lot of corruption in the US Armed Forces during the Vietnam War?'

He nodded. 'More than you'd ever guess. Since you're a student of history, you might know that by the end of the sixties a vast industry had grown up in and around the major US bases in Vietnam. The weekly turnover of the PX was greater than that of Sears Roebuck. It ran into hundreds of millions of dollars a month. Those bases became huge department stores, selling everything from women's underwear to hi-fi sets. One Hong Kong Chinese tailor had more than twenty retail outlets on the US bases. They even had night clubs with Filipino bands and Australian strippers. It was like a giant spider's web, and the spider in the middle was Bill Crum. He controlled everything from drugs and women to whisky. He operated from a villa on the outskirts of Saigon and in that villa, he lavishly entertained a great number of senior US Army officers, especially those involved with supply. It was said that Bill Crum could supply anything from a case of condoms to a brand new Abrams tank. He had girls in that villa, and drugs, and what was known as Vietnamese gold, which came in paper-thin strips. It could be moulded inside belts or suitcases or shoes. He also had a recording system which would have impressed Richard Nixon. When the war ended, he retired to Hong Kong, bought himself a yacht marina in the New Territories and converted a disused temple as a home. Naturally, he took with him his collection of documents, photographs and tapes. The problems started in the mid-seventies, when some investigative journalists from the NBC Sixty Minutes programme began to home in on him. Bill Crum was an American citizen, and the US Justice Department started extradition proceedings. It was then that Bill Crum applied pressure on certain very senior American generals, and I was hired to eliminate Bill Crum and all the proof . . . I have to say that I did a good job.'

Susanna believed him. There was no reason why he should lie. Jens looked up from his computer screen and asked Creasy: 'So what was the connection between Bill Crum and Van Luk Wan?'

'It's obvious. Van must have been working for him. In his own evil way, Bill Crum must have had loyalities and, for him, a kilo of gold was peanuts.'

Guido said: 'If Bill Crum were alive, he would be the one to have baited the trap for you. Did he have any relatives?'

'Only one. He had a daughter by a Cambodian woman. He doted on her. She was an only child.'

'Did she know it was you who killed him?' Guido asked.

'I would not have thought so. But then, looking back, I got a few things wrong. I assumed that Jake Bentsen was killed in that firefight. I also assumed that Van Luk Wan died from that bullet I put into his chest. So maybe she did know who killed her father.'

'Do you know where she is now?' Susanna asked.

Creasy pushed himself to his feet, saying: 'I've got no idea. But maybe we should start trying to find out.'

They all stood up. The Dane asked: 'Do we have a name for her?'

Creasy said: 'She was called Connie, after Bill Crum's mother.' He looked at Susanna and said: 'You've been of great help, Miss Moore, and we appreciate it. I hope you'll join us for dinner tonight. Afterwards, we'll look up some of the haunts that I frequented back in the old days, if any are still left. Maybe we'll hear a whisper or two.'

'I'd be glad to join you,' she answered diffidently. 'But maybe you guys prefer to be on your own.'

It was Guido who provided the answer. 'Come with us, and keep us out of trouble.'

CHAPTER SIXTEEN

'He's hooked!'

Van Luk Wan's face radiated malicious pleasure. Connie Crum asked: 'Are you sure?'

'Positive. My people spotted him coming through Tan Son Nut airport yesterday. I checked with immigration. He used his own name. He was accompanied by a man called Guido Arrellio. Immigration details show that he's an Italian from Naples.'

'Yes, I know about Guido Arrellio. He's Creasy's closest friend. They were in the Legion together, and later formed a mercenary partnership.'

She was silent in thought. Van asked: 'Is he also a dangerous man?'

'Yes, very. But from my information he has been retired for some years. The fact that he's been travelling with Creasy may mean that Creasy suspects he's walking into a trap. In that case Guido Arrellio may not be the only one on the scene. We have to be very careful. That bastard Creasy is not one to travel blind.' She gave Van a hard look. 'Are you sure that the man you have following Creasy is good?'

Van's voice was reassuring. 'Connie, he's the best. Very experienced. I cannot understand this part of your plan. You want Creasy to notice him and then pick him up and beat information out of him. Information we have planted. Of course the follower does not know this plan. He thinks he's just being well paid for doing a big job. The preparation was very good. He travelled to Chek and was allowed to see a little bit of our operation. He also saw the "American" at a distance, wearing foot shackles. He heard me giving orders about the American. About an area I wanted cleared of mines. He was very impressed that we had an American. I told him that we had several.'

Connie smiled. 'All true, of course. How did the Dutchman feel about having to wear those shackles?'

Van grinned. 'He was nervous. At first he refused, but I explained it would only be for a few minutes and that afterwards, he could spend an hour with Tan Sotho.'

'It's good,' Connie agreed. 'Creasy will pick him up and learn that there are Americans in that area. You are sure that the Dutchman was not close enough so that the follower could give an accurate description?'

'No. I just had him shuffle around the compound about a hundred metres away with his face in profile. The description will be of a tall, bearded, sunburnt Caucasian between forty and fifty years old.'

'It's good,' Connie repeated. 'So what's wrong with my plan?'

Van sighed and said: 'I keep telling you my man is probably the best follower in Saigon or even South East Asia. He's an ex-Intelligence officer specializing in such work. Creasy is just a mercenary. What would he know of such things? Why don't you let me put some clumsy idiot to follow Creasy, with the same information?'

Connie Crum leaned forward and said: it's one of the reasons why you work for me instead of me working for you. It's a question of never underestimating the enemy and always thinking three times before making a move. Now understand, Van, I've heard that Creasy has a sixth sense about being followed. If we sent an idiot to follow him, he'd suspect that it was a plant, and he'd be more suspicious than he is now. He would doubt the information that he extracted. On the other hand, we sent the best possible. It might take a few days for Creasy to spot him, but he will. He'll recognize an expert. And he will believe the information. The only problem is if Creasy decides not to pick up the follower. He's quite capable of just giving him the slip and disappearing.'

'Don't worry,' Van said. 'I have informers in the Continental Hotel and in most bars where he might go. They all have his photograph. We will know the moment that he leaves for Cambodia.' His voice dropped almost to a whisper and it was loaded with hatred. 'I can see his face now. It's printed on my brain. He was so confident that he fired without sighting the pistol. His face had no expression as he squeezed the trigger. He looked at me as though he was shooting a mangy dog. In his mind he was killing me for the sake of a cheap little tart. He was behaving like God, handing out his own idea of justice. One millimetre to the left, and I would have died. He shot me down and walked away.' He looked across the bare wooden table. 'Connie, I want you to make me a prom- ise, on the memory of your father. When we have Creasy, I want one hour with him alone. One hour, before you start on him.'

She stood up, brushing the dust from her backside. He followed her to the door of the wooden shack and watched as she opened the door of the Isuzu jeep.

She turned and said: 'Don't worry, Van. You'll see him suffer.'

'That I want to see . . . Where are you going now?'

She turned to look towards the west, and stretched like a cat awaking from a long sleep. 'I'm going to spend the night in Bangkok. I have an excitement in me and it must be satisfied.' Her eyes narrowed at the thought that was in her mind. 'I will take a suite at the Oriental Hotel, looking out over the river. I'll have a whirlpool bath and a strong, sensuous massage. Then in the early evening I'll put on a dress by Lagerfeld, long and clean, with noth- ing between it and my skin. I'll put Joy perfume behind my ears and below my belly button and a little lower. Then I will go down to the bar and order a champagne cocktail. There will be many Western businessmen there. They always have a drink before they go out to find a girl. I'll pick two of them.' She smiled at the thought. 'They will think they have died and gone to Heaven. I'll take them up to my suite and they will do things to me according to my wishes and my fantasies.' She held up her hands with their long, strong, red-tipped fingers. 'I will use the whole of my body on them, including my fingers.'

She climbed into the jeep and asked: 'And what will you be doing?'

He was breathing deeply. He said: 'I think I'll go and see Tan Sotho.'

CHAPTER SEVENTEEN

The bar had an unpronounceable name in Vietnamese. The sign outside was in English: 'Mai Man Bar'. It had been an old haunt for Creasy and several other unofficials during the war. He was surprised that it had survived.

He sat on a stool at the end of the bar chatting with the aged owner, 'Billy' Nguyen Huy Cuong. Guido, Jens, The Owl and Susanna sat at a corner table in the smoke-filled room. Guido was teaching them a particularly vicious form of liar dice.

It had been an interesting evening. Creasy had discovered that most of the old bars and hangouts had closed up immediately after the North Vietnamese takeover. But as the regime had become more pliable, new establishments had opened up. They had called in at several cafés and bars and Creasy had looked for familiar faces but found none. Finally he had asked the taxi driver if any of the old bars had survived and learned that 'Mai Man Bar' had never closed.

'How did you manage to stay open here?' he asked the owner.

'Billy' gave him thirty seconds of inscrutable Oriental silence, and then abruptly grinned and winked. He leaned forward.

'Because, my friend Creasy, during all the years of the Vietnam War I was a Viet Cong informer. During all the years that you guys drank in here, I used to listen to your conversations about where you had been and where you were going. I passed on that information to my Viet Cong contact. It's why a lot of those unofficials never came back from their patrols. When the North took over, I was rewarded by being allowed to keep my bar open.'

Creasy digested that, and then said: 'You let those guys give good money for your drinks and then betrayed them?'

'Oh, yes. On the whole, they were the scum of the earth being well paid to kill my people. There were rare exceptions, and you were one of them, Creasy. You never looked down on the Vietnamese. You never tortured them. You never killed anyone who wasn't trying to kill you. That was your reputation and the reason why I never betrayed you, but I have to be honest: you never gave me a chance to betray you. The others liked to boast about what they were doing and how many Viet Cong they had killed, and even how many village women and girls they had raped. You never talked about that. So you're welcome back in this bar.'

'I was no saint, Billy.'

The bar owner laughed. 'In those days this country had no saints on either side. It was just collective madness and evil.' He shrugged. 'We don't have many saints here even now; the ideals of communism were lost within a couple of years. Now we have the same corruption and the same greed. I'm seventy-five years old, Creasy, and I've never met a saint.'

Creasy took a sip of his drink and glanced at the corner table. The men were engrossed in their game of dice, but the woman was watching him. Their eyes locked for a moment; then he turned back to Billy and said: 'Talking about corruption, do you remember a policeman called Van Luk Wan?'

'Of course I do. He was the most evil of all. I heard a rumour that you shot him before you left, but he survived.'

'The rumour is true. You know where he is now?'

'For sure, he's not in Vietnam. I heard he somehow escaped.'

Creasy took a sip of his drink and then pulled out a ten-thousand-dong note and passed it across the bar. He said: 'I would be very interested in finding out where he might be now.'

The old man pushed the note back, saying: 'I will ask around. Keep your money, Creasy, for old times. Where are you staying?'

'At the Continental, Room 212. Thanks, Billy. I didn't have many good memories of Vietnam; but you're one of them.'

He picked up his glass and walked through the crowded room to the corner table. As he sat down, he glanced at Jens and The Owl and then at Susanna. He said: 'A word of severe warning: Guido has been teaching you Mexican liar dice. It looks ridiculously simple, but it takes a lifetime to play it with expertise. After a couple more sessions, Guido will start flattering you; telling you how well you play, that your gift is natural. Then he will discreetly suggest that you start playing for money instead of matchsticks. At first, just for a few cents, and of course he'll lose. He'll continue to lose for a few sessions, and the flattery will multiply until you think that you're reincarnated Einsteins and then he'll clean you out.'

He looked at his friend, who sighed dramatically and said. 'In this kind of work, a lot of time is spent sitting around. I just wanted to help pass the time.'

Creasy patted him on the shoulder. 'Of course, Guido. Just like you teach amateurs to play stud poker and backgammon. You missed your vocation. You should have been a schoolmaster.'

Guido did not answer. He was staring over Creasy's shoulder at the other side of the room. He said: 'I think we're being followed.'

Creasy did not look around. He nodded slightly and said: 'I spotted him at the last two bars.' Suddenly he hissed to Susanna, who was turning her head. 'Don't look. Just act normally.'

Jens said: 'He's probably local security. After all, this is a communist country and they're bound to keep an eye on independent travellers.'

'Maybe,' Creasy said. 'But if somebody has lured us to this country, then he could be working for them.'

'So what do we do?' Susanna asked.

'We do nothing. Just act normal.' He gave her an appraising look. 'This friend of yours, Dang Hoang Long. Do you think you could arrange for me to meet him?'

She thought about it and then answered: 'I don't see why not. I'll call him in the morning.'

Creasy glanced at his watch and said: 'It's been a long night. Let's head back to the hotel.'

Susanna had brought a light cardigan with her. As they stood up Creasy lifted it from the back of her chair and helped her on with it. She felt that it was an uncommon courtesy in this modern world. By now she had decided that he was an uncommon man.

CHAPTER EIGHTEEN

Creasy was a cautious man, especially when it came to forming an opinion on people: he was wary of instinct. But he could not help liking Dang Hoang Long. He had been shown into the old man's office five minutes earlier. The meeting had followed traditional Vietnamese courtesies; first a handshake, followed by cups of tea and sweet, sticky cakes. He expressed his appreciation for being allowed the interview.

Dang stated: 'I consider Susanna Moore to be a friend. Of course I had to grant her request. However, before doing so I asked her to give me a description of your background. I have to be honest and tell you, Mr Creasy, that you're not the kind of man I admire. You kill for money. The vast majority of Americans who came to kill Vietnamese had no choice. They were young men, almost boys. They came to our country by order of their government. They came frightened, and those who went home carried physical and mental scars that will stay with them all their lives. You, on the other hand, came by choice. You came for money.'

Creasy looked him in the eye and answered: 'I am what I am, but I came this time for a different reason. I came to look for one of those boys whose government sent them here. No one is paying me.'

The old man took a sip of his tea and asked: 'Are you telling me that you have a conscience?'

Creasy shrugged. 'That's not a word I ever thought about. Do you have a conscience, Mr Dang?'

'I like to think so.'

Creasy leaned forward and said flatly: 'Are the boat people on your conscience? Are the tens of thousands of your people who were tortured and brutalized in your so-called "re-education camps" on your conscience?'

The old man nodded. 'Yes, they are. Even though I'm a very high ranking official in my government, I had no power to stop the abuses . . . But they are on my conscience, Mr Creasy.'

Creasy sat back in his chair and stated: 'I believe you, and I will ask you in turn to believe that if I knew what a conscience really was, then I hope I have one too.'

Dang Hoang Long finally smiled. Even though the smile added more lines to his face, it made it look much younger. They had found a rapport.

'Are you having me followed?' Creasy asked.

'Of course.'

'Is he a young man with a broken nose and a scar on his forehead?'

Dang shook his head. 'No. The two people I have been using are women.' He raised an eyebrow. 'Don't you think it's strange, Mr Creasy, that when a man thinks he's being followed or watched, he always assumes that it must be another man? I always use women. Did you spot them?'

'I spotted one. Long hair, riding a new Honda moped, a blue shirt and jeans, Nike trainers. Good body.'

The old man was nodding. He said: 'She will be reprimanded. Now what can I do for you, Mr Creasy?'

'I would just like your opinion,' Creasy answered. 'You know from Miss Moore that I'm interested in a man called Van Luk

Wan. Is it possible that he's in Vietnam and if not, is it possible that he has a network of people here?'

The old man answered immediately: 'As to the first, it's doubtful, and as to the second, it's probable. Since I spoke to Susanna yesterday, I've been making more inquiries about Van Luk Wan. It's rumoured that he's in Cambodia and linked to the Khmer Rouge. He handles some of their business affairs. I do not think he'll risk coming back into Vietnam himself, but he certainly has contacts here. Perhaps your man with the broken nose and the scar belongs to him.'

Creasy stood up and held out his hand, saying: 'I'm grateful for your advice. In return for your help, I give you my word that I'll keep you informed of what I do and learn, either directly or through your friend, Susanna.'

Dang also stood up. They shook hands formally, and the Vietnamese said: 'I believe you. I'll call off my surveillance people. If you spot anyone following you, they'll not belong to me . . . Meanwhile, in some ways this is still a dangerous country, and Cambodia is even more so. I want you to watch over Susanna. She's a fine woman.' 'I'll take care of her.'

CHAPTER NINETEEN

It was the first time and it made Susanna Moore very nervous. With all the travelling and the excitement of meeting a different breed of men, it was not surprising that she had not noticed. It was only that morning when she went to take her shower and opened her toilet bag that she saw the large box of Tampax. She had packed it in Washington knowing that her period was due. Ever since puberty, she had been as regular as a Rolex.

She immediately went back into the bedroom and checked her diary. She was four days late. She sat on the bed and tried to think back, and realized that it was just possible. It had been three weeks since she last made love to her professor. For the last couple of years they had never bothered to take precautions during their rare lovemaking. Pregnancy had seemed so remote. She tried to reassure herself: maybe it was the travelling and change of climate and diet that had delayed her period. Then she felt an urgency verging on panic. She knew there was a modern drugstore on Thu Do Street. She was there in ten minutes buying a pregnancy test, and, fifteen minutes later, back in her hotel room, was studying the little stick with its two panels.

The top panel was blue, and she knew that if the bottom panel also turned blue, she was in an interesting condition. Very slowly the colour changed and she let out a deep breath: it was blue. She sat there for several minutes, then phoned down to room service and ordered a pot of coffee. She felt very strange. It was as though her body had been invaded.

She had always pushed the thought of children out of her mind. She was old-fashioned in that way: for her, children came with a happy, settled marriage. Of course she realized that at the age of thirty-four she only had a few more years to find herself in a happily married state, and as she sat on that bed in her Saigon hotel room, the prospects did not look encouraging. In the first place she was not sure about spending the rest of her life with her professor. She had never even considered him as a lifelong partner. It had somehow just drifted on. Since leaving Washington he had hardly entered her thoughts. Too much was happening, too many impressions, and she had to admit it; too much attraction to the man called Creasy.

She put down the tell-tale stick, stood up and started pacing the room. Her options were stark: either fly home and have an abortion, or become a mother. She tried to perceive herself as a mother. The picture was very blurred.

She spent half an hour trying to clarify those options and give them an element of human consideration. Then she decided that the putative father should also consider the options. She looked at her watch and calculated that it would be just after eight o'clock in the evening in Washington. Jason would be home. He always ate his evening meal at seven o'clock precisely. About now he would be lighting his pipe and putting up his feet to watch the news on TV. She gave him fifteen minutes to digest his dinner and the world's events, and then picked up the phone.

His voice was warm. She could picture him in the leather chair in the book-lined room, the telephone in one hand and his pipe in the other. Probably his cat, Thomas, was lying asleep on his lap. She felt a sudden surge of affection combined with a longing for the simple uncomplicated things in life.

After a few minutes of chatter, she simply stated: 'Jason, I've just discovered that I'm pregnant.'

The silence went on for so long that she began to think she had lost the connection. Then his low voice came, as though discussing a conspiracy: 'Are you sure?'

'Yes.'

'You've seen a doctor?'

'No, I bought a testing kit from a drugstore here. It proved positive.'

His voice went lower. 'You can buy those things in Vietnam?'

'Of course. I'm not in the middle of a jungle. This is a modern city.'

Another long silence and then, with anxiety in his voice, he asked: 'What are you going to do?'

'It's why I called you,' she said. 'We have two choices.' Unconsciously, she had emphasized the word 'we'. 'I either fly back and have an immediate abortion, or we keep the baby.'

She could hear his breathing down the line. Then he asked: 'What do you want to do?'

'I don't know. I only found out an hour ago. That's why I'm calling you. I wanted to get your reaction.'

Suddenly his voice became brusque. 'Susanna, we have to think about this in a logical way. I'm sorry that it happened. Obviously, two mature people like us, we should have taken precautions. A child at this time of life would be disruptive to say the least. You must think about your career. You're approaching the age when promotion to major is a very strong possibility. You must consider how much a child would tie you down. I know that it's a modern thing these days for a career woman to be a single parent, but I'm personally against the idea.'

She felt the anger wash over her, but she controlled her voice. 'Jason, you would be the father of that child. Of course I have the right to make my choice; but since it's your seed that is inside me, I thought it was only civilized to inform you before I made that choice.'

Another silence. Then he said: 'It's very important not to get emotional. Of course I understand that you're in a foreign city and not among friends. You did the right thing to call me. My advice is you fly back to Washington. I'll arrange a private clinic.'

The anger was like a cold stone in her stomach. She said: 'I'll think about it for a couple of weeks.'

She hung up and lost control. The tears poured unattended down her face and her shoulders shook uncontrollably. She had wanted warm words, whatever the advice. She had wanted understanding and compassion. Instead she got the cold logic of a man terrified of losing his status quo. She felt unbearably lonely.

CHAPTER TWENTY

'He's good,' Guido said. 'Very good.'

Creasy nodded in agreement.

'And he's not working for the authorities. So he's working for whoever set the bait.'

They were sitting in a pavement café on Hoa Dai Street. It was a scene of the days even before the Americans; the days when Vietnam was a French colony, and Saigon was regarded as the Paris of the East. They had breakfasted on good coffee and croissants and admired the skill of the man who had been following them for the past two days.

'He's a pro,' Creasy said. 'And he works alone. His disguises are minimal but effective. And he even changes the way he walks. Yesterday he had a limp. Today he walks normally. He never looks directly at us. He varies his distance and sometimes he just vanishes, but always turns up again. He's a pro.' There was genuine admiration in Creasy's voice.

'So what do we do about him?' Guido asked.

Creasy took a thoughtful sip of coffee and glanced again at the reflection in the plate glass window of the café. The man was sitting at a foodstore on the other side of the busy road, eating from a bowl of noodles. He wore baggy black trousers, a white T-shirt and a black, flat cap. He wore the old-style sandals made from car tyres. He melted into his milieu.

'We pick him up tonight,' Creasy said. 'We'll find out who sent him. We need to hire a car this afternoon.' He was glancing up and down the street. 'It's a strange thing,' he said. 'I never liked Saigon. It was a whore of a city in every sense. The locals sucked the blood from the Americans like a million vampires, and the Americans enjoyed it. They thought they were the masters in a sea of slaves, but it was the other way around. Deep down, nobody likes to be a whore, no matter what the rewards. There is nothing without pride. The mood is different now. Of course the Vietnamese love to trade and they are damned good at it. Of course there are still whores, and there will be more as capitalism takes over, but it's different. There is no coercion. It's a strange kind of feeling.'

Guido looked at his friend quizzically. It was not often that Creasy waxed philosophical. At least not openly. He decided to take advantage of the moment. He asked: 'What are we doing here, Creasy?'

His friend glanced at him in surprise. 'You know damn well what we're doing here. We're looking for a guy who's almost surely dead.'

Guido shook his head. 'I mean, what are we really doing here? This Jake Bentsen thing is hardly serious. At least not serious enough for you to go charging around the world, spending all that money . . . Your own money.'

Creasy lifted a hand and a waiter loomed up. Creasy gestured at the empty coffee pot and the waiter took it away. Creasy continued to gaze at the street scene until the waiter returned with a full pot. Creasy filled up both their cups and then added two lumps of sugar to his own coffee. He stirred it for a long time, and then said: 'It's a strange thing, Guido. Up until a couple of years ago I never took sugar in my coffee. I hated the taste of it. Then one night in a restaurant in Gozo the waiter gave me the wrong cup. It had sugar in it. I tasted it . . . and liked it.'

'So?'

'So things change.' He gestured. 'Saigon has changed. People change. Maybe I've changed.'

Guido grinned at him. 'You mean, you've become sweeter?'

Creasy did not smile. He said: 'Maybe I do things for different reasons these days. It's possible that I've become more curious. I'm here because I want to know who's after me and why. I guess I got a little tired of sitting in the sun in Gozo. It's why I was in Brussels in the first place. Subconsciously I was looking for some action but the options didn't appeal very much. There was a job in Bosnia. It paid well but I decided the hell with it. First of all, I have a big enough stake to last the rest of my life, and second, I felt no great desire to shoot up Serbs, Croatians or Muslims. I figure they ought to let those savages work it out by themselves. They've been doing it for a couple of thousand years. Then there were some Portuguese idiots who were trying to hire a group to go down to Angola and help Savimbe have one last crack at the government.' He snorted in derision. 'Angola, for Christ's sake! We fought there twenty years ago. It seems like it was the last century.' He took a sip of his coffee and then added another lump of sugar and gave Guido a rare smile. 'So I'm really here out of curiosity . . . Why are you really here, Guido?'

The Italian shrugged. 'I guess I was bored. I got tired of serving the same customers in the restaurant and watching the same football on TV and the same corrupt politicians with innocent faces and fat pockets.' He paused for a moment, then looked up at Creasy and said: 'Maybe I was a bit lonely. When you told me you were coming out to Asia on a mission, I thought of the old times. There were good and there were bad, but they weren't boring.' He leaned forward and almost imperceptibly jerked his head in the direction of the follower. 'So how do we take this pro tonight?'

Creasy also leaned forward. He said: 'You ask him very politely to take a car ride with you.'

Guido grinned. 'I'm always polite.'

They both looked up and then stood as they saw Susanna approach across the street, with Jens and The Owl in her wake. Creasy pulled out a chair for her. She sat down with a sigh and fanned her face with her hand.

'The heat gets to me,' she said. 'Will this place have an iced drink?'

She was wearing a lime-green, short-sleeved dress cut square across her chest. Fine beads of perspiration glinted on her shoulders and arms. Creasy beckoned for a waiter and ordered her a large, fresh orange juice on the rocks. The others ordered beer. Creasy turned to the Dane and said: 'Jens, perhaps you would look after Susanna tonight. I need to borrow The Owl.'

'It'll be a pleasure,' Jens replied. 'What's happening?'

'We're going to pick up the follower and ask him who he's working for. I know from Dang Hoang Long that he's not working for the authorities. So whoever sent him is almost certainly the person who lured us here in the first place. It's better if you and Susanna eat in the hotel tonight and stay there until we return.'

'You think he'll talk?' Susanna asked.

Creasy glanced at Guido and then answered: 'We shall persuade him to do so.'

'You'll torture him?'

Guido leaned forward. He said: 'It's not likely that we will need to. We use psychology in such things.'

'And if psychology doesn't work?'

Creasy said: 'We'll cross that bridge when we come to it. One thing is sure: we'll need to know who sent him. Otherwise we're at a dead end.'

Jens had been deep in thought. He lifted his head and said: 'Creasy, maybe he's a plant who may have disinformation.'

Creasy thought about that for just a moment and then shook his head. 'It's faintly possible, but not probable. If they wanted to plant disinformation, they would not have sent such a professional. They picked a man whom they did not expect to be noticed or caught. I think he's genuine. Anyway, we'll find out tonight.'

The drinks arrived. Susanna picked up the tall, frosted glass and rolled it across her forehead before draining half of the contents. Then she looked at Creasy and said: 'What if he doesn't speak English? After all, he's only in his thirties and it's been more than twenty years since the Americans left. Not many of the youngsters here speak English unless they work in specialist positions with the government. Since he's not working for the government, he might not speak English. How is your Vietnamese, Creasy?'

Creasy was slowly shaking his head as though in disgust with himself. He said: 'My Vietnamese is minimal. I should have thought of that. Maybe Billy Nguyen at the Mai Man Bar can find me a reliable and discreet translator. He can find most things, for a fee.'

Guido was looking sceptical. Susanna said: 'That's a risk you don't need. I had better go with you.'

There was a long silence. Then Jens remarked: 'There could be violence, and you work for the US government in a very sensitive area.'

She shrugged and answered: 'My instructions were to give you assistance. They were not specific.' She glanced at Creasy. 'What chances are there of violence?'

'Very little. Guido and I are experienced with these things. We're dealing with one man who will suspect nothing. Even if he's carrying a gun or a knife, he will have very little chance to use either.'

Guido said: 'Maybe we pick him up first and if he doesn't speak English, we'll call in Susanna.'

Creasy shook his head. 'It's too complicated. I haven't worked out the exact plan yet, but we'll have to take him out of town to a quiet spot. We have to play that part by ear. If Susanna is going to be in on it, she has to be in from the start.' He glanced again at the reflection of the figure in the window and made a decision. 'We'll go with Susanna.'

CHAPTER TWENTY-ONE

Connie Crum lay naked on the vast bed, groaning in pleasure and pain. The girl straddling her was small enough to be blown away in a gale, but she had fingers of steel and they dipped and probed into Connie's neck muscles and shoulders.

It was the start to an evening that had been planned in almost every detail. She had arrived at the hotel half an hour earlier. Chilled pink champagne and a huge bowl of fruit were waiting in her suite. She had opened the champagne and after taking a few sips had picked up the phone and ordered a masseuse. The girl had arrived dressed in a white coat and carrying a small bag. While Connie undressed, the girl had slipped off the coat, revealing a tight, trim body covered only by brief white panties. She had taken several bottles of different oils from her bag. Connie had given her a glass of champagne before lying face down on the bed. She had booked the girl for an hour. For the first forty-five minutes the girl had massaged her body with skill and strength until through the pain Connie had felt the muscles relax.

She turned her head and murmured in Thai: 'Softer now. Imagine I'm a cat.'

The girl chuckled, and her fingers changed from instruments of power to gentle, teasing strands. They glided in a continuous caress over the oiled skin.

Connie Crum's mind and body relaxed. She thought of her dead husband. He had been a hard, ruthless man, almost as ruthless as herself. Whenever she wanted something from him, she would give him a massage. The same kind of massage that she was receiving: hard at first but then soft. His mind would go numb and then she would eventually have him under her fingers and under control. In many ways he had been the perfect man for her. If only he could have kept his hands off other women, he would be alive today. Even so, she had regretted her jealous rage and, looking down at him with the knife in his heart, she had decided never to get deeply involved with any man again. In future, she would take her pleasures when she wanted them under her own conditions.

The girl's fingers had reached her buttocks. Connie moved on the bed, savouring the feeling. In her mind she reviewed her situation. She was allied to the Khmer Rouge only for profit. She was a born trader; in the chaos of war she had amassed a fortune. She had made good investments mostly in property in Japan, Europe and North America. She owned her own house at Montparnasse in Paris and had a condo on Fifth Avenue in New York. The Khmer Rouge was now beginning to disintegrate. Perhaps they would last another year or two in increasingly isolated areas. When she had finished her business with Creasy, she would pull out and make her base in Paris. She would find her way into French society, perhaps even take a nominal French husband, somebody in a position of power either in the government or in business. With her wealth and beauty she was well poised to do so. She had studied languages, philosophy and art at the Sorbonne, and she could hold her own in a conversation with any intellectual. She would be an asset to any man of power, but she would set the terms. She would allow him to have lovers and she would have her own. They would both be discreet. She would spend time in New York on her own. That would be her secret life.

The girl's fingers had moved down to her upper thighs. She leaned forward and whispered a question.

Connie shook her head. She did not want anything 'special'. She would have that later, and it would be very special and very heterosexual. She rolled over and slid off the bed. The girl packed her bottles away, slipped on her white coat and received a large tip.

Connie picked up her glass and the ice bucket with the champagne and went into the marbled bathroom. She ran a bath so hot that few humans would have attempted to enter. She sank into it with a groan and then pressed the button to set the water foaming. She laid her head back and thought again about Creasy. She had waited a long time, waited until she had the power and organization to trap him. His death would be the culmination of her past life. Her father's soul would sleep easy, the more so for knowing the extent of Creasy's suffering before he died. She sipped the champagne and sighed contentedly. Her mind came back to the present. Within an hour she would be a hunter of a different kind.

'I don't want another blow job in a massage parlour.'

He turned to his brother, Massimo. 'We have been here four days and three nights and that's all that's happened. I'm not some fat German sex-tourist who spilt out of a jumbo jet with one thing on his mind. I'm thirty-five years old, good looking, and rich. I want a little passion in my sex life!'

Massimo grinned. He was the elder by four years, and familiar with the cities of the Far East. It was Bruno's first trip. They were buying silks for the family's garment business in Milan. Both of them were married to women from the same upper level of Milan society; marriages made for position rather than love. Such trips to exotic places brought adventure into their lives in every sense. Bruno was an idealist and somewhat arrogant. He did not like to pay for sex. It hurt his pride. When he went to London or Paris or New York, he was usually able to rely on his Latin looks and charm to pick up a woman who wanted to enjoy his body as much as he wanted hers.

Massimo sighed and explained yet again: 'It's not like that here, or in Hong Kong or Tokyo. You just can't find a woman like that. Not unless you live here and get into their society and culture. Your only chance is to find a tourist, and they can't afford to stay in a hotel like this unless they are rich, old American widows.' He gestured at two blue-rinsed ladies nursing cocktails at a corner table. 'How about one of those?'

Bruno grimaced and turned his head away. He was looking into the mirror behind the bar. Suddenly he sat upright and whispered: 'Now look at that!'

Both men swivelled on their bar stools.

She entered the room as though she owned the hotel. Tall, dark-skinned; black hair and a strapless dress that clung to every curve.

'It's a Lagerfeld,' Massimo said. 'I saw it at his spring collection.'

Bruno was mesmerized. 'Forget the dress,' he murmured. 'Just look at that body.'

Connie Crum moved to a table about ten metres from the bar. As she sat down, a waiter brought her a champagne cocktail. 'She's been here before,' Bruno said. 'She didn't even have to order a drink.'

'Stop dreaming,' Massimo said. 'A woman like that doesn't go out alone. She's waiting for either her husband or her boyfriend.'

Bruno was not deterred. 'Do you think she's Thai?' he asked.

'No, she looks Eurasian. There were many created during the Vietnam War, and by the French before that. But for sure, she's rich. That's a five-thousand-dollar dress, and her diamond necklace and ring look like the real thing. So does the gold Rolex watch. She didn't buy that from a stall in the back streets.'

Connie Crum surveyed the room like a panther looking for its dinner. It was crowded, especially the long bar. Like in all the bars of luxury hotels in Bangkok, ninety per cent of the customers were men. Many were elderly and overweight, wearing expensive suits and bored expressions.

She focused on the two Italians and liked what she saw. They were not too young and not too old. They were elegantly dressed, and although the nose of the elder one was slightly overhooked, they made a handsome pair. From their looks, she guessed that they were brothers, and that thought excited her.

They had turned back to the bar and she noticed that they were both looking at her in the mirror. The body language had started. They were sitting erectly on their stools. The younger one brushed a hand through his hair and straightened the cream handkerchief in his jacket pocket. 'Fifteen minutes,' she thought. 'Then one of them will make his move.' She glanced at her watch.

After ten minutes the younger one climbed off his stool and went to the men's room. When he came back, he managed to pass by her table, giving her a close look. After a whispered conversation with his brother, he walked across to her, bowed slightly and said: 'Signorina, please allow me to introduce myself. I am Bruno Marccheti from Milano.'

She looked at her watch, smiled and said: 'You are one minute late, Bruno.'

They had dinner at the French rooftop restaurant looking over the river. Massimo was sardonically charming, Bruno was a little over-eager. They had only been seated a few minutes when she felt his leg brushing hers. She moved her leg and, because she realized that the brothers had already reached the understanding that Bruno would be given the chance, she concentrated her attention on Massimo.

She explained that she lived in Paris. Her father was a French diplomat and her mother a minor member of Cambodia's royal family. She laughingly brushed aside the notion that she had royal blood. 'Less than a millilitre,' she said. I'm only a distant cousin.'

Of course they were intrigued. Men always are, by the combination of beauty and aristocracy. And she certainly looked the part. She told them that she was in Bangkok to visit her father who was on one of those interminable peace missions. He had been called away to Phnom Penh for a couple of days. She had elected to stay and wait in the greater comfort of the Oriental Hotel. She indicated that she was a little bored. Bangkok was a man's city and it would not have been proper for her to go out and sample the nightlife alone. She was, she explained with a winsome smile, a virtual prisoner in a gilded cage. She laughed inwardly at their quick exchange of glances.

She ordered caviar followed by baby lamb provençale. They also had caviar, and then shared a Châteaubriand steak. Massimo made a great play of ordering a bottle of Château Latour 1971.

She began to work her wiles. Bruno's leg had reached further out and was again touching hers. She let it stay that way. Then she moved her right foot until it touched Massimo's ankle. Both men decided that they were making progress. Several times she leaned forward to reach for the salt or the pepper. Her dress was lowcut. She wore no bra. Their eyes moved as though they were at a tennis match. When the dessert trolley arrived, she ordered a banana split and managed to eat it with such slow provocation that Bruno's breathing quickened. His leg was moving against hers. Massimo had managed to get his left foot over her right foot and was giving her shin a gentle but insistent massage.

'Are you married?' she asked.

There was a very brief silence while they glanced at each other. Then Massimo said: 'I am married, but Bruno is in the fortunate position of being a bachelor.'

'Liar!' Connie thought. 'They both have the smell of married men. Big brother is helping out little brother, even though he's doing it reluctantly.'

They ordered coffee and Cognacs and the waiter brought over a box of cigars. Both men selected Havanas. As the waiter turned away, she called him back and picked out a black Brazilian cheroot. The men looked on with scarcely concealed surprise as she clipped the end and dipped it into her glass of cognac. She then put it between her red lips and leaned forward to accept a light from the waiter.

'It's one of my rare pleasures,' she explained. 'A fine meal followed by a rough cigar.'

The two men composed themselves. Bruno asked: 'Are those your only pleasures?'

She blew smoke at him and smiled to take away the offence. 'Not at all, Bruno. Before dinner I enjoyed a wonderful massage and then spent half an hour in the whirlpool bath. I just love the feeling of that water pumping over my body.' She glanced at Massimo, whose eyes were a little misty in thought. 'I find it almost as pleasant as sex,' she said.

His eyes came into focus. 'Almost?'

'Yes, Massimo. I'm a healthy woman. I like a massage, I like a whirlpool bath, I like fine wines and rough cigars . . . I also like men. In fact, I need them. I need them as much as I need food. It has been a week since I left my husband in Paris. It is as though I had not eaten for a week. My body is hungry.'

Her voice was almost a whisper. Both men had leaned forward to catch her words. Bruno found his voice.

'I'm an Italian. It would be a stain on my country if I were to allow such a beautiful lady to remain hungry in any way at all.'

'Yes, it would be a shame,' Massimo murmured, as though in some pain.

She smiled at both of them and said: 'You are such gentlemen, but I have a problem.'

'A problem?' they chorused in true concern.

'Yes. For the past two hours I have been trying to decide which of you I would like to help me with my appetite. I regret to tell you that the choice is such that I have not been able to make a decision.'

The two men looked at each other with the disappointment apparent on their faces. But then she said: 'Just a few weeks ago in Paris I was trying to decide whether I was going to buy this dress or another one. For a woman, that is a terrible decision to make. So I indulged myself. I bought both of them.'

She pushed back her chair and stood up, smoothing her dress down her hips. She said: 'I'm in the Maugham Suite. Perhaps you would like to join me in half an hour?' She reached forward and with a slender finger touched the top of the wine bottle. 'Maybe you could arrange to have them send up another bottle? 1971 was such a good year.'

She turned and walked through the restaurant to the door. They watched in silence. Then Massimo said: it's going to be an interesting night, little brother!'

CHAPTER
TWENTY-TWO

Susanna dialled a number, hoping that Elliot Friedman had not yet left home for the office. It should have made no difference, but she wanted to talk to him in a very unofficial way and phoning him at the office somehow made it official.

His wife, Julia, answered the phone. 'Has he left?' Susanna asked.

'No, he's just finishing his waffles.' Susanna heard Julia shout through to the kitchen, and half a minute later Elliot was mumbling: 'Hello' through a mouthful.

'I'm kind of reporting in,' she said. 'Just to give you a background. I have nothing specific. I'm in contact with Creasy and his group and tonight we're making an operational move. I've offered my help as an interpreter. I want to clear that with you.'

At the other end of the line the munching stopped and Elliot asked: 'What kind of an operation?'

'I cannot say over an open line, but Creasy is moving down the road and he may have to talk to a Vietnamese who has no English-.'

'May it be dangerous?'

'Possible, but not probable.'

'When did you last take a holiday?'

'A what?'

'A holiday. When did you last take a holiday?'

'What the hell . . . ?'

His voice was stern. 'Susanna. Think back and tell me when you last took a holiday.'

She thought about it and then said: it was eight months ago. I went to stay with my cousin in California for a week.'

'OK. So as of now, you're on holiday for two weeks. When I get to the office, I'll send a fax to the hotel confirming that fact. And, Susanna, what you do on your holiday has got nothing to do with the department. As of the moment you receive that fax, you're no longer on official business. What you do in your own time is your business. If you get in trouble, don't come running to me.'

She laughed down the phone. 'OK, boss . . . Sometimes you're not just beautiful, you can also be intelligent! I'll phone you at home later and let you know what happened.'

'OK, Susanna. I've always admired your common sense. Keep using it. '

As she cradled the phone, she heard a tap on the door. She moved across the room and opened it. Creasy stood there. He said: 'I need to have a talk with you in private.'

She stood back, gestured a welcome and pointed at the minibar. 'Can I get you a drink?'

He shook his head. 'It will only take a few minutes, but there are some things you have to understand.'

She sat down on a chair in the corner, saying: 'Go ahead.'

He started pacing the room and, without looking at her, started talking.

'You invited yourself into this thing. I'm not unhappy about that, but you need to understand the reality. What you'll see tonight will not be pretty. I have to terrify a man. I don't like doing it. You'll watch me do it and you'll think I enjoy it for the sole reason that he has to think I enjoy it. If he's not convinced, he will not talk. The alternative would be for myself and Guido to torture him. You know my history, so you know that I'm no saint: but when we do this kind of work, if you're going to remain a human being, you have to have a bottom line. My bottom line is that I never killed anybody who wasn't trying to kill me. And I never tortured anybody. Except once, a long time ago, and he deserved it. What I'm going to do to this follower may seem to you to be a form of torture, but for me it is not. I'm just going to give him one hell of a fright. It will shock you. But within that shock, keep something clear in your mind. After I get the information from the follower, I should logically kill him. Most people in my profession would do that. Otherwise the people who hired him could find out that he talked. No matter what happens I'll not kill him. So while you might be disgusted by my actions, try to remember two things: first of all, he's earning his money in a risky business, and second, I gave him his life. Try to remember that. Try to keep in mind that I'm not a monster.'

He had not looked at her at all, but she could sense the importance of his words to his own mind. In a moment of revelation, she felt sorry for him. He was not a man who was comfortable explaining himself.

He had sat down on the bed and was watching her. She felt like a priest in a confessional. Without thinking, she stood up and moved to the bed and sat beside him. She picked up his huge right hand in hers and looked at it. There were mottled scars across the back.

'How did you get these?' she asked.

'It was a long time ago. I was a prisoner. An interrogator was asking me questions. He smoked a lot. There was no ashtray.'

She looked up at him. 'Did you talk?'

'No. The problem was I didn't have any answers. But he did not believe that.'

She released his hand. He stood up and moved to the door. She said: 'Creasy, I appreciate what you said to me. But I can tell you that I never believed you were an evil man. Violent, yes. Dispassionate, certainly. But not evil. I may not like what I see tonight, but I will try to understand it.'

His hand was on the door. He turned and gave a half smile. Then his face was serious. 'Did something happen to you, Susanna?'

'What do you mean?'

'Today, at the café, I was watching. You were very preoccupied, as though something was on your mind. Have you got a problem?'

She smiled and shook her head.

'You asked me to understand you, Creasy. Now try to understand me. I normally work in an office, totally absorbed in files and data. Now I find myself in Saigon in company with a bunch of killers. It's not exactly a normal situation. If I seem different, it's because I am different. I have to make my own adjustments.'

He was looking into her eyes, holding them as though trying to judge her. Then he glanced at his watch and said: 'We'll leave in an hour.'

CHAPTER
TWENTY-THREE

If she had combed the hotel bars and Bangkok for a month, she would not have found a more perfect pair. They had the vanity inherent in every Italian male. But still they were nervous, perhaps because they were in a situation which they had never faced before. And they were also visibly excited. The waiter had preceded them with the bottle of Château Latour. She poured the wine in the spacious lounge. She had left the bedroom door open, and their gaze was constantly drawn to the Emperor-size bed which was bathed in a strange, glowing, flickering light. They clinked their glasses and she proposed the toast.

'To pleasure!'

'To pleasure,' they murmured.

She gestured at the two armchairs, and sat back herself on the settee. 'To be perfect,' she said, 'pleasure has to be prepared. We're going to spend this one night together and never see each other again. That is part of the pleasure. There are no consequences.' She looked at Massimo. 'Have you and your brother ever made love to one woman together?'

His tongue moved over dry lips as he shook his head.

She turned to the younger brother. 'How would you go about it, Bruno?'

He took a sip of his wine. He glanced at his brother and answered: 'Perhaps we should take it in turns.'

She lifted her head and laughed. 'How boring! Since you have so little experience, I shall be the choreographer tonight. We will make a dance to remember. And at the end of it, the moment of pure pleasure will come at the same time for all of us. You'll be guided by me. You'll do exactly what I tell you. If you fail to do that, the evening will end immediately, and I'll go and look for men who are truly men. In my experience only a real man has the capacity to be guided in pleasure by a woman. If you were not here at this moment, you would be out with a couple of whores, instructing them to your own desires. This will not be like that. Tonight you'll discover the reality of pleasure.'

She drained her glass and in one flowing movement stood up, reached behind her and unzipped her dress. The silk fell to her ankles. She allowed them to look at her naked body for half a minute, then she said: 'Follow me.'

And she walked into the bedroom.

There were candles on every flat surface and the air was filled with the scent of musk and incense. She pointed to the foot of the bed.

'Massimo, sit there. You'll watch and do nothing.'

She turned to Bruno. 'Take off all your clothes.'

She eased herself onto the bed and pushed the pillows high behind her head. They did as instructed. Bruno had a thin, wiry body with thick black hair on his chest and his arms. He already had an erection. She patted the bed beside her and he moved and lay down. She took his penis in her left hand while her eyes were fixed on his brother at the end of the bed. She said: 'When I was eighteen years old, I was a student in Paris. I decided that it was important for a woman of my nature to have certain skills. I conferred with my mother and she agreed. She hired the most famous call-girl in Paris to teach me those skills. I have two degrees from the Sorbonne University, in languages and philosophy. But I have a more important degree from a lady called Lucette. Let me show you, Massimo.'

She leant over and ran her tongue from Bruno's chin down his chest and stomach, and took his penis into her mouth. It was large and long. Very slowly, she took it all in her mouth, deeper and deeper, until her lips were touching his scrotum. Bruno moaned in his throat while his elder brother looked on in disbelief. She lifted her head and looked again at Massimo.

'Be patient,' she said. 'You'll have your turn.'

She turned her attention back to Bruno's penis and ten seconds later pulled away as he ejaculated and rolled over.

She laughed, again looking at Massimo. 'He's just a boy,' she said. 'He's never had an orgasm so quickly in his life.' She patted Bruno on the bottom. 'Go into the bathroom and take a cold shower and then drink a glass of that good wine. You'll be ready again in half an hour. Meanwhile, I'll play with your brother.'

Massimo was older and wiser. As he stepped out of his clothes, he said: 'It was a clever trick, but I saw your right hand. It went between his buttocks and inside him. You massaged his prostate gland. It's an old trick for a busy whore with a long line of customers.'

She laughed in appreciation. 'You have been to the East before,' she said. 'But it's a good thing for a young man to learn the ways of the world. Your brother will not be so confident again. If he had paid a thousand dollars for that experience, he would be disappointed now. Let's find out how you handle things.'

She lifted her hands and touched both her nipples. 'The left one is more sensitive than the right. I want you to start slowly, just with the tip of your tongue. Take your time. We have hours in front of us.'

He eased on to the bed and moved up along her body and tried to kiss her lips. She turned her face away.

'The left nipple. That's where you start. The rest will come later.'

Bruno came out of the bathroom towelling himself. His penis was flaccid. He stood and watched his brother leaning over the woman. She was watching him, and her eyes dropped to his penis. It was growing again.

'Go into the lounge,' she said, 'and drink some wine. You can watch from the door.'

He remained standing there. Abruptly she grabbed Massimo's hair, pulled his head away from her nipples and spat out the words: 'Take your kid brother and get out of here! You know the rules!'

Massimo pulled his head away and cursed his brother in Italian. Bruno scurried into the lounge.

'Let it be the last time!' Connie said. 'Now I want your tongue inside me, very slowly and very carefully.'

Massimo lasted for fifteen minutes. Several times he tried to enter her, but each time she stopped him with a single word. Finally she made him stand by the bed and she simply used her hand while looking into his eyes. He tried to hold back but it wasn't possible. Bruno stood at the bedroom door with a glass in his hand, watching mesmerized. The sperm came across her breasts and she rubbed it into her skin, never taking her eyes away from Massimo's.

'That was the hors d'oeuvre,' she said. 'Now we will also take a glass of wine, and then we will see if the combination of two brothers can do better than the single parts.'

They were instruments and she was the player. She played on Bruno as though he were a drum, while Massimo was a violin. She positioned them and used them. She used their hands, their mouths and their penises. She knew exactly when they were about to have an orgasm, and each time she stopped them, either with a sharp flick of her finger or a painful squeeze of their testicles. They moaned and writhed while she laughed. They were unable to differentiate between pleasure and pain. Finally she took a small bottle of scented oil from the bedside table. She gave it to Massimo and then she straddled his younger brother and eased him inside her. She turned and looked over her shoulder at the older brother.

'Put the oil on your penis,' she said. 'We're going to make a sandwich.'

She felt the pain as he entered her from behind. Then she screamed with pleasure.

'We will not be going home tomorrow,' Massimo said.

'Why not?' Bruno asked. They were standing in the bathroom.

'Look at your back,' Massimo said, pointing at the mirror.

Bruno turned and looked, and saw the parallel scratches on his back and the blood oozing from them.

'I have the same,' Massimo said. 'It'll take at least a week to heal. Our wives would not understand if they saw those marks.' 'I never felt anything,' Bruno said. 'Neither did I, but we got clawed by a cat!'

CHAPTER TWENTY-FOUR

Susanna felt no fear. Probably because the whole operation was mounted in such a matter-of-fact way. It was as though Creasy, Guido and The Owl were simply going about a routine task. She sat beside The Owl in a rented Toyota van. They were stationary at the side of a narrow road with the lights and engine turned off. The Owl explained it to her.

'Creasy is drinking in a bar two hundred metres behind us. In three minutes, he'll leave that bar and walk down this road.' He pointed to a narrow alley to the left. 'Guido is waiting in that alley. The follower will be behind Creasy, at about sixty metres. He will be on this side of the road, because there is more light on the other side. Just before he gets to the alley, I will jump out and shout something at him. He will turn, Guido will take him from behind. We will put him in the back of the van, pick up Creasy and head out of town.'

'That simple?' she asked.

'Yes, that simple. Guido is very fast. Even if the follower has a gun or a knife, he won't have time to use them.'

It was that simple. Three minutes later she watched Creasy amble down the road on the other side from the van. A minute after that a small, dark figure passed them on the left-hand side. The Owl was holding the door slightly ajar.

He jumped out and called: 'Monsieur!'

The figure turned and, a second later, a dark shadow loomed up behind it. There was a dull thump and then no sound at all until she heard the side door of the van slide shut. The Owl jumped back into the front seat and casually turned the key. The van moved forward a hundred metres and Creasy emerged from the shadows and also went into the back. The Owl turned off onto To Doe Street and slowly drove out of town.

The journey lasted half an hour, and during that time Susanna's trepidation grew. She kept recalling Creasy's words back at the hotel and tried to find comfort in them; but deep down she knew that he and Guido and The Owl were very hard people. She hoped that the follower would not be stupid. He must realize his position and talk.

They turned off onto a dirt track and slowly moved through heavy forest to the slow-moving river. The Owl pulled up beside a small wooden jetty. There was an almost-full moon. As she climbed out, she could hear the sounds of the forest: crickets chirping and birds calling in the trees above them. As she walked around the van, the side door slid open. Creasy jumped out. He turned and reached up and lifted the figure of the follower out of the van.

It was a very slight figure, dressed in black jeans and a dark-blue shirt. His arms and feet were bound with black tape. He had a rope tied under his armpits and a large stone was tied to his feet. His mouth was shut by a strip of tape. She could see the fear in his eyes. Guido also jumped down, and together they carried the Vietnamese onto the small jetty. Susanna and The Owl followed. She said to Creasy: 'What are you going to do?'

He answered: 'It's lucky we brought you along. He does not speak English. Tell him that in a few minutes I'm going to ask him some questions. But first I'm going to give him a little demonstration . . . Just to concentrate his mind.' He nodded to Guido.

It happened very abruptly. Creasy took the end of the rope. Guido picked up the Vietnamese as though he were a child, and dropped him into the river. Susanna started forward but The Owl put an arm across her.

'Just wait,' he said.

The Vietnamese disappeared under the water, dragged down by the weight of the stone. Seconds ticked by. For Susanna, each one felt like an eternity. She started shouting at Creasy.

'For God's sake, he'll drown! What are you doing?!'

Creasy held up a hand. 'Just wait,' he said. He was looking at his watch.

Guido was looking at the angle of the rope. He said: 'He's on the bottom. I guess one minute will be enough.'

'We'll make it two minutes,' Creasy said. 'Be ready to pump him out.'

For Susanna, those two minutes felt like two months. She tried to move forward again, but The Owl had both his arms around her. He was surprisingly strong.

Then Creasy and Guido were hauling up the rope. The Vietnamese came to the surface shedding water, his whole body shuddering. They pulled him up onto the wooden planks. Creasy ripped the tape from his mouth and pushed him onto his stomach. The water was pouring from his nostrils. Very quickly Guido straddled him and placed the palms of his hands on his back, then started to press rhythmically. Water poured out of his mouth and his body shook as he coughed chokingly.

Creasy turned to Susanna. He had a plastic wallet in his hand. He opened it and said: 'His name is Tran Quock Cong. He's forty-three years old and has a wife and two young daughters. He lives in Cholon. I want to know who hired him to follow us, and when.'

Guido had picked up the Vietnamese, who was dragging air into his lungs. Creasy said to Susanna: 'First tell him that if he does not answer our questions, he will go back to the bottom of the river. And that's where he will die.'

It took a minute for her to compose herself. She felt hatred for Creasy and Guido, who loomed like monsters over the frail Oriental.

'You said you wouldn't torture him, Creasy! What do you call that?!'

It was Guido who answered. 'Sometimes you have to be cruel to be kind. We gave him a shock and a bath. I could break his arms and his legs and all his fingers and his toes, and pull out all his teeth. Hopefully, that will not now be necessary. Pull yourself together and ask him the questions.'

'Fuck you!' she said, and turned away.

Before she even reached the end of the jetty, Creasy's voice stopped her.

'His life is in your hands. If I can't talk to him, I have to kill him. Otherwise, whoever sent him will know that he's been compromised.'

She turned. 'Could you kill him, Creasy? How would you do it?'

'I'd strangle him and then drop him back in the river. This is no picnic, Susanna! Either talk to him or wait in the van.'

Slowly she walked back down the jetty, knowing that she would never look at Creasy or Guido or The Owl with anything less than abhorrence. She was in the company of animals. Her one thought now was to save a life.

The Vietnamese was on his feet, leaning back against Guido's chest. His eyes were dull. She spoke to him in Vietnamese.

'You're in great danger. If you don't answer these men's questions, they'll certainly kill you!'

Slowly, his eyes focused on her. 'What do they want to know?'

She replied: 'Who you are, who hired you and why.'

Creasy had taken two faded photographs from the wallet. He showed them to her. They were of two young girls, one about five and one about three years old. He said: 'Tell him also that after he has drowned, I'll go to his house and kill his daughters as well.'

She could see Creasy's eyes in the moonlight, and she believed him. Now there were three lives in her hands. She spoke to the Vietnamese and something extraordinary happened. He started to laugh hysterically. From behind, Guido smacked him hard across the face, knocking him sideways and onto his knees. Slowly he picked himself up. He started talking to Susanna and gesturing at Creasy. She translated.

'That is exactly the same threat that he received from the people who hired him. They told him that if he talked to you or anybody else, they would kill him and his daughters.'

'Shit!' The word came out of Creasy's mouth as an explosion. He walked down the jetty, continuing to curse under his breath. He stood at the end of the jetty for more than two minutes, then turned and walked slowly back.

'Untie him,' he said to Guido. 'And the stone from his feet.'

Guido followed the instruction while Creasy paced up and down the jetty. The Vietnamese rubbed the wrists of his freed hands. The fear was still in his eyes as they followed Creasy's every movement. Finally, Creasy turned and walked up to the slight figure. He reached up his hands and gripped him by his shoulders. Then he said to Susanna: 'Translate exactly everything I say.'

He was looking to the Vietnamese man's eyes. He said: 'I would not have killed you, and I do not make war on children. The people you work for have no such qualms.' He paused while Susanna translated. Then he went on. 'You're caught between a rock and a hard place. Now you'll tell me what I want to know, and then, in return, I will give you the gift of your children's lives. After you've talked to me, you will continue to follow us for the next forty-eight hours and continue to report to your masters about our movements. Within those forty-eight hours, I'll bring two men to Saigon who will guard you and your family. The choice is yours. You can talk to me and have protection, or you can walk away now.'

Susanna finished the translation. Creasy dropped his hands from the Vietnamese man's shoulders and stood back. The only sounds came from the forest. The Vietnamese was looking down to the dark, worn planks of the jetty. Slowly, he lifted his head and looked at Creasy, and then asked a question.

'Who are these men who will protect me and my children?'

Susanna translated, and then translated Creasy's answer.

'They are men like me.'

The Vietnamese said: 'I will talk to you.'

CHAPTER
TWENTY-FIVE

'So you do have a heart.'

Creasy gave her a shrug.

'Susanna, about two years ago I was visiting Jens in Copenhagen and I had some trouble with an old wound. Jens sent me off to the hospital and they gave me a full check-up, including an ultrasound scan. It was amazing. I was looking at a television monitor and I could see all my insides, my lungs, liver, kidneys, intestines . . . And suddenly, I saw it. I asked the doctor: "What the hell is that?" He said: "That's your heart!"' Creasy grinned. 'So yes, I do have one. Occasionally it works. I'm sorry that we put you through that scene earlier, but it was necessary. You were the psychological conduit to Tran Quock Cong. If you didn't believe what I was saying, then neither would he.'

'You had no intention of drowning him or killing his children?'

'I told you before. I don't kill people who are not trying to kill me.'

They were in Creasy's room at the Continental Hotel. Jens was tapping at the keys of his computer. Beside him was a large-scale map of Indo-China. Guido was on the telephone. The Owl was encased in the earphones of his Walkman. Tran Quock Cong was sitting at a bar across the road, watching the hotel entrance.

Guido cradled the phone and stood up. He said: 'OK. Maxie got hold of René in Brussels. They're catching a flight out of Paris in the morning. They arrive at Tan Son Nut airport the following

morning at ten a.m. They're flying club class, so they'll be rested ...
But Creasy, they're going to need weapons.'

'Yes, they will. And so will we. I'll talk to Billy at the Mai Man
Bar. He has the connections.'

'Who are these people?' Susanna asked.

'Old friends,' Creasy answered. 'Maxie Macdonald is an
ex-Rhodesian. He fought in the war there with the elite Selous
Scouts, one of the toughest units in any army anywhere. René
Callard is a Belgian. He was with me and Guido in the French
Foreign Legion. Now he's a specialist bodyguard. Tran Quock
Cong and his family will be safer than if they were holed up in
Fort Knox.' He turned to the Dane. 'So what do we have, Jens?'

The Dane stretched his shoulders and then studied the screen
of his computer and assumed his policeman's tone.

'Tran Quock Cong, born September 1958 in a village near
Hui. He only had primary-school education. His parents were
killed during an American bombing raid when he was twelve
years old. He found his way to Saigon and became one of the
thousands of street urchins feeding himself by being a pickpocket
and petty thief. When the communists took over, he became an
informer for the secret police and was trained by them in surveillance techniques. He remains an informer but does private work
on the side. Three weeks ago he was approached by a man called
Cong Hung. That is probably a false name. He was offered a job
to follow a foreigner who was expected to arrive in Saigon about
two weeks later. He was given a thousand US dollars in cash and
told to travel to Phnom Penh and check into the Quai Ban guest
house. He did so and was contacted by a Cambodian woman
called Pan Chamnan, probably also a false name. She took him
by train to the town of Sisophon near the Thai border, and from
there they were taken by Land Rover on a two-hour journey
during which Tran Quock Cong was blindfolded. It was a dirt
road. They arrived at an army camp in the forest, near a village.

Tran Quock Cong estimates that they were travelling due north, and looking up a map later, thinks that they may have been near a village called Chek. It was a Khmer Rouge camp. There he met a man who called himself Ha Minh Hien, who from his description is almost certainly your friend Van Luk Wan. He was given a photograph of yourself. It was taken at least twenty years ago but showed the scars on your face that you still carry. He was given a further two thousand dollars in cash and a portable Samsung fax machine and a fax number in Phnom Penh. He was to send his reports to that fax number with the prefix code word of CALAN. He was to send his reports daily at six p m. He spent a day and a night at the camp, during which time he overheard several conversations indicating that the Khmer Rouge were holding several American prisoners who were put to work clearing mines. The following morning he saw one of them at a distance. He wore leg shackles which restricted his movements. He was bearded, aged between forty and fifty years old. Before he was driven back blindfolded to Sisophon, he was told by the man calling himself Ha Minh Hien that if he failed on his job, he and his wife and two daughters would be killed.

The Dane looked up at Creasy. 'I've checked the area in Cambodia and confirm that it's a Khmer Rouge stronghold.' He glanced down at the map. 'It's only twenty miles from the Thai border. As far as the Cambodian army is concerned, it's a no-go area.'

Susanna stood up and moved to the phone, saying: 'I have to call my boss in Washington. If there are Americans there, they must be MIAs.'

'Hold on,' Creasy said, 'if you pass that information on to your boss, what will he do?'

'He'll send in agents, maybe even come himself. This is the first real sighting we've had for years.'

'What will those agents do?'

'They'll try to infiltrate the area.'

Creasy glanced at Guido, and then said to her: 'That could be a major disaster. The last thing I want is a bunch of enthusiasts running around that area. If there are MIAs there, the Khmer Rouge can always whisk them away within minutes.'

'It's my duty,' she said.

Guido spoke up. 'Fuck your duty, Susanna! You were told to co-operate with us. You also told us that you're now officially on holiday. I suggest you let us work out a plan and then if we need any back-up, we can call on your department.'

'It's the best way,' Jens agreed. 'First we need more information. I want to trace the fax number in Cambodia. Now that we have Tran Quock Cong on our side, it's possible we can set up a dummy operation and flush these people out. At least the Phnom Penh cell. In this kind of operation it's necessary to move step by step.' He looked at Creasy. 'I think that Tran Quock Cong was an unknowing plant. They expected you to pick him up. It's the next step in their carefully organized paper chase.'

Creasy was shaking his head, it doesn't make sense, Jens. The guy is an expert. If they were going for a set-up, they would have put an amateur in there to be sure I spotted him. And they would not have blindfolded him on the way to that camp.'

'They were very clever,' Jens said. 'They only blindfolded him ten minutes after they left the town of Sisophon. At that time, by looking at the sun, he would have known the direction. Whoever wants you knows you well. They know that you would pick up even an expert. But they don't know you as well as I do. They would assume that after picking him up and extracting his information, you would kill him so that he could not warn them. Now I think the advantage is with us.' He looked at Susanna. 'You're the only one able to communicate with him. Do you really think that he believes Creasy can protect him?'

She had sat down again. 'Yes,' she answered. 'He believes that Creasy will keep his word.'

'Then that's our advantage,' Creasy said. 'And it's all we have. Jens, tomorrow I want you to travel with The Owl to Phnom Penh and try to trace that fax number. Also, get as much information as you can about the area surrounding the village of Chek. It'll be useful to know some details about the local Khmer Rouge commander and how many men he has and the size of the area he controls.' He turned to Guido. 'In the morning I want you to go and see Billy Chan at the Mai Man Bar. I'll give you a note for him. He'll plug you into the Black Market and you'll buy us some machinery. We need at least two SMGs, four hand-guns, and some grenades and whatever else you think might be useful. There's probably a lot of Russian machinery around. AK47s will be fine, unless you come across Uzis. The Chinese made a very good version of the Soviet Tokarev pistols. They must be all over this country. Try to get the type 51, with plenty of spare mags.'

He turned to Susanna. 'I want you to pick up Maxie and René from the airport and give them each a pistol that Guido will buy Take them to Tran's home together with enough tinned food and bottled water to last a week. Bring them up to date on what's happened and hire three mobile phones. Give one to Maxie, I'll have one and so will you so we can keep the communication network. You can do that through the hotel reception.'

'And what will you be doing?' Susanna asked.

'I'll be doing some sightseeing,' Creasy answered. 'Tran will be faxing the movements of a typical tourist. Once Jens has done the groundwork in Phnom Penh, we all move into Cambodia.' He glanced at his watch and stood up. 'Maybe the puppy is alive, but for sure he's no longer a puppy. Not after twenty-five years as a prisoner of the Vietnamese and the Khmer Rouge.'

CHAPTER TWENTY-SIX

She would have recognized them even without a description. She picked them out as they came through customs: two men carrying canvas bags, small enough to be carried into an airliner's cabin. One was of medium height, stocky and broad-shouldered; a square face with sandy hair. The other was dark and tall and elegant with a suntan and jet-black hair. Physically they were different, but in their walk and behaviour, they were the same. They moved with an awareness, a constant shifting of the gaze, a strange caution, as though they were walking into a battlefield.

Susanna stepped forward, introduced herself and stated: 'Creasy asked me to pick you up and take you to the place.'

She was under immediate scrutiny; cold eyes evaluating. Then the Belgian held out his hand.

'I am René Callard. This is my colleague Maxie.'

Callard sat in the front passenger seat, Maxie in the back. As they drove towards Cholon, it was the Rhodesian who asked the questions.

'You have the machinery?'

'Yes . . . In the bag on the seat next to you.'

'What is it?'

Susanna drew a breath, never having realized that she would ever be uttering such words. 'Two Chinese-made Tokarev pistols with six spare mags. And six hundred rounds. A Nokia mobile phone and also the twenty square metres of fishing net you requested.'

'Supplies?'

'Enough food and bottled water for a week.'

'The family?'

'They are stocked up with enough food for a month. They have their instructions.'

She got a grunt of approval from behind. René asked: 'The others?'

'Jens and The Owl left for Phnom Penh yesterday. Creasy is acting as a tourist. Guido has vanished.'

'Vanished?'

'Yes, I don't know where he is. Creasy didn't tell me.'

She had noticed in the mirror that Maxie was constantly glancing through the rear window, but the Belgian never turned his head. He was watching the road ahead. They were not tense, but they were totally alert. Maxie said to her: 'When we get to within five hundred metres of this guy Tran's house, pull over and stop. Keep the engine running.'

For the first time, René glanced over his shoulder. He asked: 'What do you think Guido is up to?'

Maxie chuckled. 'He's roaming. He does it well. You and I will be inside that house. Guido will be outside. Miss Moore, does Guido have a mobile phone?'

'Yes. He will be in touch . . . And, under the circumstances, you can call me Susanna.'

She felt a light tap on the shoulder as he said: 'Thank you. So far, so good. I assume that the family has been fully briefed and will not do anything stupid.'

'Yes, Maxie. They are in great fear for their lives.'

'OK. This is the procedure: first we park five hundred metres away for a few minutes, so René and I can check that we're not being followed. Then you drive to within ten metres of the house so we can recce the vicinity. After that we move in. You follow ten minutes later . . . I gather the Trans don't speak English?'

'Very little.'

'Then you must brief them for us, and emphasize that they must follow the procedures exactly. Let them know that if they do something stupid or outside the procedures, René and I will stop protecting them and start protecting ourselves. We won't shed a tear at their funeral.'

She found herself talking in the same staccato manner. 'Understood. They will get a full situation report.'

She drove across the bridge, and five minutes later eased the car to a stop at the side of the road. Maxie reached from behind and adjusted the rear-view mirror so that he could survey the road behind. It was a busy road. Cars, buses, tri-shaws and bicycles, together with a lot of pedestrians. René was looking forward and to both sides. They sat absolutely still. Susanna managed to stifle a sneeze.

Finally Maxie said: 'OK. Move closer.'

She engaged first gear and, as they moved forward, listened to their conversation.

Maxie said: 'Lot of movement, René. It's a bag of worms.'

'Yeah. It's going to be inside work. Seal the place off. It's a reaction job. There's no place to stand off or cover forward.'

Again Susanna pulled the car to the curb. She pointed.

'The house is down that side street. Exactly fifty-five metres on the left-hand side. The front door is painted black. Mrs Tran and the children are waiting.'

A minute passed and then Maxie muttered: 'Let's go.'

She watched them amble down to the side street and then turn into it, carrying their two bags and the bag of machinery. The busy hubbub continued around her, and she felt it a little strange that life should be so normal after she had just injected two such men into the community.

Ten minutes later she locked the car and followed them. The door was opened by René. He had already changed from his slacks and sports jacket into black jeans, a black polo-neck shirt and black sneakers.

Mrs Tran and her two daughters were sitting apprehensively on the sofa, watching Maxie go about his work. He had also changed into black clothing. Susanna pulled up a chair next to the sofa and watched with interest.

Maxie was cutting up sections of fishing net and then fixing them across the windows. René had a roll of white marker tape in one hand. The other hand was held up in front of his eyes as he moved around the room looking through each window. In his turn, he started unrolling the tape and sticking it into lines on the wooden floor. Susanna asked: 'Can you tell me what you're doing, so I can explain to Mrs Tran?'

Maxie turned and said: 'The netting over the windows is anti-grenade. Its mesh is fine enough not to be noticed from the outside. If someone lobs a grenade through the window, it will bounce back outside.' He gestured at René. 'But obviously, it won't stop a bullet. So René is checking lines of fire.' He pointed at one of the windows. 'For example if there should be a sniper in a building across the street, he will have a limited view into the room. We have to make sure that the angles are right. Also the lighting. When we're finished, I'll explain everything.'

She glanced at Mrs Tran and gave her a little background. The Vietnamese woman listened intently, as did the two young girls. They were like little dolls with round faces and black, bobbed hair. She thought they were adorable. Abruptly, she was conscious of her own condition and the need to make a decision. She forced it out of her mind and turned back to watch the two men.

René had finished laying his lines of tape and was unscrewing the light bulb from a red, ornate lampshade hanging from the ceiling. Maxie was testing the tension of the netting. Satisfied, he said to Susanna: 'We'll do the other rooms in a minute.' He pointed at the lines of tape. 'These are passage lines. When Mrs Tran and the girls move around this room and the others, they must always follow those lines. Then they're not exposed to sniper fire through the windows. We'll take out the bulbs from any lights that illuminate the wrong areas. We'll build a safe area in the bathroom.' He reached down into his canvas bag and pulled out several small black boxes attached to long, thin wires. 'After dark we'll rig these outside. They make up an infra-red alarm system. If anyone approaches the doors or windows, a buzzer will go off in all the rooms. Immediately Mrs Tran and the girls will go to the bathroom and stay on the floor until René or I tell them to flush the toilet.' He grinned. 'That's the password for them. All clear - "flush the toilet".'

She translated that, expecting the woman to be amused. But she simply nodded silently and then asked: 'Will I be safe with these two men?'

Susanna glanced at them and then answered: 'They will do their very best to protect you and your daughters.'

The woman shook her head. 'I didn't mean that. We're going to be sort of locked up together for many days and nights. What if they get drunk and try to rape me?'

Susanna started an answer, but then stopped and put the question to the two men.

They showed no offence. Maxie said: 'First of all, while in this house, we will drink no alcohol.' He glanced at René. 'And secondly, if it will reassure her, you can tell her that we are both gay.'

She looked at them both and then translated to the woman.

For the first time, Mrs Tran smiled. Then she laughed and said: 'Of course they are not gay. But now I trust them. Please tell them thank you, and welcome to my house.'

CHAPTER
TWENTY-SEVEN

She had seen the scars on his face, but not those on his body. And her eyes were drawn to them in morbid fascination. It seemed almost impossible to be able to place even a fingertip on his torso without covering a scar.

She had tapped on the door of his room a few minutes earlier. He had only been wearing shorts; the air-conditioning in the hotel had broken down yet again, and on a windless evening the room was as hot as an oven.

He poured them both a glass of cold water from a flask and listened intently as she briefed him about the arrival of Maxie and René, and their preparations at Tran's house.

'It was reassuring,' she said. 'They seem to be very competent.'

He gave her one of his rare, brief smiles. 'The fact that they're alive is proof of their competence. It all comes from experience. You can take a twenty-year-old athlete and turn him into a bodyguard by training him in the martial arts and the use of a variety of weapons. He can become a total expert physically, and to some extent, mentally. But the only time he gets actual experience is when someone tries to kidnap or kill his charge. And then you have a situation of a highly trained man or woman having to do a job at which they've had no experience. It's like training a company of soldiers and then sending them into battle without experienced officers or sergeants. The minute the firefight starts, their training goes out the window. It's ironic. René and Maxie both passed fifty years old. There's no protective organization I know of who would think of hiring fifty-year-old bodyguards. And yet those two are the best in the business.'

She was looking at the scars again. She gestured at his body and asked: 'Do they have as many scars as you?'

'They have enough,' he said. 'To my knowledge, René was wounded several times in Algeria when he was in the Legion. And again in the Congo. Maxie was once left for dead on the Zambian border during the Rhodesian war. He dragged himself ten miles back into Rhodesia. He was in hospital for over three months. The point is, Susanna, that they've been through it all many times.'

'Why do you do it?'

He shrugged. 'It's all we know. I joined the Marines when I was seventeen to get away from a lousy life at home. I've never known anything else except being a soldier of one kind or another. The same applies to Maxie and René, and of course to Guido. There's nothing romantic about it. We've been called the dogs of war and the orphans of society. Maybe the truth lies somewhere in between. Mercenaries have a bad reputation and usually it's deserved. By its nature the profession attracts very low-life types, but they're not all bad. The best time of my life was in the Legion. It was like the family that I'd never had before. The same applied to René and Guido. We were brothers in that family.'

'You had to retire?' she asked.

'No. No soldier ever has to retire from the Foreign Legion. If he wants to stay on after his fighting age, then they give him other duties or he goes to their vineyards in France. Under normal circumstances, he's never forced out of the family.'

'So why did the three of you leave?'

'It was at the end of the Algerian war, when de Gaulle decided to give the Algerians their independence. Some of the generals and other officers rebelled, including those commanding our own parachute regiment. Legionnaires always follow their officers. When the rebellion failed, our regiment was disbanded. De Gaulle was very vengeful, and perhaps with good reason. At one point we were within forty-eight hours of parachuting onto Paris.' He shook his head at the memory. 'It was madness, but it was a mad time.'

Abruptly, he stood up, walked to the window and tried to force it even wider to let in a shred more air. He looked down at the buzzing street below and said over his shoulder: 'So they kicked us out.'

He turned. She could see the discomfort on his face. He was a taciturn man not given to long monologues and definitely averse to showing his own feelings.

'End of speech,' he said, 'and change of subject. Tomorrow I'm heading to Phnom Penh. I don't think we'll make any more progress here. Guido will stay on for a couple more days to keep an outside eye on Tran's house and on Tran himself.'

'Is that what he's doing now?'

He nodded. 'I think we can trust Tran, but you can never be sure. In this country there are many wheels within wheels. And there may be more than one puppeteer pulling the strings.' He moved back to his chair and sat down and said: 'I'm grateful for your help. Your introduction to Dang Hoang Long was very useful. I'm sorry you had to go through that unpleasantness at the river.'

She hardly heard his last words because her mind was forced back to a decision she had put off for the last two days. The speed of events and their emotional impact had allowed her to push her own personal problem to the back of her mind. But she would soon have to face it. She must have been lost in her thoughts for a long time because she suddenly heard his voice.

'Are you all right, Susanna?'

Her head jerked up. 'Yes, I'm fine. I was just thinking about something.'

'It must have been something sad.'

'Why do you say that?'

'It shows on your face. It's been that way now for the past couple of days. You're not the same person. Has something happened?'

Abruptly, she realized that his tone of voice had changed. The hardness had left it. For a moment she felt an urge to tell him everything. Maybe it was because he was twenty years older than her and so much more experienced. But then her eyes looked at the scarred body and face, and her mind asked the question: What would such a man know of the emotions of a woman who realizes that a child is about to grow inside her? What would he know about the disappointments of a man she thought she might love and who might love her? What would he know about anything, apart from weapons and killing? His world was as far from hers as a planet a million light years away.

She stood up and smoothed her skirt, saying: 'I'm fine, Creasy. I'll probably stay on a couple more days and then head back to Washington. I hope everything goes well for you in Cambodia . . . for all of you. I'm glad I was a little help.'

She went back to her room and took a cold shower, wrapped herself in a towel and lay on the bed. She could not seem to focus her thoughts in any clear direction. Slowly, it became apparent that she had reached a crossroads in her life. She was of an age and in a condition that required one of life's decisions. She felt lonely and even abandoned. She pushed herself up against the headboard. She made a decision. It was an easy one. She would decide tomorrow. She would have dinner in the hotel and drink a good bottle of wine, sleep late and then decide.

The phone rang. It was Creasy. His deep voice said: 'I just had a fax from Jens. He has made good progress and I will definitely be leaving in the morning. Now let me tell you something: when I was here all those years ago, a Frenchman called Jean Godard ran a restaurant on Co Ban Street. He served the best French food in Indo-China. Of course he was forced out when the communists took over and he went back to France. But I heard today that he's back and has been allowed to rent his own premises. I'm going there for dinner tonight. If you have no plans, why not be my guest and give me a chance to thank you properly for your help?'

She thought for only a moment before she answered: 'You don't have to thank me. I was only doing my duty . . . But I'll be very happy to join you for dinner.'

CHAPTER
TWENTY-EIGHT

Mr Ponnosan lifted the lid of the box and, in spite of himself, felt and heard the slight gasp he let out. There were no opals this time, nor any other gemstones. Only the six large pieces of jade. They were of a size he had never seen before. He composed himself and then looked up at the smiling face of Connie Crum across the table. It was the same setting as the previous few occasions. The wooden house in the jungle, a bare room and the two black-clad young women standing at her shoulders with their holstered pistols.

He had done well on the last three trades, earning a profit of more than fifty per cent. This was the big one. He studied the tiny 'windows' cut into the stones. They revealed the creamy white of Imperial jade, and he knew they must have come from the northern mountains of Burma. He was not a great expert in jade, but he could recognize what he was now turning in his fingers. He tried to keep his face expressionless as he asked: 'What do you want for them?'

She leaned forwards. Her voice was cold and crisp.

'Four hundred thousand dollars. And I'm not going to bargain. If you're not interested, I'll take them to Bangkok myself.'

He looked again at the grey lumps of stone.

'It's a great deal of money,' he muttered.

'No,' she answered. 'Not for that jade. You would not be here if you had not made a good profit on the previous occasions. You know the rarity of such jade. And you know that it normally goes straight from Rangoon to Hong Kong for auction. I will take nothing less than four hundred thousand . . . not a cent. You know very well that you can double your money.'

The two young women were watching his eyes. They could see the greed in them. Abruptly he closed the box and nodded his head, then reached for his money belt.

As he walked out the door in his Italian silk suit, clutching the box, Connie Crum looked up at one of the girls and grinned like a cat that has just had a lobster put before it. Then she went back to counting the money.

Van Luk Wan came in and raised his eyebrows at the small mountains of thousand-dollar bills.

'You made a good trade?' he asked.

She gave him her cat smile.

'I sure did! Mr Ponnosan won't be coming back. When he arrives in Bangkok and shows those stones to a real expert, he'll discover that he paid four hundred thousand dollars for Alaskan jadeite worth no more than fifty bucks!' She stretched and yawned. 'I don't know what gives me more pleasure: an orgasm, or ripping off a complaisant Thai business man.'

Van grinned, but his eyes never left the pile of money. He asked: 'Did you have a good time in Bangkok?'

She almost purred at the memory. 'A very good time! It has been an excellent week.'

'It's going to be better,' Van said. 'I just had the news that the Dane and the Frenchman arrived in Phnom Penh. They checked into the Cambodiana Hotel an hour ago.'

Slowly, she sat back in her chair. The money was forgotten. She said: 'So he caught the follower?'

'Obviously. But that Creasy is clever or rich. The follower is still sending in reports. So he was turned. Creasy is still in Saigon. And his friend, Guido Arrellio, has disappeared.'

She was nodding her head thoughtfully.

'Yes, he's clever. He sends in an advance guard to dig around for information while he keeps up a facade. He will go to Phnom Penh soon and then we begin the next stage.' Her eyes narrowed. 'You threatened the follower with the death of his family if he talked?'

'Yes. It made our deception more authentic.'

'Good. As soon as Creasy has left Saigon, arrange for the follower's family to be killed.' 'Is it necessary?'

'Of course. We must be seen to keep our threats. It will become known. It will strike fear.'

CHAPTER
TWENTY-NINE

They were never shown a menu.

The old patron of the bistro had greeted Creasy with a kiss on both cheeks and a bear hug, and Susanna with a kiss on her hand. Then he had waved them to a corner table.

They could have been in the neighbourhood bistro in a Paris suburb; check tablecloths, old mirrors and pictures on the walls. Simple home-cooked food. They ate a thick fish soup followed by a rack of baby lamb and then French cheeses and local fruit. There was one difference: there were lighted candles on the tables, a thing one does not often see in Paris. The wine was good and Susanna drank too much of it.

Apart from a little small talk, there had been no conversation. The bistro was busy but not noisy. The music coming out of the loudspeakers was French and muted; Yves Montand and then Edith Piaf singing '*Je ne regrette rien*'. As the song started, she noticed something strange. Creasy turned his head towards the bar, behind which the patron sat on a high stool. She saw the old man raise his right hand in a brief salute. She saw Creasy return it.

'What was that about?' she asked.

He hesitated for a moment, and then explained. 'It's a footprint of history. Jean is an ex-Legionnaire. He fought at Dien Bien Phu and then stayed on. He knows the Legion's history and my part in it. In Algeria, when the rebellion failed, my regiment, the second REP, blew up our barracks and marched out to oblivion.

As we marched we sang . . . we sang "*Je ne regrette rien*". That song was stamped into our minds. When Edith Piaf died, the Legion sent an honour guard to her funeral. Every year on the anniversary of her death, flowers are laid on her grave in Paris with a card that simply states "*La Légion*".

There was a catch in his voice, and Susanna felt strangely moved. It was a contradiction that such men could have such emotions; but then she realized the connection. The life of Edith Piaf and the life of a Legionnaire were somehow similar. The 'sparrow' had been as much an orphan as all of them.

She knew from the Interpol file she had read back in Washington that Creasy had been married twice. His first wife and only child had died on Pan Am 103 over Lockerbie; his second wife had been blown to bits in a car bomb in London. She realized that just being close to him constituted an act of danger. Maybe it was the wine, or that fact, which sent a surge through her. She looked at his battered, candlelit face with its eyelids which seemed to droop against cigarette smoke, although he did not smoke; his grey, closely cropped hair and his inbuilt air of menace. With a shock, she realized that he affected her sexually.

Into her confusion, he said: 'I can't remember ever having dinner in such romantic circumstances with a captain of the US Army.'

She laughed and said: 'Maybe I should have come in uniform.'

Solemnly, he shook his head. 'I would never like to see you in uniform. That dress suits you perfectly. You have a strange beauty, Susanna. At first glance, you are quite severe, but as time goes by, it softens and develops.'

She felt absurdly pleased at the compliment. It had been a long time since she had received one.

'Is there a woman in your life now?' she asked.

'No. I seem to be a liability to women.'

'Creasy, that's understandable. You don't exactly work nine to five in an office.'

He leaned forwards, resting his elbows on the table. His voice dropped a decibel.

'Let's talk about you, Susanna. To stay alive, I have to be alert and observant. I've watched you these last few days and something has happened. You may not believe it, but I care for you. At first I thought it was the business with the follower at the river. Now I think it's something different.'

Maybe it was the ambience of the room, but she just blurted it out.

'Three days ago, I discovered I was pregnant.'

He did not react, except to pick up his glass and take a sip of wine. Then he said: 'You may as well tell me all about it. I'm not your father or your boss or your lover. I'm just a friend.'

So she talked. After listening in silence for fifteen minutes, Creasy said: 'In this case, having an abortion is like running away.'

'It's my choice, Creasy.'

'Of course it is. But it would be a tragedy.'

'How can you say that?'

'Because you need a baby.'

'A baby without a father?'

'A father can be useful, but isn't essential. If a child has the love of the mother, it can be enough.' He sighed reflectively. 'Yes, I'm old fashioned and unrepentant about it. I agree with abortion under some circumstances, but you admit that when you conceived that child you were, in a way, in love with that guy in Washington. The fact that he doesn't want to know any more does not make that concept ugly or wrong. The fact that you phoned him when you knew you were pregnant and the fact that you still haven't made the decision of what to do about it, means only one thing: there is a part of you that wants that baby. What we have to find out is how big that part is. In essence, we have to find out how strong your maternal instinct is.'

She sat back and laughed. Then she asked: 'Creasy, you keep saying "we". How can you find out how strong my maternal instincts are?'

'I have a way,' he answered. 'After we leave here, I'll find out.'

She was both curious and a little piqued.

'What are you going to do? Take me down to the river, half-drown me and then ask me how strong my maternal instincts are?'

He shrugged. 'In a different way, that is what I'm going to do.'

It was a big room. It gave an impression of a white mist. The impression came from rows of mosquito nets hanging from the ceiling and covering the cots and beds. The young nun walked between them as they crossed the room, explaining to Susanna about the workings of the orphanage. Near them were the sounds of crying. The nun moved to the cot and lifted the net and picked up a baby and crooned gently to it. It was a girl, only a few months old, but her features were already formed. She looked like an oriental doll, with narrow eyes and the beginnings of jet-black hair.

Another baby started to cry. The nun turned to Susanna and said: 'Please hold this one for a moment.'

Susanna took the tiny bundle and cradled it in her arms. She looked down at the little face and murmured silly words. The baby stopped crying. Susanna lifted her head to Creasy and said: 'You bastard!'

CHAPTER THIRTY

It was hard for Jens to realize that he was in a country which only a decade earlier had witnessed one of history's greatest acts of inhumanity.

He sat with The Owl on the patio of a bungalow in the gardens of the Cambodiana Inn. It could have been a scene from Eden. It was just after midnight and a full moon hung like a lantern above them and illuminated the bougainvillaea which tumbled down the walls of the bungalow. There was the low, throbbing sound of thousands of insects, and the air was heavy with the scent of a tropical night.

The Dane was satisfied. They had eaten a delicious local meal at a small open-air restaurant by the river. Together they had drunk an excellent bottle of claret selected by The Owl, and on returning to the bungalow, The Owl had produced a bottle of duty-free Hennessy XO. In the meantime, Jens had phoned his wife Birgitte and spoken at expensive length to her and his daughter. That alone would have put him in a good mood, but his night was made perfect by the fact that during the afternoon he had worked well at his profession.

They had arrived from Saigon in the late morning. And by early afternoon, they had discovered the source of the fax number to which Tran Quock Cong had sent his reports. The Owl had been very impressed, which made Jens even more satisfied. They had gone from the airport straight to the offices of the Khmer Telecommunications Corporation. Jens produced one of his bogus business cards and presented it to the receptionist, gave her a charming smile and asked for an appointment with the technical executive. He was slightly astonished to be ushered into the office of a tall, sunburnt Australian who, after shaking hands, asked: 'What's the problem, mate?'

'What's an Australian doing here?' Jens countered.

The Australian went to a fridge in the corner, took out three cold cans of frosted lager and, having proven Australian hospitality, explained that his company was co-operating with the Khmer government to repair and upgrade telecommunications in the country. He pointed a finger upwards and remarked: 'Everything comes and goes through a Russian satellite up there. You can phone or fax the world, but it's damn near impossible to get a call through to the next town.'

Jens explained his problem. He was an exporter from Copenhagen specializing in meat products, and through a trade organization had been put in touch with a Khmer company. For the past months they had been in fax communication and potential business looked promising. So, while on a business trip to Saigon and Hong Kong, he had decided to drop in at Phnom Penh and pursue the matter. The problem was that his briefcase had been stolen at Saigon airport, and it contained the relevant files. He could not even remember the complicated name of the Khmer company, but he could remember the fax number.

The Australian was very helpful. He punched the number into the computer on his desk, hit a button on the console, looked at the screen and said: 'Bingo! It's one of three faxes located at the business centre of the Cambodiana Hotel.'

Jens also had his Notebook computer out. He tapped in that information and then asked: 'Is there any way you can find out who has been using that particular fax?'

The Australian shook his head and said: 'That information is held by the hotel itself. The manager is a Frenchman called Marcel Duprey. He might help and he might not. He's a bit officious. You know what the French are like.'

Jens had grinned, and gestured at The Owl. 'I know exactly. This one is French as well!'

The Australian was not at all put out. He just reached forwards, patted The Owl on the shoulder and remarked: 'Some French are OK. I had a cracker of a French girlfriend once.'

'Is it a good hotel?' Jens asked.

'Yes, it's the best and the biggest. It's right on the river. It's air-conditioned and has a great bar and good food. If you're going to stay there, opt for the adjacent Cambodiana Inn, which has its own bungalows. Mind you, it's going to cost you an arm and a leg.'

Jens stood up, saying: 'That's OK. Business has been good lately. Maybe we'll see you in the bar down there some time, and return your hospitality. Many thanks!'

The rest was straightforward. They checked into their bungalow and then made a recce into the hotel's business centre. It was very up to date, with the three fax machines, telex, phones, computers and a very charming Cambodian-French manageress. Jens signed in for a week, and explained that he would be expecting some important faxes that evening between five and seven. She told him to relax in his bungalow and she would have them sent over as soon as they arrived. He demurred, explaining that they would be of a highly confidential nature and that he would prefer to wait himself during that period in the business centre. She fully understood and told him that he could order food and drinks from room service.

So he waited inside the centre while The Owl waited outside the hotel with a taxi standing by. The centre was very quiet. Between five and five thirty, three Chinese businessmen came in to send and receive faxes. At a quarter to six Jens ordered coffee and a ham sandwich. At five to six, a tall, slim Cambodian man came through the door, wearing a smart business suit and carrying a briefcase. He nodded politely to Jens and took a seat at a table near the fax machines. Jens munched away at his sandwich and read a three-week-old Time Magazine. At precisely two minutes past six, the centre fax machine came to life. Both he and the Cambodian jumped up and approached it.

'I'm expecting a fax at this time,' Jens explained.

The Cambodian smiled and said: 'Me too.'

They watched as the paper curled out. The Cambodian turned it and read the postscript.

'It's for me,' he said, and with a subtle movement placed his body in front of the machine, but not before Jens had seen the word CALAN at the head of the paper. He went back to his seat and picked up the magazine, raising it so he could watch the Cambodian over the top.

The Cambodian only glanced at the fax before tucking it into his briefcase and strolling out. Jens followed him through the lobby and watched as he went through the entrance, down the steps and into the back of a waiting black Mercedes. Jens looked across the road and nodded at the Owl, who immediately jumped into his waiting taxi.

The Owl was back at the bungalow twenty minutes later, and reported: 'He went into a building on Achar Hemcheay Boulevard. It's the offices of a company called Lucit Trade Company.'

And so Jens went back to the business centre and sent a fax back to Creasy at the hotel in Saigon. Then they went out for a well-deserved dinner.

CHAPTER THIRTY-ONE

They decided to have a nightcap in the hotel bar. She had been silent during the taxi ride back, but now she felt the need to talk. They sat on stools at the end of the bar, which was almost deserted. Creasy was a good listener. She told him about her early childhood and life as an army brat, when she and her mother had followed her father to postings in Germany, Japan and Guam. Then he had been posted to Vietnam and she and her mother had returned to the States.

It had been difficult for her at school because, due to her travels and experiences, she had been mentally older than the other children in her classes. Even though she had done well at her lessons, she had become isolated and increasingly drawn to her mother.

Then had come the terrible day when they were told that her father was missing in action. He had been a senior combat Intelligence officer at Chu Lay and one day, as the Khe San disaster was looming, he took a helicopter to that isolated base. On its return the helicopter was shot down by a SAM missile over heavily forested Viet Cong territory. The pilot just had time to radio that they were hit and that he was trying to make an emergency landing. The helicopter and its occupants were never found, even after the end of the war when the Vietnamese government was co-operating with the Americans.

'My mother always believed he was alive somewhere,' she said. 'She believed that until her death from cancer ten years later.'

He had been taking small sips of his vodka-tonic, holding the glass with both hands and leaning forwards with his elbows on the bar. He glanced at her and asked: 'Did you also believe it?'

'Not really. Of course I hoped and I prayed, and I guess that I voiced my belief mainly to support my mother. Every year on his birthday, she used to make a dinner of his favourite food and lay a place for him at the table. It was as though he might walk in the door any moment. On those nights I could never sleep. I would hear my mother crying in the next bedroom. The day before she died, she asked me to continue that practice. I never did. The day I buried her, I also buried any thoughts of a live father.'

Again, Creasy just glanced at her as she continued.

'I joined the Army because it was the only life I knew. When I had the chance to join the MIA department, I jumped at it. I was well suited to the work.' She smiled briefly. 'I'm very good at talking to relatives, to try and console them. In fact, so good that they made me a captain.'

Still looking at his glass, Creasy said: 'They made you a captain because you are intelligent and damn good at your work. The Vietnamese and Khmer languages are among the most difficult anywhere, but you learned to speak them both, and also a bit of Lao. When I was here in the war, I met dozens of US Army Intelligence officers and CIA men and so-called specialists. You could count on the fingers of one hand those of them who spoke Vietnamese with any competence. It was a farce. They had to rely on ARVN interpreters, many of whom were VC sympathizers. The level of military intelligence was appalling.' He shrugged and, without looking at her, said: 'That's no slur on your father.'

'No, it's not,' she agreed. 'My father was a linguist. He spoke good German and Japanese and was fast mastering Vietnamese before he went missing. I read his file. It's why he went to Khe

San. He didn't believe the reports he was getting from the Marine Intelligence officers.'

Creasy had finished his drink, and as though by magic the bartender appeared and refilled his glass. Susanna declined another one. She was feeling a little light-headed from the wine at dinner and from the emotional experiences afterwards. As the bartender moved away she said: 'Perhaps the isolation, you might even call it loneliness, has made me ambitious. My father was made colonel when he was forty-two. He was tipped to go on to be a general. Since he couldn't make it, I'm going to.'

She looked at him and saw a half-smile on his face. He lifted his glass in a toast and said: 'I'll drink to that! I only made sergeant myself, but sergeants can always judge officers. You'll make it to general. I hope you'll still talk to me when you get your first star up.'

She smiled at the thought, and then said seriously: 'You would have made a fantastic senior officer. I can hardly believe what's happened during the last few days. It's only been ten days since Jake Bentsen's father approached you in Brussels. Only a week since your name popped up on our computers in Washington. Now here we are in Saigon. You have a defensive team around our informer and his family, and your advanced team is in Phnom Penh and are already feeding back information. I've met both teams and I'm impressed. You know how to pick the right men for the right jobs.'

'That's just instinct,' he said. 'I've known them all for years and they've proved themselves.' He took a hand from his glass and lightly touched her on her arm. 'Also we had your help. We'll miss you.'

There was a silence, and then she turned full-square on the bar stool and said: 'You're not going to miss me. I took a decision driving back in the taxi. OK, you forced that decision. I'm not going back to Washington. I'm not going to have an abortion.

Right now I'm on official holiday. I want to stay with the team. I want to go with you to Phnom Penh tomorrow.'

Creasy shook his head. 'The situation is different. We're being sucked into what could be a violent party. I'm not taking a pregnant woman into that.'

She laughed. 'All I have is a seed inside me. It will be weeks before I even begin to feel pregnant. Right now it's only in the head, not in the body. At the speed you're going, this mission will probably be concluded in a couple of weeks. I have an instinct about that. I'm going with you. We have an office in Phnom Penh which could be useful. And don't forget that I also speak the language.'

He was shaking his head. She went on.

'Besides, if I don't go with you, I'll feel duty-bound to report to Washington that there have been recent, reported sightings of American MIAs.'

'That's blackmail!'

She laughed. 'Look who's talking! Who was it that hijacked me to an orphanage a couple of hours ago?'

'That wasn't blackmail. That was just an exercise in mental suggestion.'

'Whatever it was, I want to see this thing through. Apart from anything else, it's my job.'

She watched his face as he considered. Then he gave her a brief nod.

'OK, you're staying. But early tomorrow morning, you have to use your influence with your friend Dang Hoang Long to pull some strings and get you a visa to Cambodia. It can usually take up to a few days, but I'm sure he can fix it quickly. Then we'll go by road.'

'What about Guido?'

'He'll follow in a couple of days. If those people are going to hit the follower's family, they'll do it as soon as we leave Saigon. So Guido will keep an eye on the outside while Maxie and René are inside.'

'What will we find in Phnom Penh?'

He drained the last of his vodka, turned to her and said: 'We continue to follow the paper trail as laid down for us. For sure it won't end in Phnom Penh.'

'Where will it end?'

'I don't know. But it will end in death. Theirs or mine. It always does . . .' He pushed himself up from the stool. 'I don't know why they want me, but it's not to give me a kiss on the cheek . . . Let's get some sleep.'

Once again, the lift was out of order. As they walked up the stairs, she said: 'I'm sorry I got a bit emotional down there. I guess I talked too much. It's not like me. Maybe it was the wine . . . Maybe it's because today is the twenty-seventh.'

They had reached the corridor. He asked: 'What does that mean?'

They were at the door of her room. She said: 'It's the date of my father's birthday.'

They both had their keys in their hands. He turned and looked at her with his brooding eyes. She put her key in the lock. He said: 'Susanna, if you don't want to be alone tonight, you can sleep with me.'

Her laugh was almost hysterical.

'I've heard a lot of come-on lines in my life, but that's a great one!'

'It's not a line. I'm not inviting you to bed to make love. And I'm not being sentimental. You're a long way from home and the man who you thought might love you. Right now you're a lonely human being. Go in there and lie awake half the night, if you want. Or else come with me and sleep.' He gave another of his almost smiles. 'I have that effect on women.'

She looked at him for a long time, and then slowly pulled the key out of the lock.

CHAPTER THIRTY-TWO

They only had to wait ten minutes at the Moc Bai Border Crossing. Creasy had got out of the car with the passports in one hand and a folded hundred-dollar bill in the other. 'Nothing changes,' he grunted as he got back into the car and started the engine.

'It never will change,' Susanna said, 'while government officials get paid less than subsistence rate.'

The road was potholed to such an extent that Creasy had to weave his way between them. The countryside was flat and wet, with paddy fields stretching out on each side of the road. Traffic was sparse; a few beaten-up old trucks and occasionally a UN vehicle.

'What time will we reach Phnom Penh?' she asked.

'With the condition of this road, it's hard to say. But not before late afternoon.'

They had hardly spoken since leaving the hotel at dawn, and then it had only been to exchange comments and observations. She glanced at his profile and said quietly: 'I suppose I should apologize for this morning.'

'Apologize for what?'

'For what happened this morning.'

He gave her a quick, puzzled look and said: 'Well, this morning we got up, had coffee and croissants, loaded up the car and headed off to Phnom Penh.'

'I mean before that. I mean before we got up.'

His eyes were concentrating on the road again. He said: 'All I remember is going to bed well after midnight and having to wake up at five thirty with a bit of a thick head.'

She laughed inwardly. 'I guess I must have been dreaming.'

'It happens, Susanna, especially after a few glasses of good red wine.'

She had not been dreaming. They had got into the huge double bed and gone to sleep separately; but it must have been about four in the morning when she woke up to find her arms around him and her head in the crook of his shoulder. He was fast asleep, breathing deeply. Strangely for a man like him he had explained that he could never sleep in total darkness, so the bathroom light was on and the door ajar. She lifted her head and studied his face and felt both a warm compassion and a growing desire. He was a man who kept his word. He had not tried to seduce her; just offered his close company on a lonely night. Slowly, she began to move her hands over his body and to kiss him gently on his cheek. The kisses moved gradually to his lips, and she could feel his body begin to move with the rhythm of them. They spoke not a word, but for the next half-hour made slow and very gentle love. She was always the leader, which was rare in her limited love life. At the end of it, she drifted back to sleep, again with her arms around him. It was only an hour's sleep, but it was perfect.

As they bumped along the road she tried to collect and evaluate her feelings. Had she fallen in love with him, or had it been only a moment of unexpected passion? He was a man poles apart from her late lamented professor. They might have come from different planets. She had never been attracted to hard, tough men. It was always the mind that first sparked her attention.

She tried to move her mind off the subject, to concentrate on the scenery around her and the peasants in the fields, with their conical hats, the occasional water buffalo and the fruit-selling children by the roadside, some of whom had either one or no legs, thanks to the millions of mines scattered around the country.

But her mind was obstinate, coming back to the man beside her. She realized what he was doing. On the one hand he was saving her blushes, and on the other hand he was putting up an invisible wall between them; at least, that was what she thought he was doing. She decided just to let time pass and see what developed. Meanwhile, for the first time in days her mind and body were tranquil. It had been a combination of sharing both a problem and some good lovemaking.

Briskly she asked: 'When do we eat?'

He looked up from the road and glanced at his watch. 'With luck we should reach the Mekong River at Neak Lung in about an hour. I want to get there first to make sure that the ferry is running. We'll eat on the other side. There used to be a market there with lots of foodstores. I remember eating some of the best freshwater fish in that market. Then we press on to Phnom Penh. There's a lot to do.'

'How will you proceed?'

He avoided another massive pothole, and answered: 'By now, Jens should have found out who is behind the Lucit Trade Company. And The Owl will have done a full-scale recce of the building. It's possible he and I will break in there tonight and take a look around.'

She thought about that for a moment, and then asked: 'Isn't it a bit dangerous? Two foreigners in a city like Phnom Penh to go breaking and entering. I would have thought that was a job for experts.'

He grunted in amusement. 'I'm no amateur when it comes to breaking into places, and The Owl is a real pro. Before joining Jens, he spent most of his life in the mob in Marseille. He can pick a lock easier than most people blow their noses. With a bit of luck we'll get into that office and out again without anyone ever know-ing. Then, depending on what we find, we'll go on from there.'

The ferry at Neak Lung was operating. As they crossed the five kilometres of muddy, slow-moving water, Susanna reflected that it represented a crossing-point in her life. This time, she would not leave Indo-China the same woman as when she had entered it.

CHAPTER
THIRTY-THREE

At first sight it looked like a Swiss Army knife with a myriad of little blades and gadgets. But as he opened them all out, The Owl explained that they were all tools for different kinds of locks, together with blades for prising open window catches and the like. She was intrigued.

'How did you find such a thing in Phnom Penh?'

It was the first time she had seen The Owl laugh.

'This is made by the finest craftsman in Marseille,' he said. 'An Arab called Gadra. He supplies the top lock-picks all over Europe and North Africa. He's very professional and buys locks and safes from the biggest manufacturers for his own little trading company. Then he makes the tools to unlock them.' He held up the instrument. 'This is made from the hardest steel and cost me more than a hundred thousand French francs. I travel with it in the same way other people travel with a toothbrush or a passport.'

He was obviously proud of his skills. He went out of the front door of the bungalow and told her to lock it from the inside. It was a modern Mortice lock. Within twenty seconds he was back inside, smiling broadly. Susanna said with mock severity: 'So it's no use locking my bedroom door tonight.'

The Owl's expression immediately changed. He said sternly: 'Susanna, you don't have to worry about your virtue here. For us, you're not a woman. You're a person working with us.'

She digested that back-handed compliment and walked back into the lounge. Creasy and Jens were sitting at a table, poring over several bits of paper. She looked over Creasy's shoulder. He glanced up and explained: 'Jens was able to find out the name of the current directors of the Lucit Trade Company. Apparently it specializes in gemstones, in particular the different-coloured sapphires that come from Battambang province near the Thai border. We know that because they have a sign outside.' He pointed to another piece of paper. 'This is an external diagram of the building. There's a front door on to the main road and a back door up an alley. There are no external signs of alarms. The Owl and I will go in the back door some time tonight. The directors are all Cambodians and their names are meaningless at this time.' He gave the Dane an encouraging punch on the shoulder. 'But Jens is nothing if not a good detective. With the help of a little bribe, he got the original records from when the company was founded in 1965. Would you believe, we discovered that the major shareholder at that time was a certain William Crum.'

For a second Susanna was confused. Then she remembered. 'That's the man you assassinated in Hong Kong?'

Creasy stood up, saying: 'One and the same.'

Jens also stood and stretched his shoulders. He said: 'There's one thing I didn't tell you. When The Owl followed the man with the fax back to the Lucit Trade Company, he noticed that no evasive action was taken.'

'Why should there be?' Susanna asked. 'After all, he's a Cambodian in his own country. Why should he suspect that he's being followed?'

Jens supplied the answer. 'Because I checked with a new-found Australian friend and discovered that the Lucit Trade Company has its own fax machine. So it's suspicious that they use a public fax in a hotel for such confidential matters.'

'It's part of the paper chase,' Creasy said.

Susanna thought about that, then felt a twinge of concern. She said: 'In that case, they could well be waiting for you in that office tonight. It could be very dangerous.'

Creasy shook his head. 'I doubt it. Just as I doubt there'll be any internal alarms in that building and for that matter, any gemstones. Just a filing cabinet or two. Because gemstone dealers in this part of the world don't keep their stock in their offices. They usually keep gemstones under their mothers' mattresses.'

'Then what do you expect to find?' Susanna asked. Creasy glanced at the Dane and answered: 'Another piece of paper.'

CHAPTER THIRTY-FOUR

The follower Tran Quock Cong returned to his family and discovered that his wife and two daughters had domesticated two wild creatures.

At least they were wild in his eyes, living outside of a normal society. The one called René was sitting by his younger daughter's bed singing a lullaby in French. The one called Maxie was in the kitchen preparing a chicken curry. Tran said to his wife: 'They don't exactly look ready to protect us from a bunch of assassins.' His voice carried a tone of rebuke.

She quickly pointed out the fishnet screens over the windows and the tape lines over the floor, the small metal box on the table and the two pistols which lay within reach of the two men. She explained to her husband how he must move around the house, and that if there was an attack, he must grab the elder daughter while she grabbed the younger and quickly move into the bathroom and lie on the floor.

'Where do they sleep?' he asked.

She pointed to a single mattress on the floor by the front door.

He asked: 'They both sleep on that?'

'While one is asleep, the other one is awake... They are good men.'

He gave a short laugh. 'They are killers, like their boss.'

She shook her head. 'Young children have an instinct, and the children became their friends even though they could not talk to them.'

The children slept while the adults ate Maxie's curry. Without a common language, it should have been a strained meal. But the atmosphere was relaxed and the sign language plentiful. Maxie was proud of his prowess with curry. He had made a big pot of it, expecting it to be enough for tomorrow's lunch; but within an hour it had been consumed. After the meal Tran tried to offer them some brandy, but Maxie raised his palm upwards, pointed to his gun and gestured with his hand as if sighting. Tran understood that they would not drink while they were at work. With many gestures of thanks, he and his wife went up to join the children in bed. Maxie pulled out a deck of cards and he and René sat down to play yet another game of gin rummy.

Seventy metres away from the house, Guido sat in the rented van. He had arrived two hours earlier and he would stay there until dawn. The night was dark and the street was quiet, with only one lamp casting dim shadows. He was not sleepy because on such occasions he took a Dexedrine tablet every four hours. It kept him awake, but it also kept his mind racing, and it had the odd side-effect of arousing him physically. He decided that it was time he found himself a girlfriend. He began to picture her mentally. She would preferably be Italian from his home town of Naples. She would have a face full of character, with a full mouth and slightly slanted eyes. Her body would be full and long and big-chested. And her legs would curve from her waist to her toes. She would have a lot of passion and a mind as quick as his own. She would also make pasta like a god.

Suddenly, he laughed inwardly. He had just painted a mental picture of Sophia Loren.

He tried to give himself a stern talking-to, but then realized that the subconscious part of his brain was telling him a practical truth. His life at the Pensione in Naples had become lonely. Of course he sometimes went out on the town and found a woman, but it was always only a fleeting affair. He had never considered taking a woman into his life since his wife had died fifteen years before. It would have seemed like a betrayal. But his subconscious was telling him that he would grow old lonely. It was why he was now sitting in this van in a city in Indo-China craving the company of old friends, especially Creasy. He needed companionship. He wanted to be part of the team. When this job was over and he returned to Naples, he would look around him with different eyes. He would open his mind to new possibilities. He would look at women differently. He would not go hunting for a woman. It was not his way. But if one came into his life he would be receptive, even if she was not exactly Sophia Loren.

Time must have passed more quickly than he imagined, because when he saw four men moving past the van on the other side of the road and glanced at his watch, it was just after three a.m. He watched them for only a few seconds, then picked up the mobile phone from the seat beside him and punched a number. He let it ring four times, then switched off the phone and reached for his pistol.

In the house René was asleep on the mattress, snoring gently. Maxie was at the table playing solitaire. The mobile phone was on the table next to the cards and the pistol. As it rang, Maxie reached for the pistol, listening. Then the pistol was in his hand and he was moving. He kicked René's foot gently and as the Belgian's eyes opened, he whispered to him. From a deep sleep, René came awake and alive in an instant. He scooped up his pistol and headed for the stairs. Maxie moved back to the table and turned it on its side, crouching behind it. From upstairs he heard the soft movements of the Tran family being shepherded to the bathroom. Two minutes passed, and then the black metal box beside him gave a soft beep. And then another one. The photocell beam had been broken. Maxie slipped off the safety catch of his pistol.

It started and ended in less than thirty seconds.

The window across the room shattered, but Maxie did not take his eyes from the door. He heard a thump on it and guessed it was a clamp explosive. He ducked his head behind the upturned table. Then his eardrums were compressed by the explosion, and then by another one as the grenade exploded on the ground outside the window. He shuffled to his right, raising his pistol. The door had been blown in. Two black-clad men were crowding through it. 'Amateurs,' he thought. 'They should have tossed a grenade through.'

They both held pistols, but were getting in each other's way. He shot them both in the chest and then glided across the room and put his back against the wall alongside the door. A third man ran in, hurdling the two bodies. Maxie shot him in the back while from the foot of the stairs René shot him in the chest.

'There's one more,' Maxie shouted.

They heard the sound of running footsteps outside, then two shots, and then silence.

'Guido got him,' René said. 'Let's go!'

René scooped up the black box and the mobile phone while Maxie grabbed his precious cards. The pistols went into their shoulder holsters.

Maxie ran up the stairs to the bathroom and spent half a minute reassuring the Trans the danger was over. He smiled at the children, ruffled their hair, and turned away. Ten seconds later they were out of the door, into the revving van and on their way to the safe house.

'Do you think they may try again?' René asked.

Guido chuckled, and answered: 'Not after they've seen what happened to their A-team.'

CHAPTER THIRTY-FIVE

Creasy held the thin beam of his torch on the lock while The Owl picked it. They both wore black raincoats with deep pockets, and transparent surgical gloves. It was a modern Chubb lock and it took The Owl a full two minutes to open it. Creasy listened patiently to his mutterings and then heard a grunt of satisfaction. The Owl dropped his implement into his raincoat pocket and gently eased open the door, shining his torch through.

Creasy waited outside, looking down the alley with the gun held loosely in his hand. He waited for three minutes until he heard a low whistle from inside the building. He went in and closed the door quietly behind him. The light from his torch showed The Owl waiting at the top of a short flight of wooden steps. Creasy moved up them and The Owl whispered: 'There are no alarms that I can see.' He pointed his torch to a door that was ajar. 'That's the secretary's office. Beyond there is a small meeting room which opens on to what must be the manager's office.'

Creasy pushed open the door. His torch revealed a desk and a chair, two metal filing cabinets and a fax machine. On the desk was a modern IBM PC and a printer. Creasy moved to the filing cabinets. They were locked but The Owl had them both opened very quickly.

Inside were the business files of a gem trader. It took Creasy just ten minutes to learn that the Lucit Trade Company only had three customers. Two were in France, one in Paris and the other in Lyon; the other was a Chinese company in Hong Kong. Creasy quickly leafed through the correspondence in French. The letters to the Hong Kong company were in English and were equally innocuous. He took a small pad and a ballpoint from his pocket, and made a note of the companies' names.

They moved through into the meeting room, which was bare except for a table and six chairs. They continued to the manager's office which was very plush, with Persian carpets on the floor contrasting with Scandinavian-style furniture, a wide pine desk with a leather chair and a grouping of a coffee table and three chairs. There were abstract paintings on the walls.

The desk had four drawers, all locked. They found the slim file in the third drawer, inside a metal box. Creasy quickly leafed through it and then stopped at a sheaf of eight-by-ten photographs. He looked at the first one and grunted to himself as if in confirmation. Quickly he laid the photographs and the pages of the file onto the carpet, and then took a small camera and separate flash from his pocket. The Owl aimed the beam of his torch at the photographs and papers for added light.

Four minutes later, The Owl was relocking the back door and they slipped away into the dark.

CHAPTER THIRTY-SIX

It was a new acquisition and Connie Crum was very proud of it. It arrived from Bangkok early in the morning and sat on the table like something out of the next century. Even the placid faces of her two female bodyguards were animated with interest as she explained how it worked to Van Luk Wan.

'It's what foreign correspondents use, and also international aid agencies, to communicate from remote areas of the world.' She pointed upwards with one elegant finger. 'It works through a satellite, and from here or anywhere else I can phone to anyone in the world.'

Van was impressed. 'How much does it weigh?'

She looked in the instruction book. 'Twelve and a half kilos. It has been around for a few years now, but the early ones were very heavy. They get lighter every year. The agent told me that in five years' time they'll be about half the size of a briefcase and weigh only two or three kilos. I bought two. One is being sent to Tuk Luy and will be there tomorrow. It works from rechargeable batteries.' She pointed to a row of buttons and a crystal display. 'These buttons are for preset numbers. I had the agent programme in the ones I use most.' She looked at her watch, 'it's nine thirty now. Sok San will have arrived in his office.' She turned and smiled at Van, like a child about to play with a new toy. 'Let's surprise him with a phone call. He knows that I'm supposed to be at Chek and he also knows that we don't have telephones here.'

She reached forward and flicked two switches on the side of the matt black metal box. With a soft thump, an aerial started to extend upwards and stopped at a height of about two metres, almost reaching the roof of the hut. A red light then appeared at the top left-hand corner. She waited for half a minute and then picked up the handset and pressed the first of the row of buttons. A number flashed up onto the small screen. It had many digits. She swung her long hair away from her face and placed the phone against her ear. The box emitted a series of musical tones and then went silent. She tapped her right foot on the wooden floor as she waited, explaining to Van: 'The signal is bouncing off the satellite to an earth station in Phnom Penh and is then fed into their telephone grid.'

Half a minute passed. Then suddenly she was talking excitedly and laughing. 'Yes, it is me. Yes, I am in Chek. No, they haven't put a telephone line in. It's just that I have upgraded our communications equipment from carrier pigeon to satellite communication . . . Do you have anything to report?'

She listened. Van Luk Wan watched her face turn from happy amusement to sharp alertness. She listened for several minutes without interruption, then said authoritatively: 'Don't leave your office. I'll call you back within an hour.'

She clipped the phone back onto the box and stood thoughtfully looking at it. Then she said to Van: 'Two things happened last night. In Saigon, your entire hit team got wiped out in a gun battle at the follower's home. The follower and his family escaped unhurt.'

'I don't understand,' Van said. 'My instructions were that they were not to attack until Creasy had left for Phnom Penh.'

'He did leave for Phnom Penh. According to Sok San he arrived there with the girl in the afternoon. It must have been the Italian Arrellio . . . or somebody else he brought in.' Her expression was now very hard. 'He's a clever bastard! The follower must have told him of the threat to his family. And so he turned the follower by promising him protection.'

They looked at each other in silence. Then Van said: 'That man moves quickly.'

'Yes, he does. Last night the office of the Lucit Trade Company was entered and searched.'

'Are you sure?'

For a moment anger flamed in her eyes. Then she took a breath and said: 'Of course I'm sure. Sok San was carefully instructed. The past few nights pieces of cotton thread were lightly fixed to doors, cabinets and drawers, all of which were locked. This morning all these threads were displaced. Creasy went through that office and then relocked everything after him.'

'Was anything missing?'

'Of course not. He's too clever for that. But we can assume that he checked every file.' She was tapping her foot again impatiently.

Van said: 'But wasn't that the intention?'

'Yes, it was; but not so quickly. From the moment that Creasy arrived in Saigon, I expected it to take him a week or ten days. I'm not ready for him yet and the date is not right. We must find a way to keep him in Phnom Penh for a few more days. Meanwhile, we leave for Tuk Luy in two hours.'

She reached again for the telephone.

CHAPTER
THIRTY-SEVEN

It was a rare luxury. She lay on the sunbed by the hotel pool with a tall glass of chilled, fresh orange juice by her side, reading a novel by P. D. James.

It had not crossed her mind to pack a swimsuit, but the hotel boutique had a wide selection, all from Paris and all wildly expensive. It had pained her to pay nearly three hundred dollars, even if the skimpy bikini did have a designer label on it. But the pain had eased when she looked in the mirror, and eased further when she walked out to the pool and saw the heads turn.

Creasy and The Owl were sleeping off the night's work, while Jens had gone off to try to get Creasy's film developed.

The night before, she had waited up with Jens. He had produced a pocket-size backgammon set, but after she had lost half a dozen times, he tactfully put it away. They had just talked. She found herself liking the Dane. He had a dry sense of humour and a charming self-deprecation which contrasted with what she already knew was a razor-sharp brain. He told her the story of how he and The Owl had first met Creasy. It sounded like a hilarious adventure instead of a war against a deadly gang of drug dealers and white slavers. He also talked about his wife, Birgitte, and their young daughter, and she saw the fondness in his eyes. It was obvious that while he was enjoying himself in this exotic place, he was missing his family. She liked men like that.

Creasy and The Owl returned at three a.m. They had the air of a couple of men returning from a visit to a good nightclub rather than from a dangerous act in a dangerous city. But she noticed that Creasy took a rare drink, and so did The Owl. Creasy quickly briefed them and then handed over a tiny roll of film to Jens.

She was very excited, but tried to keep it from her face. In the years that she had worked in the department, this was the closest she had ever come to solving a case. Keeping her voice calm, she asked Creasy: 'Are you sure it was Jake Bentsen in the photograph?'

He nodded firmly. 'Of course it showed him much older, but I'll never forget that face . . . It was Jake Bentsen.'

'And there were two other Americans?'

He shrugged. 'There were two other Caucasians, but they weren't waving the Stars and Stripes.'

At that moment she saw the lines of exhaustion around his eyes. She felt a sudden sympathy. He was a fit man, but not young. In the previous twenty-four hours, he had made love to her and then driven for hours along one of the worst roads in the world. He had finally gone out in the middle of the night and risked his life.

'You need sleep,' she said.

Creasy nodded. 'We all do.' He looked at the Dane. 'Jens, you have to try to get that film developed in confidence. And you have to be there while it's being developed and be sure that nobody else sees the prints.'

Jens looked at the film in the palm of his hands and then slipped it into his pocket, saying: 'I'll put my mind to it.'

She caught the eye of a white-jacketed waiter and ordered a fresh fruit salad. When it arrived, she laughed in astonishment. It was a large bowl set inside an even bigger bowl filled with ice. It contained at least ten different kinds of tropical fruit, some of which she had never seen before. She had only managed to eat half of it when she saw The Owl on the other side of the swimming pool. He looked so incongruous in this luxury setting. He wore baggy grey trousers, a dark-blue shirt buttoned to his neck and, even in the tropical heat, a black woollen cardigan. His eyes were moving over the recumbent bodies, obviously looking for her. She watched as he walked around the pool and saw his eyes focus on her and then move away. She put down the bowl of fruit, sat up and called out: 'Here!'

His eyes swung back to her and he stopped abruptly. She stood up, asking: 'What is it?'

He was embarrassed. 'I'm sorry, Susanna, I didn't recognize you.' He waved a hand at her. 'I mean, I never saw you like that before.'

Sternly, she said: 'I am a woman, you know.'

'So I see.' He took a deep breath. 'And I might say, Mademoiselle, a very beautiful one.'

She inclined her head to acknowledge the compliment and asked: 'What's happening?'

'Jens is back. I just woke Creasy. We have a meeting in fifteen minutes.'

She was immediately alert. 'Did he get the film developed?'

She thought she saw a slight smile as he said: 'Of course, Mademoiselle.'

She washed off the suntan oil at the poolside shower and strolled back through the luxuriant garden to the bungalow. Creasy was finishing off a late breakfast of croissants, ham and cheese. He looked refreshed. Jens and The Owl were at the other end of the table, leaning over the photographs. From somewhere, Jens had managed to find a large magnifying glass.

Creasy gestured at the photographs and said: 'Take a look, Susanna.'

The two men made room for her and she looked down at the large-grain prints. Three of them were photographs of photographs. Jens pointed at one of them and she leaned closer. It was black and white. It showed three men. One was tall and fair-haired, wearing only khaki shorts. He was holding a dark, round object in his hands. The other two men were short and Oriental. They wore Khmer Rouge uniforms and they had rifles slung over their shoulders. They stood on each side of the taller man. They were smiling at the camera. She had studied Jake Bentsen's file back in Washington. She too recognized the face. It was not smiling.

The other two photographs were of similar Caucasians, each bracketed by two Khmer soldiers. Jens handed her the magnifying glass and she studied them. Bentsen had been clean-shaven, but these two men wore heavy beards. She studied the faces for a long time and they told her nothing. But she knew instinctively that they were Americans.

She looked again at the photograph of Bentsen. Directly behind him in the distant background was a low hill with a building on its crest. She brought the photograph closer under the magnifying glass and saw that the building was a temple, typical of the many thousands scattered around Cambodia. She looked at the other photographs. There were six of them, all depicting lines of handwritten Vietnamese.

Creasy pushed away his empty plate and said: 'Can you read that, Susanna?'

She picked up one of the photographs and held it under the magnifying glass. After studying it for a minute, she looked up and said: 'I can decipher most of it.'

'Good,' Creasy said. 'Then that's a first step. Jens, please find Susanna a pad of paper, and as she finishes each page, put the information into your computer.'

Jens lifted his briefcase onto the table, opened it up and produced a yellow legal pad and a felt-tip pen. She asked him: 'How on earth did you get that film developed so quickly?'

He shrugged modestly. 'I'm a detective, Susanna. And to be a good detective, one needs to be a bit of a psychologist. I knew that the manager of this hotel is French and of course the French always love a good intrigue, especially when it's a matter of the heart. And particularly if it involves a scandal, no matter how small. So I arranged for a meeting with the manager, Monsieur Marcel Duprey, who has been here three years and of course has many contacts in the city. And I simply explained my problem.'

'Your problem?'

'Yes, of course. A clandestine love affair between a Danish female army officer on assignment here with the UNTAC - which is United Nations Transitional Authority in Cambodia - and an Australian major attached to the same mission. Obviously, someone in that mission dislikes the Australian to the extent that he or she sent an anonymous letter to the woman's husband in Copenhagen, who happens to be a wealthy businessman, much older than his wife. At that point I gave Marcel Duprey my business card which identifies me as a private detective, and explained that her husband hired me and my colleague to come to Phnom Penh and check the details contained in that anonymous letter. That was what my colleague was doing last night. He managed to get compromising photographs of the couple concerned. Naturally, before flying back to Denmark, I needed to get the film discreetly developed and enlarged to be sure that the photos are clear enough.' He gave her a conspiratorial wink. 'Marcel Duprey was suitably intrigued. And since he knows many officers in Phnom Penh attached to UNTAC, he asked me who the lovers might be. Naturally, I gave him a polite little lecture on client confidentiality inasmuch as it applies to both hotel managers and private detectives. He kindly phoned a close friend at the French embassy, where they happen to have their own dark room. The rest, as they say, was plain sailing.'

Susanna looked up at Creasy, who said: 'As well as having to be psychologists, private detectives also have to be damned good liars!'

At that moment they were interrupted by a tap on the door. While The Owl went to answer it, Jens quickly shuffled the photographs together and slipped them into his briefcase. The Owl returned with an envelope and handed it to Jens. Inside was a slip of fax paper. The Dane read the two lines and then passed it on to Creasy who in turn read it and passed it on to Susanna. It read: 'The deal was concluded satisfactorily very early this morning. Our traders are returning home and I will join you shortly.' It was signed Henry.

She looked up. 'I assume that Henry is Guido and that the traders are Maxie and René?'

'Yes. Guido should be here by tonight or tomorrow.'

Jens had put the photographs back on the table. Creasy reached out and picked up the photograph of Bentsen, studied it and said quietly: 'The clue lies in the temple. We have to find out where it is. And for that, we need an expert to identify it.' He looked up. 'In the meantime, Susanna, we need that translation.'

CHAPTER
THIRTY-EIGHT

It took her an hour to translate the writing on the photographs. As she was finishing the last page, Guido arrived, and again she noticed the strange ritual. As Creasy greeted him, he kissed him hard on the side of his face, close to the mouth. She had asked Jens about that, and he had explained that it was the custom between mercenaries of that era. A sort of symbolism. Guido greeted Jens and The Owl warmly, but not in the same way. He gave her a kiss on both cheeks and an envelope, saying: 'Messages for you which came to the hotel after you left.'

There were three messages, all from Jason Woodward. The first one read: 'Please call me.' The second read: 'Please call me urgently.' The third read: 'Please call me very urgently. I love you.'

She looked at that last message for a long time, and then crushed the papers up in her hand and dropped them into the waste-basket beside her chair.

Guido's face was as drawn and exhausted as Creasy's had been the night before. She listened as he briefed the three men on the events in Saigon. He himself had managed to get an early connecting flight via Bangkok. René and Maxie would stay holed up in the safe house for a few days, and then either head home or come on to Phnom Penh if they were needed.

Creasy brought him up to date on what had happened in Phnom Penh, and showed him the photographs. While Guido studied them, Susanna finished off the translation, handed the last sheet to Jens, and said to Creasy: 'It was a correspondence between the leader of a group of irregular Vietnamese militia and an officer of the Khmer Rouge who, at the time, was based in Battambang.' She could not keep the catch from her voice as she said: 'It involved the sale of three American prisoners of war who were held by the Vietnamese. The price for one of them was two taels of gold. The price for the other two was three taels. The difference in value was because the two were experts in minelaying and clearance.' She sat down and they could all see the sadness permeating her face.

Quietly, Creasy asked: 'Were they identified?'

'Not by name. Only by dogtag numbers.'

Jens was transcribing the last page into his computer. He looked up and said: 'The buyer and seller were not identified by name either. Only by code words. The Vietnamese was known as a Commander Tanon and the Cambodian by the name of Commander Indravarnam.'

Susanna laughed without humour and said: it's the name of a famous Khmer emperor who reigned in the ninth century.' She turned to Creasy. 'I have no choice now, since I have dogtag numbers.'

Creasy was nodding thoughtfully. He said: 'Yes, but I want you to give me time. Just forty-eight hours. I want to try to identify the place where those photographs were taken.'

She started to argue, but Creasy held up his hand. 'Susanna, be fair. I let you come on to Phnom Penh with us. Right now you could be on your way back to the States knowing nothing. Give me the forty-eight hours. If these men are still alive, those hours could be crucial to them.'

Jens had finished on his computer. He closed the lid and joined the debate.

'Susanna, in the last few days we've made great progress. The danger is that if you inform your boss, you'll involve the Phnom Penh government, which is a web of corruption. The Khmer

Rouge have their own agents in very high places. If they find out that the American government suspects there may be American MIAs in the country, then the evidence could be quickly obliterated . . . which means six feet under the ground.'

All their eyes were watching her. Irrationally, she thought to herself that the past two days had all been about making decisions. She sighed and said: 'It means that as an officer, I'm breaking my code of duty . . . But OK, forty-eight hours.' Guido stood up and asked: 'Where do I sleep?' Jens gave him a key and said: 'That's for the bungalow next door.'

He picked up his canvas bag with a curt nod and walked out.

CHAPTER
THIRTY-NINE

The Toyota Landcruiser pulled into the compound in a cloud of dust. It was followed by two covered trucks. Piet de Witt watched as Connie Crum jumped out of the jeep and strode towards him. She was carrying a leather folder and an air of urgency, but she greeted him warmly and said: 'I hear you've been doing good work. But now I need you to go into top gear.'

With the scent of her perfume in his nostrils, he followed her into the building, as she shouted out for cold drinks and something to eat. Her clothes and face were covered with dust. As they sat down side by side at a long table, she asked: 'Piet, how many mines do you think you and your team have cleared in the last six months?'

By chance, he had been calculating that the night before.

'About twelve and a half thousand.'

She turned and gave him her most engaging smile. 'That's wonderful. But now I want you to lay a few thousand.'

At first he was struck speechless. Then he asked with incredulity: 'You want me to put them back in the ground?'

'No, no. Not those old ones.' She gestured behind her at the door. 'In those two trucks out there I've got two thousand Czech PP-M1-SR bounding fragmentation pressure mines and fifteen hundred PMN2. Soviet blast anti-tank mines. I want you to lay the most concentrated antipersonnel minefield in the history of warfare. And Piet, I want you and your team to lay that minefield within the next four days.'

He drew a breath to protest, but before he could say anything, she had reached into her pocket and laid a small ebony inlaid box in front of him. It was a work of art and obviously centuries old. 'It's a bonus for you,' she said. 'Open it.'

With huge but gentle fingers, he prised open the lid. Inside were three perfect sapphires, one white, one yellow and one jet black. Piet de Witt knew about gemstones and he knew that these were the very best from the Cardamom Mountains. He knew that each one would fetch at least twenty thousand dollars. He picked them up and rolled them in his fingers, and then in a rough voice asked: 'Where do you want your minefield?'

She opened the leather folder and took out a detailed map of an area east of Tuk Luy. It was in the upper foothills of the Cardamom Mountains and not far from the mines which had given up the sapphires in his hand. She put her finger on the map.

'This is a walled temple. I want that minefield to surround it with only one very narrow access path. The density should be one mine every two square metres on the outer perimeter, increasing to two mines every two square metres on the inner perimeter.'

'Jesus,' he muttered. 'You don't want anyone getting into that temple.'

Her voice turned grim as she said: 'I don't want anyone getting in or getting out.'

A soldier brought a tray of food consisting of rice, fish and pork, together with bottles of chilled mineral water and Coca Cola. They ate while the Dutchman studied the map and calculated. Finally he said: 'The minefield will have a radius of four hundred metres from the centre of the temple. I'll intersperse the PP-M1-SRs with the PMN2s. If you want it ready in four days, we may have to work under lights. Which means we'll need a generator up there.'

'You'll get everything you need,' she said.

His curiosity finally broke through. 'Why that temple?' he asked.

She sat back in her chair, dabbing at her lips with a lace hand-kerchief. 'It's not just a temple,' she said, it's a shrine. And that's all you need to know. I have twenty of my best men up there guarding it. Neither you nor any of your men will pass through the walls at any time, on pain of death. You understand that, Piet de Witt?'

He picked up the ebony box and slipped it into his pocket. 'I always follow orders,' he said.

CHAPTER FORTY

The manager's office was plush, full of leather chairs and rosewood furniture. Across one wall was a huge aquarium brightly coloured by darting tropical fish.

'It soothes me,' the manager explained to Jens. 'Managing a big hotel in this country, at this time, can be very stressful. You can't imagine the problems of getting supplies and trained staff. Did you know that when the Khmer Rouge took over, every single man or woman who had worked in a hotel was automatically executed? As were most of the intelligentsia and bureaucracy. I had to start from scratch. Every time I want to tear my head off, I sit back in my chair and watch my fish.'

'You do a wonderful job,' Jens said in all sincerity. 'The food and service are excellent and very unexpected.'

Monsieur Duprey preened himself slightly. 'I spent the past twenty years opening hotels in Third World countries. It's my speciality. My work here will be finished in another six months, and then I move on to open a new hotel in Vientianne.'

Jens was curious. 'Don't you get restless, not having a permanent base?'

The Frenchman shook his head. 'Not at all. When I have things running smoothly, I get bored. Sometimes I go and take over a hotel which is losing money and turn it round. I'm a sort of hotel doctor. I get called in by all the big chains. If Hilton have a problem with a hotel in India or Zambia or Timbuktu, they always call for Doctor Duprey.' He leaned forward, as if imparting a great secret. 'And do you know what I do?'

Jens was genuinely interested. 'Please tell me.'

'I fire the head chef, the assistant manager, the front office manager, the housekeeper, the reservations manager. And that's all. Even in a hotel with a staff of a thousand or more, I only ever fire at most five people, always at the very top. Then I promote their assistants and teach them. I don't worry about profit for the first three months. After that I start to use my computer.'

Now the Dane was fascinated. They had reached common ground. He asked: 'How do you use your computer?'

Duprey smiled contentedly. 'I have special software. It's programmed to give me daily figures on every profit centre, the rooms, the restaurant, the bars, room service, laundry service, international telephone surcharges, etcetera. And then I start to cut away at the costs. And I always watch the magic ratio; costs against occupancy.' He chuckled at a thought, and asked: 'Do you know the highest occupancy rate of any hotel in the world, Mr Jensen?'

The Dane shook his head.

'Six hundred and fifty per cent,' Duprey stated with a smile, and then burst out laughing at the puzzled look on Jens' face. 'It's the Phu Tey Hotel in Bangkok. You see, it's a brothel and on average, they rent their rooms out six-point-five times in every twenty-four hours.' He sighed in mock misery. 'The dream of every hotelier. Anyway, back to business. What can I do for you? Was your visit to my friend at the Embassy successful?'

Jens straightened in his seat.

'Yes, it was, Monsieur Duprey. But I have to ask a further favour of you, calling your friend Pierre again. I need an enlargement of a section of one of the photographs.'

'An enlargement?'

Jens winked and lowered his voice. 'Exactly. You see, for the evidence in divorce proceedings, we need proof of actual penetration. You understand that it was a miniature camera.'

Now it was the Frenchman's turn to be fascinated. He pushed his leather seat back, stood up and started pacing the carpeted floor.

'Computer enhancement,' he said. 'That would do the trick. Pierre is a fanatic with computers.' He came to his desk and punched a button on his telephone console. When his secretary answered, he said: 'Get me Pierre Lacroix at the Embassy.' While he waited, he smiled at the Dane and said: 'Computer enhancement... That's the answer.'

The Dane felt very much at home.

CHAPTER FORTY-ONE

'We all do stupid things sometimes. Life would be boring if we always made the right decisions.'

Creasy spoke the words defensively, and they made no impression on Guido.

The two men were sitting on the patio of Creasy's bungalow drinking cold Tiger beer and having a mild argument.

'It's been every step of the way,' Guido said. 'From the moment that dogtag was delivered in San Diego, I've never seen anything so precise.' He ticked off the incidents on the fingers of his left hand. 'The dogtag, the description and drawing by Mrs Bentsen of Van Luk Wan, the follower in Saigon with his information of having seen a captive Caucasian near Tuk Luy, the fax number here in Phnom Penh.' He had run out of fingers on his left hand, so he moved on to his right hand. 'The file at the office of the Lucit Trade Company containing the photograph of Jake Bentsen.'

He looked up at his friend. 'Whoever is behind this is extremely clever and well organized. And they well understand your capabilities. They knew you would catch the follower in Saigon, they knew you would trace the fax number and they knew you would break into that office and find that file. It all comes down to one man who is long dead. A powerful man who had great influence in Indo-China. You have to do two things, my friend. The first is to track down the ex-associates and the family, if any, of Bill Crum. The second thing you have to do is call in the Americans.' He gestured at the luxuriant gardens around the bungalow. 'You sit here in a dangerous paradise under the control of clever and probably evil people. They are drawing you on for a purpose. If they wanted you simply dead, they could have hired a sniper in Saigon or even here.' He pointed to a cluster of sugar-palm trees fifty metres away. 'There could be a sniper right there at this moment drawing a bead on your forehead.'

Creasy took a sip of his beer and said: 'It's logical; but it's also logical that they don't want me dead yet. My instinct tells me that we're coming to the final phase. You're right about Bill Crum. He was probably the most evil man I ever met, and I've met many. We know that he paid to get Van Luk Wan out of Vietnam. We have to try to find out who is controlling Van. We need to find the puppet master. Bill Crum spent the last years of his life in Hong Kong. The answer might lie there. I'm going to send Jens and The Owl to Hong Kong and see what they can dig up. As for bringing in the Americans, I'll keep it in mind and make a decision when we fully understand the next step. Anyway, it's better that Jens is out of the country. Things are going to get violent and he's not equipped for violence.'

Guido stood up and started pacing up and down the patio. He said: 'That brings me to something else. Maxie and René will stay in Saigon for a few more days before heading home. It's better that you order them to wait there or even bring them into Cambodia very quietly as back-up. I also think you should send the girl home. I know she's useful with her languages, but she's very exposed.'

Creasy said: 'Sit down, Guido. It's like watching a tennis match with you walking up and down. I have a problem with the girl.'

Guido sat down with the curiosity showing on his face. He said: 'Don't tell me that you've fallen in love with her.'

'No, although she's a fine woman and attractive in a very special way. She's a captain in the US Army and right now she's doing her job, which is to help us track down American MIAs. If she's at risk, that's her duty and she understands it.'

'So what's the problem?'

'The problem is her father.'

'Her father?'

'Yes. As you know, he was a colonel in the US Army Intelligence in Vietnam. He was reported missing in action near Khe San after a helicopter crash. The problem is that there was no crash.'

'How do you know?'

It was Creasy's turn to stand up and start pacing. His face was troubled. He said: 'When I took that assignment to kill Bill Crum in Hong Kong, part of the job was to destroy any files in that converted temple at Sai Kung. Before I destroyed them, I read them. It was a kind of insurance. I had been hired by senior US officers who were implicated in Bill Crum's web of corruption. There were fourteen files with details of fourteen officers. I made a note of all the names. One of them was a Colonel Bruce Moore of Army Intelligence . . . Guido, Susanna's father worked for Bill Crum. It seems that towards the end he developed a conscience. There was a memo in that file from Bill Crum to General Wayne Thomas, who was also on Crum's payroll. It ordered Thomas to have the colonel killed and make it look like an accident. General Thomas had a lot of influence. He was a senior liaison officer with the ARVN. A week after Crum's memo, he sent a handwritten memo back. It was an evil piece of paper, probably written with great pleasure. It explained how he had arranged for Colonel Moore to be flown to Khe San in an ARVN helicopter. During the flight the colonel was overpowered and tied up and tossed out of the helicopter at ten thousand feet without a parachute. It was very easy for General Thomas to fake an accident report.' Creasy moved back to his chair and sat down. He said: 'So my problem is: do I tell Susanna the truth, or do I go on letting her think that her father died a hero?'

The two men sat in silence, with only the background noise of the crickets in the bushes. Then the Italian spoke firmly.

'You tell her nothing. Too often in life the truth can do more damage than a lie. Besides, maybe the man was a hero. It takes guts to walk away from temptation. Bill Crum had him killed because he thought he was going to upset his organization. Let her live with her memories.'

Creasy gave him a slow smile and a nod of agreement. 'It's the romance, Signor Guido. Your Italian blood. There's another problem with that woman.'

Guido rolled his eyes theatrically, then remarked: 'Women and problems go hand in hand. What is it?'

Creasy waited to give effect to his words. Then he said: 'First of all, she has fallen in love with me. And secondly, she's pregnant.'

The Italian lifted his head, laughed and asked: 'How do you do these things, Creasy?'

'I didn't do it. The father is a Professor of Political Science at Georgetown University in Washington. She's only a few weeks pregnant and he wants her to have an abortion.'

Guido's expression turned sombre. He asked: 'What does Susanna want?'

Creasy shrugged. 'She doesn't know. She's confused. I think she wants to have the child. After she told me about it, I took her to an orphanage in Saigon. I watched her hold a two-week-old baby. I was looking at a woman who wants to be a mother.'

Guido was studying his friend's face. He asked: 'Is old Creasy getting a little sentimental?'

Creasy shook his head. 'Not at all. But she's part of our group. I have a concern for you and for Jens and The Owl and I have a concern for her. We live in a dirty world, all of us. It's probably our destiny. You and I have seen more death and destruction than is good for any human being. You remember the faces of the children in Biafra and Angola, in Vietnam, bewildered, frightened, and all too often dying. It's a strange thing, Guido, but when Susanna talked about having an abortion, I seemed to see all those thousands and thousands of faces in front of me. I gave her a hard time about it. Maybe I was wrong. It's her life.'

'You were right,' Guido said emphatically. 'It's not because I'm a Catholic. I don't know her well, but I like her. If she has an abortion, it will scar her life. I'll tell her myself.'

'You can tell her now,' Creasy said, gesturing with his chin. Guido turned to look. She was walking across the lawn towards them, wearing only a bikini. Her gown was thrown over one shoulder.

'She's beautiful,' the Italian murmured.

'Yes, she is, and not only on the outside. We will not discuss her father. But maybe a second opinion about her child would be useful.'

Both men stood up, and Guido went behind the chair and moved it to the table for her. She gave him a smile of thanks and sat down. 'What can I get you to drink?' the Italian asked.

'A Coke, please. And lots of ice.'

Guido went into the bungalow. Bluntly, Creasy said to her: 'I told Guido about your condition. Don't get upset. He's my closest friend. It so happens that you're under my protection on this mission, and if anything happens to me, Guido will take over. I will tell no-one else and neither will he. You can talk to Guido as you talk to me. And you can rely on him under any circumstances. We both think that things are going to get violent soon. He wants me to call in the Americans as back-up and I'm considering it. I'm just waiting for the opposition to make their next move.'

She absorbed all of that without any change of expression. Then she started to say something, but Guido came out onto the patio with the glass in his hand and said immediately: 'Susanna, you must have the baby. I'll be the godfather.' He grinned mischievously. 'And any child with a godfather from Naples is guaranteed a perfect future.'

Again she started to say something, but this time she was interrupted by Jens and The Owl coming up the path. Jens put his briefcase on the table, opened it and took out four eight-by-ten photographs. He spread them on the table with the air of a conjuror producing a rabbit out of a hat. They all craned forward to look. All the photographs showed the same thing: a blurred foreground, but in the background the very distinct shape of a temple.

The Dane said: 'What we have to do next is find a temple expert.'

CHAPTER FORTY-TWO

The Dutchman worked as he moved slowly backwards, scooping out the earth with a small, sharpened shovel and then gently placing the mines one after the other in a pattern that zigzagged the length of the white, pegged-down tape. As each mine was laid, activated and covered, he rolled the tape up. The Khmer Rouge soldier stood behind him holding a lamp high and casting a pool of light. It was after midnight and the air had cooled, But Piet de Witt still sweated: it was that kind of work. He glanced to his left and then to his right. There were other pools of light and other mine-layers at work.

Piet de Witt covered the last mine and stood up, stretching his aching limbs. He shouted an order that they would stop for the night and start again at first light.

As late as it was he would pay a visit to Tan Sotho. It was always that way after putting his life on the line. He needed the release of a soft woman. He needed to celebrate the fact that he would see the sun rise in the morning.

CHAPTER
FORTY-THREE

It was spontaneous. They had all eaten together from room service in one of the bungalows and enjoyed a surprisingly relaxed dinner. Afterwards, Jens and The Owl went into town, not hunting for girls or nightlife, but to ask around in a very casual way and try to get a lead on a Buddhist temple expert. Susanna sat with Creasy and Guido on the patio, sipping a brandy and listening to them reminisce about old times and old comrades. Their minds were so close together that they communicated in a strange abbreviated manner. She listened as Guido asked a one-word question.

'Denard?'

'Sailing smooth.'

'Still copped out of France?'

'No. They gave him a pardon.'

'Only fair. He always worked on the side for CND.'

'True. Even in the Comoros.'

'Retired?'

'Who knows. He's probably casting an eye on Guadeloupe or Saint Bart's. He always wanted to be an emperor.'

Susanna did not feel outside the conversation, even though most of it was incomprehensible. More and more, as the days passed, she felt a part of this strange group of men. She had never known that in her life. Even during her army training she had never made friends easily. She realized that even though these four men had different nationalities and different personalities, they were in many ways very similar. They relished what they were doing. They woke up each morning not knowing what life would bring.

She realized that Creasy was exerting an ever-growing influence over her. She could not define it as love, although the physical attraction was very strong. It was more a question of companionship. She felt good when he was nearby. She enjoyed his dry sense of humour and the depth of his mind. She had noticed that he kept himself completely in touch with world events, always looking for newspapers and weekly magazines and every day listening at least twice to the news on the BBC World Service. During their discussions she had noticed a strange combination of conservatism and liberalism. That night during dinner he had teased Jens, telling him that Denmark was probably the only truly communist nation left on earth. The Dane had been indignant, but Creasy had pointed out that the true ideals of communism had never been realized in Russia or China or even Cuba. In a strange way their real ideals had possibly evolved in Denmark. The community looked after its own. It was a contradiction. The people had a free and inventive spirit and yet they conformed to the good of the whole. They paid massive taxes with surprisingly little complaint because their tax money was spent sensibly for the community. There were very few rich and very few poor. Jens had started arguing. Creasy had held up a hand and said: 'I've travelled the world, Jens. And since I've met you, I've spent some time in Denmark. The quality of life there is the highest I've ever seen. Be proud of your country.'

That had silenced Jens. Then Creasy teased Guido about Italy.

'A nation of peacocks,' he said. 'A recent survey showed that Italian men spend forty per cent of their disposable incomes on clothes.' He glanced at his friend, who was dressed immaculately in an Armani suit. 'In your case I suspect you spend sixty per cent.'

Guido took the ribbing good-naturedly, and answered: it's a sign of civilization. The Americans and the English have no style. We hate to pay taxes, we like rich food and plump women. We live in the sun and dream dreams. We are, on the whole, chaotically happy.'

The Owl joined the conversation. 'If you talk about civilization, France is the heart and the soul. We have the greatest food, the most beautiful women, the finest wines, the most delicious cheeses and the fastest trains. The Danes are well organized, the Italians have a superficial style, the Americans have Hollywood. But la France has flair.' He turned to look at Susanna. With a twinkle in his eyes he asked: 'What has America given the world except John Wayne?'

She felt her patriotism welling up and answered: 'We gave the world the blues and the jazz. Louis Armstrong, Ella Fitzgerald, Brubeck and Miller. That music is unique and it came from America. You can have your Mozarts and Beethovens and Verdis. We have our own culture and we're proud of it. And we don't need some snivelling Frenchman lecturing to us about culture.'

The Owl beamed with delight.

It had been a good evening. Eventually Guido drained his glass and stood up, saying that he had a meeting with his bed. Susanna poured herself a little more Cognac and Creasy poured himself the last of the red wine.

'How do you choose them?' she asked.

'Choose?'

'Yes. Among all the hard men that you must have known, how do you choose people like those . . . and even René and Maxie? They are good men. I guess they may have done terrible things, but they strike me as decent men.'

The question gave him pause for serious thought. He swirled the glass of wine, looking down at it, and then answered: 'It's not a matter of choice, Susanna. Life is like being in a fairground and riding the dodgem cars. You bump into people all the time. I guess that sometimes the bumps are not so bad. Jake Bentsen was like that. I bumped into him in Vietnam. He was just a scared kid putting on a brave face. But I liked him. When I met his parents I knew why. They're good people. I guess that's why I'm here. I have enough money saved and invested not to have to work any more at my trade. I want to find out what happened to Jake Bentsen, not just because of my own curiosity, but because back in San Diego there's an old couple who deserve an answer. It's not a question of sentiment or even emotion. It's a question of balancing out.'

'Balancing out what?'

He sighed reflectively. 'Balancing out my own life. I've done a lot of things and not all of them to be proud of. I've done jobs for money that put me outside of what decent people would call proper behaviour. It's not a real excuse, but I had no choice. I was in the fairground getting bashed up by all the dodgem cars. For most of my life the main criterion was survival. Perhaps instinctively, I'm trying to redress the balance. I'm in danger here . . . We all are. I could leave in the morning and go back to my old farmhouse in Gozo and swim in warm seas and eat good food and enjoy the friends that I have there.' He shrugged. 'But maybe I wouldn't sleep so good. I want to be able to tell that couple in San Diego that their son is either dead or alive. If he's alive, I want to take him home. I've been called a dog of war and I accept it. But old dogs have their own loyalties. And this dog wants to rest in peace.'

'What will you do after this?' she asked. 'Just go home and retire?'

He laughed quietly, as though at an often-heard joke.

'I've been trying to do that for the last ten years. I decided to retire after a stint with the Rhodesian army back in the late seventies. I was drinking too much and I got right out of shape, mentally and physically. I turned up at Guido's pensione in Naples one night with no horizon in my life at all. He arranged to get me a job as a bodyguard to the young daughter of an Italian industrialist. I did a lousy job. She was kidnapped and later killed: but in the months before that, I had fallen in love with that child. Not physically, you understand. She was only eleven. But she came into my life and changed it. I was badly shot up in the kidnapping and nearly died. I went to Gozo and spent two months getting physically fit again. Then I went back to Italy and killed a lot of people . . . the Mafia gang who had been responsible. I didn't do it for money. I did it for myself. The girl's name was Pinta. Since then, at periodic times, there have been other Pintas in my life.' He smiled wryly. 'In a sense Jake Bentsen was a Pinta . . . I guess there will always be Pintas turning up somewhere; and that's good. It gives a purpose to my life. It gives me always an unseen horizon.'

'Do you ever get lonely?' she asked.

'Not really. I live in my own head. I have conversations with myself. Perhaps there are occasions sometimes in the night.' He gestured out into the darkness. 'They say that Cambodia was a killing field, and that's true. But I've been in many killing fields. Sometimes a memory brings loneliness, and that's always late in the night.'

'Not tonight,' she said softly. 'Tonight I will stay with you. After all, you recently did the same for me.'

She woke at first light. Her body was entwined with his. Her mood was serene. The lovemaking had been long and gentle. She was watching his face as his eyes opened. He moved slightly and kissed her on her chin and murmured: 'It was very good.'

'What was?'

'The lovemaking. It was perfect.'

'What are you talking about?'

His eyes opened wider. 'I'm talking about last night. I'm talking about the meal and the conversation, and afterwards the lovemaking. It was perfect.'

She gave him a puzzled look. 'I don't know what you're talking about. We just slept together, that's all.'

He pulled her close and chuckled into the nape of her neck.

CHAPTER
FORTY-FOUR

'You're crazy!' Creasy said.

'I'm totally sane,' Jens answered. 'Trust me.'

Creasy sighed. He was sitting in the passenger seat of the rented Toyota. Jens was driving. They were on a bumpy road running parallel to the east bank of the Mekong River.

'An ex-colonel in the Australian army?'

'Exactly.'

'And he's now a Buddhist monk?'

'That's right. And he lives like a hermit outside the village of Prek. He's our man.'

'How come?'

'He was captured by the Japanese during World War Two, in Burma. He survived the war and afterwards got himself demobbed in Thailand. He took up the Buddhist faith and studied it for the next twenty years and became a monk. In the early sixties he moved to Cambodia and became so learned in the faith that the local people venerated him to the point where he became considered among the three holiest monks in the country. When the Khmer Rouge took over, he was taken by his followers back into Thailand. He returned to Cambodia four years ago. He's eighty-eight years old now and he's looked upon as the holiest man in this country. He's an expert on Buddhism, and in particular its history and its temples. However, he's a recluse. I'm not sure he'll even talk to you. We can but try.'

'How did you get on to him?'

'I was talking to an American in the bar last night. A place called the No Problem Bar. It's a place where the expatriates hang out. The American is doing field work at Angkor Wat. He's a postgraduate student in Eastern Archaeology and a convert to Buddhism. One of those nutcases with long hair and a beard and bangles on his wrists. But he knows his stuff. This Australian ex-colonel, now monk, is called Chum Bun Rong. The American tells me that he's a living, breathing encyclopedia on Buddhist temples. The trouble is he doesn't like talking to people. I'm not crazy, but maybe this guy is.'

They passed through the small, dusty village of Prek. Jens stopped the car, consulted a hand-drawn map, and then pointed to a rickety wooden house on stilts which hung precariously over the river bank.

'That's got to be it,' he said. 'How shall we play it?'

Creasy looked at the house and muttered: 'You carry the rice and the fruit, and I'll carry the photographs. We don't say a single word. You give him the rice and food and I hold the photographs in front of his face. If he's such a fucking expert, he'll get curious.'

It worked. They climbed the wooden steps and pushed open the squeaking door. The old man was sitting in the lotus position in the corner of a totally bare room. He wore dirty, saffron-coloured robes. He was completely bald. His face was as lined and as dark as the wooden walls. Jens placed the wicker basket containing the rice and the fruit by the door. Creasy moved forward and placed the four photographs on the floor in front of the old man. Then he retreated back to the door. The old man ignored the wicker basket and Jens. His eyes remained steadily on Creasy's face. Perhaps three minutes passed with the only sound the river beneath them. Then very slowly, the old man's gaze lowered to the photographs.

CHAPTER
FORTY-FIVE

'We're going to need help from the Americans,' Creasy stated. 'But it has to be selective help.' He looked up at Susanna and then pointed at the photographs. 'That temple lies in the heart of a Khmer Rouge stronghold.'

'Was the monk sure?' Susanna asked.

'Oh yes. He's almost ninety but he's as bright as a button. He was also surprised to see that photograph. Before the Khmer Rouge took over there were more than thirty thousand temples in this country. They destroyed more than two-thirds of them. That monk could not understand why this one was saved.'

Guido looked down on the photographs. He said: 'If there were thirty thousand of them, many must have looked alike. How can he be sure where this one is sited?'

'He was very sure,' Creasy answered. 'During the nineteen-fifties and sixties he visited that temple many times and prayed in it. It was built by Jayavarman the seventh between 1181 and 1193. The architecture has particularly strong Indian influences. The monk was in no doubt.'

Susanna asked: 'Apart from being very old, what else was he like?'

'The most striking thing,' Creasy answered, 'was his accent. It was as though he had never left Sydney. But he had no curiosity about the outside world. He was very serene, but also a little frightening.'

'In what way?'

'I was with Jens, but he only talked to me. He looked at my face for a long time and then told me that I was in great danger. And that the danger was represented in the form of a woman.'

'That's all?'

'Yes. I suppose it's nothing. But the man had a strange influence on me. I'm not religious or superstitious, but somehow he had a presence, and an air of deep understanding.'

'Is that why you want to call in the Americans?' Guido asked.

Creasy shook his head. 'No, that's not the reason. This well-laid trail is going to end at that temple. It lies four kilometres to the southeast of a village called Tuk Luy, which is the headquarters of the largest concentration of Khmer Rouge troops in Western Cambodia. There's no way that I can simply drive over there and take a look. I need help to get in and before that, I need good intelligence of what's happening in the area.' He glanced at Susanna. 'Since it's possible that there are American MIAs there, I take it that assistance will be forthcoming?'

'Of course. I'll phone Colonel Friedman and he'll set things in motion. I'd better do that from my Embassy on a secure line. What will you need?'

Creasy sighed and answered: 'I have no idea yet. But the first thing is to get information on the whole area southeast of Battambang and particularly the Cardamom Mountains. I'll need detailed maps and, if possible, satellite surveys. I'm sure the CIA will have them. I'll also need to know the level of Khmer Rouge concentrations and, if possible, the names of local commanders. I don't want to have to go through any Cambodian officials. That's too risky because many of them still have secret ties with the Khmer Rouge.'

Susanna glanced at her watch and made a calculation. She said: 'It's eight o'clock in the evening in Washington. Elliot will be home. I'll call him there. I'll get the address of the American Embassy and then take a taxi.'

Jens was sitting at his computer. He punched at the keys and then read from the screen: 'The address is 27 EO Street 240. The ambassador is called Henry Gates and the CIA resident is probably a senior military attaché whose name is William B. Garner. Aged forty-two, married with two children, and plays a lot of tennis.'

'I'm impressed,' she said. 'How do you get this stuff?'

He just gave her an enigmatic smile and answered: That's my job.' He looked at Creasy and said: 'I'm wondering if Colonel Friedman has enough seniority to pull the right strings.'

Susanna answered that query. 'Yes, he does. And if he runs into any problems, he'll make a call to Senator Grainger, who can pull just about any string in America.'

She was interrupted by a knock on the door. The Owl opened it and came back with an envelope.

'It's from reception,' he said, 'and addressed to you.'

She opened it. Inside was a single sheet of paper with a typed message which read:

I have information of interest to you. I will send it to the hotel on Thursday afternoon. It is important that your associates do nothing in the meantime.

It was unsigned. She passed it to Creasy who read it and then showed it to Jens, Guido and The Owl.

'Let me see the envelope,' Creasy said.

She passed it to him. It was addressed to Captain Susanna Moore, US Army, MIA Department, care of Cambodiana Hotel, Bungalow 4.

Creasy looked at the envelope for a long time as though it was conveying information, then passed it to Jens. The Dane took the magnifying glass from his briefcase and carefully studied both the envelope and the letter. Then he stated: 'It was printed on a modern laser printer with high resolution.'

From behind him The Owl said: 'There was one in the office of the Lucit Trade Company. A Japanese OKI.'

Creasy took the sheet of paper back and said: 'It's another piece of the paper trail . . . but why do they want us to wait until Thursday?'

Nobody had an answer. Creasy said to Susanna: 'Make your call to your boss anyway.' He turned to Jens. 'In the meantime, I want you and The Owl to get to Hong Kong as soon as possible and start looking into the background of Bill Crum's last years. It would be good to know something before Thursday afternoon.'

Susanna picked up the photographs and put them into the folder along with her translation of the correspondence, and then said: 'I should be back in about an hour. If Jens needs a secure link from Hong Kong, I could arrange that through our Consulate there to our embassy here.'

'It could be useful,' Creasy agreed. He was still looking at the printed message. 'Maybe they're stalling,' he said. 'Maybe we're moving too fast for them.'

CHAPTER FORTY-SIX

Moira Friedman had made a beef casserole with fresh spring vegetables. Following a long-established ritual, she carried the pot to the table and lifted the top. Elliot leaned forward, inhaled the aroma and spoke the often-repeated words: 'You are beautiful, creative and the light of my life.'

He was about to ladle himself a large portion when the phone rang. In exasperation, he rolled his eyes at his wife and said: 'Whoever it is, I'll get them to call me back.'

It was not to be. She heard him say: 'Hi, Susanna. Where are you?' Then he listened intently for a couple of minutes and reached for a pad and pencil. He made some notes and said: 'Wire me the photographs, all of them, including your transcripts.'

Moira Friedman could hear the excitement in his voice. He said: 'I'll be at the office in twenty minutes. And I'll have State communicate with our Ambassador with orders to co-operate with you in every way. I'll arrange for them to set up a mobile SAT phone for you so you don't have to go to the Embassy too often.' He listened again and then said: 'I don't think I'll need Grainger, not with those photographs. It's the first break we've had in years. But I'll keep Grainger informed anyway. Maybe I'll send someone out there as back-up for you.' He listened again, then nodded and answered: 'OK, I'll hold my fire until Thursday night your time. Just wait there at the Embassy and I'll call you back when I've talked to the guys at State. By the way, your friend, Professor

Woodward, has been calling the office two or three times a day trying to get hold of you. He seems agitated . . . OK, I'll tell him you'll be in touch in due course. Be careful out there. It's a dangerous place.' He listened again and then chuckled. 'Yes, I guess you are. OK, wait for my return call.'

He cradled the phone and returned to his wife. 'That was Susanna Moore calling from Phnom Penh. She's there with a bunch of mercenaries and she's got photographs of what may be three MIAs being held captive by the Khmer Rouge. One she's certain about. I have to check the dogtag numbers of the other two.' He made a forlorn gesture at the casserole dish. 'Sorry, honey. You'll have to keep that warm. I'm going to be late at the office.'

She was not upset. She knew the frustrations of his work and she could see the excitement in his eyes. She walked over, kissed him and said: 'On your way, Elliot. Call me if you have a chance.'

CHAPTER
FORTY-SEVEN

Ambassador Gates was not a happy man. He was a career officer, and quite reasonably liked to do things by the book. He sat in his office with the Stars and Stripes hanging behind him and a photograph of the President on the wall. He said: 'Captain Moore, I understand the importance of anything relating to our MIAs and I'm ready to help you in any way I can. I just had the Assistant Secretary of State on the phone telling me to do just that. But can't you tell me anything more? It's all so vague. There may be some Americans held by the Khmer Rouge and you're mounting some kind of an operation to find out and, if possible, to rescue them. Is that all you can say?'

Susanna answered: 'I'm sorry, Mr Ambassador. It's all I can tell you at this stage. I'm working undercover with some very unofficial people who demand the utmost security and secrecy.'

'The CIA?'

She smiled and shook her head. 'Hardly that. I can tell you that we have a strong lead and that the people I'm working with are very competent.'

'Are they Americans?'

She shook her head. 'I think that one was once, but it's an international group. And I must ask you not to probe any further. I hope I can give you more information by the end of the week. In the meantime, I understand that you can issue me with a mobile satellite phone and fax. Over the coming days I may request that certain necessary items be brought in to Phnom Penh by the diplomatic pouch.'

'Like what?'

'I don't know yet, but they could include weapons and communications equipment.'

'Weapons!'

'Yes, Mr Ambassador. My colleagues may have to go into Khmer Rouge territory and it would be rather stupid to walk in with a white flag.'

He was a tall, thin man with an austere face. But a lifetime of diplomacy had not broken his sense of humour. He gave her a smile and stood up, saying: 'We're at your disposal, Captain. I take it that I won't have to smuggle in a detachment of Abrams tanks or a battery of Cruise missiles?'

She also stood up, returning his smile. 'No, sir. It would be small arms and ammunition and perhaps secure radio transmitters and receivers. I'm sorry I can't tell you more at this moment. But I can tell you that events have been developing rapidly and seem likely to continue doing so.'

'Where are you staying?' he asked.

'At the Cambodiana Hotel. But my colleagues and my superiors would be very upset if the Embassy were to arrange any kind of surveillance. And I can assure you, Mr Ambassador, that if that happens, my colleagues would very quickly be aware of it.'

'It won't happen,' he answered. 'But understand one thing, Captain. I represent our government in this country and I would prefer not to have any nasty surprises.' He pressed a button on a console on his desk and a moment later a young man knocked on the door and entered. The Ambassador said to him: 'Mark, please issue Captain Moore with the communications equipment she needs and instruct her how to use it.'

He held out his hand and Susanna shook it.

'Thank you, Mr Ambassador.'

'You're welcome, Captain . . . Be careful. We don't want any more MIAs.'

CHAPTER
FORTY-EIGHT

They stood at the bottom of the gently sloping hill looking up at the outline of the temple. Connie Crum was in the centre. The Dutchman was on her left and Van Luk Wan on her right. The Dutchman pointed to the bright red line of string that zigzagged up the hill to the entrance of the temple wall.

'That string is laid exactly in the centre of the mine-free pathway, which is one metre wide. It changes direction three times. You'll have to learn to take bearings which I'll point out. That means you take a bearing on an object nearby and line it up with a tree or a mountain peak in the distance. There'll be three such bearings, and only the people who know them will be able to get in and out of the temple compound.' He pointed to the members of his team, who were about fifty metres from the temple wall. 'The minefield will be completed by nightfall tomorrow. So in the afternoon I'll show you the bearings and then we take away the string.'

Connie Crum patted him encouragingly on his shoulder. She said: 'You've done well, Piet. I assume that all of your team know the bearings.'

'Of course.'

She turned to Van and said: 'I want every member of the team to be given a bonus of two hundred US dollars tomorrow night.'

'On their behalf, I thank you,' the Dutchman said. 'For them it's a fortune.'

She smiled cynically. 'And they'll spend it on drink and women. That's the circle of their lives. I won't keep you any longer, Piet. Van and I will return tomorrow, at five in the afternoon. Again, well done!'

The Dutchman walked up the hill, very carefully following the line of the red string. Connie watched him in silence and then said: 'Tomorrow, when the last mine is laid and those men have come out, I want them all shot.'

The Vietnamese showed no surprise. He said: 'Before or after I give them the two hundred dollars each?'

She laughed. 'Before, of course. And the Dutchman we put into handcuffs and leg irons. His work will be finished tomorrow, and I haven't decided what to do with him.'

Piet de Win reached the interior perimeter of the growing minefield and stood behind his team, watching them work. He had trained them well; but of course some were better and quicker than others. His best man could lay and set a mine every three minutes. He turned and measured the approximate distance to the compound wall. It was about forty metres. He did a quick calculation in his mind and then relaxed. The minefield would be ready. They would not even have to work under floodlights tonight. That was dangerous work, and he was glad they didn't have to do it. In the evening he would drive into Tuk Luy and buy some fresh fish in the market and then take it to Tan Sotho. They would make love and afterwards she would cook the fish with saffron and rice in the way he liked so much. And he would teach the young boy a little more English. It had become a routine two or three times a week, the lovemaking, the food and the hour-long lesson. The boy was only three years old, but he was bright and a quick learner. The Dutchman laughed inwardly at the thought of himself being a teacher. Who would believe that?

CHAPTER
FORTY-NINE

Jens and The Owl shared a large room at the New World Hotel looking out over the harbour. Both of them had been to Hong Kong before a few years ago on a previous assignment with Creasy, and had been massively impressed. The city and its harbour literally buzzed with people and activity. Across the water in Victoria, skyscrapers rose like stalagmites. From the balcony Jens could count over twenty ferries plying back and forth. It was bliss. He had been a ferry buff since he was a small child. He had sat on his parents' patio at Helsingor watching the ferries passing through Oresund Strait. Much to the chagrin of his wife Birgitte, his idea of a restful holiday was taking one of the big Swedish ferries that plied the Baltic. She could never understand it since he would spend most of his time in the bar drinking beer with Schnapps chasers. He had even joined the Ferry Appreciation Club and he and other ferry fanatics would go on trips and get profoundly drunk.

He had been looking out over the harbour for half an hour. The Owl was lying on his bed with his Walkman by his side and the earphones clamped to his head. He was silently conducting Beethoven's fifth symphony. Jens tore his eyes away from the view, glanced at his watch and shouted: 'Let's go! We'll take the Star Ferry to Victoria and pay a visit to the business registrations office. I want to find out who's behind the Cuontum Import-Export Agency.'

Reluctantly, The Owl switched off Beethoven and stood up. Jens opened his briefcase and from one of its pockets took out a stack of business cards. He flicked through them and selected one, saying: 'Today I'll be Svend Torp, managing director of the Viking Credit Rating Agency.'

Twenty minutes later they were at the inquiries counter of the business registrations office, and Jens was charming the middle-aged Chinese woman in charge. She studied his card as he told her that he wanted to see the records of the Cuontum Import-Export Agency. It was a routine inquiry on behalf of a Danish company who were about to start trading with it.

She went off into a back room and returned three minutes later with a blue file tied with a black ribbon. She explained that he could only take photocopies of the statutory directors and shareholders list. Being a private company, it did not need to file its annual balance sheets, but it did need to record changes on the board of directors and major shareholders.

He went immediately to the back of the file and noted that there were only two directors who had founded the company. One was William Crum and the other Tam Wok Lam LD. He flicked through the pages and noted that in March 1977, William Crum had ceased to be a director and that Connie Lon Crum had been appointed to the board four years later. Her address was given as care of the other director, Tam Wok Lam, in a building on Ice House Street. There had been no other changes on the board since the company was first formed in 1962.

He turned the file around, pointed and asked the woman: 'What does LD signify?'

She looked at the name and said: it signifies that Mr Tam is a lawyer. In fact, he's a very prominent lawyer in Hong Kong with many business interests. He also sits on the Legislative Council, appointed there by the Governor. He's a very respectable person.'

'That's good to know,' Jens said. He closed the file. 'Thank you for your help. I don't need to make any photocopies.'

Outside on the busy street, Jens turned to The Owl and said: 'I need to learn a little bit about gemstones, especially those that originate from Indo-China. Let's go and find a jeweller. And then, maybe, we'll go and talk to Mr Tam. But before that I have to phone a friend in Copenhagen.' He smiled cheerfully. 'Then, this evening, I'm going to ride a few of those ferries. Do you know that they have eighteen different destination points from the island to the mainland?'

'I didn't know that,' The Owl answered. 'It's a very serious gap in my knowledge of trivia.'

'A very serious gap,' Jens said severely.

The Dane ended up buying a small sapphire ring for Birgitte. It cost him two thousand Hong Kong dollars, but he considered it money well spent, since he had deliberated for over an hour with the shop's owner, examined most of his stock, and gleaned a great deal of information about the various gemstones and their sources.

They made the five-minute ferry journey back to the hotel and Jens phoned a good and old friend in the police department. He needed to know the name of a jewellery importer in Denmark who on the surface appeared reputable, but was maybe a little shady in the background. Someone who would deal in gemstones as a front for money laundering. His friend promised to phone him back soonest, and for the next half hour Jens watched the ferries while The Owl conducted Beethoven.

CHAPTER FIFTY

It was the most luxuriously appointed office that Jens had ever been in. A deep Tientsin carpet covered the floor, the walls were panelled with mahogany and the furniture was comprised of leather and carved ebony. On the desk was an intricately carved ornament of ivory. The man behind the desk was short and bald and dressed in an immaculately cut dark suit. He rose as Jens entered the room and took the proffered business card which had been printed only an hour before. It indicated that Jens was a Mr Lars Petersen of the Odense Import Company in Denmark. Mr Tam offered Jens a seat, and a girl brought in a pot of jasmine tea and two gilded cups.

As Jens described his business, the Chinese man sipped at his tea and watched him intently. Then he asked: 'Why have you come to me, Mr Petersen? Why did you not go directly to the Cuontum Import-Export Agency and see Mr Fu, the manager?'

'For two reasons,' Jens answered. 'Firstly, I discovered that it's always better to discuss business with the organ grinder than with the monkey. And secondly, I prefer dealing with lawyers.'

Mr Tam smiled and nodded slightly. 'But how did you know that I was connected in any way with the Cuontum Agency?'

'I make it a rule to always find out who are the directors and the shareholders of the companies I deal with. Then I require information about their reputations. I was at the business registrations office earlier and noticed that you were one of the two directors, along with a Miss Connie Lon Crum. You are also a fifty per cent shareholder.'

'That's correct. I founded the company with Connie Crum's father. After his death, she acquired his shares and the directorship.'

'That was in 1977, wasn't it?'

'Yes, I believe so. Mr Crum died in 1977 and left his shares in the company to his daughter, Connie. She became a director some years later, when she reached the minimum age of twenty-one.'

'Yes, I noticed that from the records. Now, Mr Tam, I've only been in Hong Kong a short time, and I know of your fine reputation. But I know nothing about Miss Crum. And there is another important factor. I am mainly interested in buying Cambodian sapphires. Naturally, over the past years, the supply has been very erratic.'

Mr Tam nodded in agreement, and said: 'That's the strength of our company. You may know that most of the sapphires come from the Cardamom Mountains and that area is largely controlled by the Khmer Rouge. Miss Crum's mother was Cambodian and it happens that she has close connections with the people operating in the Cardamom mountain range.'

'You mean with the Khmer Rouge?'

'No, no,' Mr Tam answered with a slight smile. 'I would never even suggest that. She spends a lot of her time in Paris and in Bangkok. But because of her connections, she does have an influence in south-west Cambodia, and that influence means that the Cuontum Trading Agency has a regular supply of top quality sapphires. You need have no worry about that. I'm sure that Mr Fu can help you. He carries considerable stock. Would you like me to make an appointment for you?'

'Not just yet,' the Dane answered. 'First I would like to discuss financial matters with you.'

Mr Tam was immediately alert. 'Financial matters?'

'Yes. You might know, Mr Tam, that import duty and taxes are very high in Denmark. My company intends to import a very significant amount of sapphires over the next few years. Of course you would understand in this business that such stones are a financial commodity easily transported.'

'Of course.'

'We'll need to come to an arrangement with the Cuontum Agency so that the stated value of the stones we import would be somewhat different from the real value.'

'I understand, Mr Petersen. It's quite common and it's not a problem in Hong Kong, which is a free port. I assume that you would pay the invoice value by irrevocable letter of credit?'

'Certainly. And the difference will be paid before shipment into any bank account you nominate anywhere in the world.'

'Very reasonable,' Mr Tam said and then gave a conspiratorial smile. 'Although business taxes in Hong Kong are quite low, it's still painful having to pay them. The arrangement will suit us. When would you like to see Mr Fu and inspect his stock?'

'Not for a couple of days. I only arrived in Hong Kong this morning and it makes good business sense to get over the jetlag before sitting down to what I know will be tough negotiations. I plan to do a little sightseeing before getting down to business, and perhaps go to Macau for a day trip.'

The Chinese man stood up and said: 'You're a practical man, Mr Petersen. I suggest you phone Mr Fu when you're rested. In the meantime, I'll brief him on our conversation. And I look forward to a long and profitable relationship.'

'What will happen,' The Owl asked, 'if Mr Tam checks with the Odense Import Company?'

They were sitting in the Captain's Bar at the Mandarin Hotel, round the corner from the lawyer's office.

Jens answered: it's no problem. My friend in the police headquarters in Copenhagen has twisted a couple of arms down in Odense. If they get a fax from Mr Tam, they'll send a fax back stating that Lars Petersen is their purchasing director and he's currently travelling on business in the Far East.'

He took a contented sip of his Carlsberg beer. He had not ordered it out of patriotism; he just preferred it to the local San Miguel. He looked around the crowded room and muttered: 'Connie Crum, aged thirty-four, daughter of Bill Crum. She's the one stalking Creasy.'

CHAPTER FIFTY-ONE

Creasy listened and then said: 'It's good work, Jens. Well done! I want you to go to Bangkok and try to dig up some information on her there. Meanwhile, Susanna will see what the American Embassy might have or be able to find out.'

He hung up the phone, turned to Susanna and Guido and said: 'Bill Crum had a daughter by a Cambodian mother. She's thirty-four years old and is apparently well connected to the Khmer Rouge. From what Jens told me, she could even be part of that organization. She spends time in Bangkok and Paris and presumably also in south-western Cambodia. Jens and The Owl will leave for Bangkok this afternoon and try to get more information about her. In the meantime, Susanna, I'd like you to talk to your ambassador again. The CIA may have a file on her and it's almost certain that they have satellite surveillance photographs of the whole of Cambodia. It would be useful to see some pictures of the area where that temple is located. I'll give you a map grid reference.'

She picked up the phone, called the Embassy and arranged a meeting with the Ambassador in twenty minutes.

After she had left, Guido stated: 'This is a matter of revenge, and it has been very cleverly arranged. The woman must know that you killed her father. She's three-quarters Oriental and we both know that Oriental people have long memories and huge patience. She has waited a long time and whatever she has in mind for you will not be pleasant. I think you should get the hell out of here . . .'

Creasy shook his head. 'You know damn well I won't do that! Their organization is superb. It stretches from Cambodia all the way to San Diego. She obviously has a lot of money and influence. It's not in my nature to run and hide and even if I did, she would find me. In a matter like this it's her life or mine. She's planning to kill me for sure. My guess is that first she wants to talk to me. She wants to tell me why she's doing it and she wants to watch my face. I've no other choice but to go down the trail that she's laid so cleverly. If she's one per cent as evil as her father, killing her will not bother my conscience a bit.'

Guido was probably the only person in the world who could truly understand Creasy's mind. He said: 'Then I'm going to call in some back-up in the shape of Maxie and René. If you're even dreaming of going into Khmer Rouge territory, you're going to need firepower and you're going to need information. Whatever satellite photographs the CIA may have are probably not going to be enough. They will just represent routine surveillance of a wide area which is heavily forested.' He pointed at the phone. 'I think you're going to have to phone Senator Grainger. The Ambassador here will co-operate with Susanna, but you need more than mere co-operation.'

Abruptly, the Italian smiled. 'It's like old times,' he said. 'I already feel ten years younger.'

CHAPTER FIFTY-TWO

'Don't ask me,' Colonel Jonas Chapman said to his co-pilot. 'We just fly the damn thing. The fucking onboard computers know more than I do. The orders come from the top, A1 priority. We overfly Manila and then pretend to be a civilian aircraft en route to Bangkok. We make a slight diversion over south-west Cambodia at twenty thousand feet and there the computers trigger the cameras at prearranged co-ordinates. And before we even land at the base in Thailand, the photographs will be on their way to whoever wants to have a look at that little piece of South East Asia. We'll finish the checks. Get taxi clearance and start up the engines.'

Five minutes later the AWAC (plus 246/7) surveillance plane with its giant radar dome and its crew of fourteen experts lifted off the US Air Force runway on the Pacific island of Guam. After they had levelled off at 42,000 feet and set up the computers, Colonel Chapman and his co-pilot sat back in their seats and began drinking the first of many beakers of black coffee. They would not touch the controls for the next five hours.

'It takes me back,' Chapman said reflectively. 'I was on B52S at the end of the 'Nam war. My first assignment. We used to do the round trip from Guam to the Ho Chi Minh trail, and also to eastern Cambodia. I was just a kid and all fired up, but I can tell you that after twenty-five missions, I was bored out of my skull. It was a ten-hour round trip and everything was co-ordinated from our base in

Chiang Mai. We had about one thousand guys up there enjoying the hash and the massage girls and playing around with computers which got signals from airdropped sensors that supposedly could tell the difference between the passing of a column of Viet Cong troops on foot or in trucks. They were crazy days.' He glanced at his much younger co-pilot, it was a sort of a ritual. When we were over our programmed position, the computer would trigger the bomb release. The B52 would elevate about fifty feet. Then there would be a silence after which all the crew would chorus reverently: "Sorry about that!"' He smiled at the memory. 'The trouble is that often as not the damned Viet Cong would have found the sensors and moved them half a mile away from the trail. We must have dropped millions of tons on nothing in the jungle or on innocent villages. We lost that fucking war because of technology.'

'What do you think this mission is about?' the co-pilot asked.

'Who the hell knows? Maybe some general wants some nice photographs for his office walls.' He cursed again. 'I had to cancel a round of golf this afternoon. Now tell me, Lieutenant, what comes first? A game of golf or taking pretty pictures over Cambodia?'

The co-pilot smiled ruefully. 'Don't complain, Colonel. I had to give up a lunch date and an interesting afternoon with a pair of big tits from the base hospital.'

The colonel chuckled. 'Ah, well. I guess our country comes first.' He glanced at the computer screen to his left. 'We hit the Manila beacon within an hour. It's going to be real exciting because at that moment, this plane banks three degrees to the north while we sit and drink coffee and contemplate our navels . . . I was born fifty years too late. Imagine what it was like, wrestling with a Mustang or a Flying Fortress over Tokyo or Berlin. That was real flying.'

The lieutenant smiled. He was only twenty-three years old, but he had heard the same lament at least a hundred times.

CHAPTER FIFTY-THREE

The minefield was finished and the Dutchman was proud of it.

He led the way out, with his team of ten men following exactly in his footsteps. They made the last zigzag and approached the waiting canvas-topped truck. A Khmer Rouge officer was standing at its rear. He pointed and shouted an order in Khmer which Piet de Witt could not understand. His team could, and the men quickly lined up and stood to attention. The officer moved to the side and gestured for de Witt to come and stand beside him. The Dutchman did so, a little puzzled. And then he realized that the officer would be making a speech of praise for the many dangerous hours that his men had spent laying that incredibly dense minefield without a single accident.

The officer turned and shouted another order. The canvas back of the truck dropped down and the Dutchman saw the machine gun and simultaneously watched the flame spit from its muzzle and then heard the crackling rattle as the bullets cut down his team. He stood rooted to the spot in horror, watching the bodies twist and fall. One of them scrambled away amidst the screams, but in his terror went the wrong way. The first mine at the outer perimeter blew him high into the air.

The Dutchman turned, his hands coming up in a reflex action to strangle the officer: but the officer was holding a pistol pointed at the Dutchman's forehead. 'It was necessary,' he said.

CHAPTER FIFTY-FOUR

He was young, handsome, intelligent and obviously very expert at this work.

Creasy didn't like him. Maybe it was because he was cocky; maybe it was because he was so obviously trying to impress Susanna; maybe it was because he brought bad news. He had arrived from the American embassy ten minutes before and spread out the photographs on the dining-room table in the cottage. Naturally, being CIA, he was dressed in a dark suit, a plain tie and a button-down shirt.

'You would need at least a batallion,' he said, 'with tanks and heavy artillery.' He pointed at one of the photographs. 'There are at least one thousand Khmer Rouge soldiers in that area within a radius of twenty kilometres from that temple. The government troops don't even contemplate the idea of going in there.' He pointed to another photograph. 'That's the small town of Tuk Luy, which is the main headquarters of the Khmer Rouge in the area.'

Creasy was only listening to him with one ear. He and Guido were studying the photographs intently. Some had been taken two months earlier from a satellite, and the others a few hours ago from the AWAC plane out of Guam. They were very high definition, and the CIA man had brought a device that could be placed over the photographs and give them a three-dimensional aspect. It was easy to pick out buildings, vehicles and individuals.

The temple itself measured thirty metres by eighteen and was in remarkably good condition. It was surrounded by a high wall with a diameter of about a hundred metres. There was only one gate, and the two guards standing just inside it were clearly visible. Several of the photographs had been taken using heat-imaging film and were simply a kaleidoscope of different colours.

The CIA man explained, 'They show different vegetation and different kinds of soil and even minerals.' He pointed to one. 'That was taken by a satellite two months ago when we did a complete coverage of the area. The darker red is forest. The lighter red is grassland. And the pink shows paddy fields. Now, there's something interesting here.' He leaned forward and pulled the photographs directly under Creasy's eyes. 'This was taken from the AWAC today. Of course all the photographs were sent simultaneously to Washington for expert analysis.' He put his finger on a photograph. 'This is your temple.' He pushed another photograph alongside. 'This is your temple taken from the satellite two months ago . . . Notice the difference.'

There was an obvious difference. On the photograph taken from the AWAC, a pale grey area circled the temple. It was not present on the earlier photograph.

What is it?' Creasy asked.

The CIA man seemed to savour the moment. After an over-dramatic pause, he said: 'Our boys at Langley tell us that it's a minefield, and a very extraordinary one. There are hundreds or even thousands of minefields all over Cambodia, laid by the Khmer Rouge, by the Vietnamese during their occupation, and by the present government. It's estimated that there are more than five million mines, but none of those minefields ever showed up on satellite or aerial photographs. That minefield is extremely dense and so it had to be laid by experts. And it must have been laid within the last two months.'

Susanna remarked: 'Maybe by our American MIAs . . .'

Creasy said: 'It's a possibility. Jake Bentsen was an ordinance specialist, but not that experienced by the time he got hit in that firefight. But still, he could have learned a lot within the last twenty-six years.'

'Could be,' Guido said. 'But then I can't get something out of my mind. The follower in Saigon told us that the white man he had seen was referred to as "the Dutchman". What would a Dutchman be doing there right among the Khmer Rouge?'

'It could be a mercenary,' Creasy said. 'There hasn't been much work around for the last ten years, except in Bosnia-Herzegovina and Chechenya. I've heard rumours that a few mercenaries are working in this area and also in Burma . . . A Dutchman,' he mused. And then abruptly lifted his head and said to Guido: 'A Dutchman, that was what we always called the Afrikaaners. There are very few Netherland mercenaries, but there were plenty of Afrikaaners.'

The Italian was nodding, and he began to count them off on his fingers. 'Joey Bock, Renne de Beer, Janik Jarensfeld, Piet de Witt. From what I hear, they're all still active.'

Susanna said to Creasy: 'Why don't we do what my boss did when we wanted information on you? He contacted Interpol in Paris where they keep very extensive files on all active mercenaries. Something might turn up.' She turned to the Italian. 'Guido, please write down all the names you and Creasy can remember of Dutch or South African Afrikaaner mercenaries.' She gestured at the CIA man. 'Mr Jennings can then fax Interpol from the Embassy. From our experience in the MIA department, you'll get a reply within twenty-four hours.'

Creasy nodded to Guido, who immediately started writing names on a sheet of paper. Creasy was again looking at the photographs and the indication of the minefield.

'It fits the pattern,' he said. 'She expects me to attack that temple and she's laid a minefield in preparation.' He turned to the CIA man and asked: 'Do you have any agents in the area?' 'Negative.'

'Does the Cambodian army have any agents?' 'If they do, they're not telling us. Anyway, they would be an unreliable source. We have a guy in Battambang, which is a hundred and fifty miles from that temple. He's a Thai businessman, but frankly, I think he just takes our monthly cheque and sends us reports from the local newspaper. He's probably also in the pay of the Khmer Rouge.'

Susanna had turned away from the table and was pouring coffee into four cups. Over her shoulder she said: 'Mr Jennings, how many agents do you have in the country?'

The American smiled and answered: 'Please call me Mark. I'm sorry, Miss Moore, the answer to your question is of course classified.'

She brought him a cup of coffee and gave him a sweet smile and said: 'Well, Mark, it will only take me one phone call to Washington to get it unclassified. We may have three MIAs in that area. Your orders are to co-operate with me fully. If I make that phone call, I will preface my conversation by stating that the co-operation from Mr Mark Jennings is seriously lacking in quality.' She gestured at Creasy and Guido. 'For the last few days these two men have been risking their lives trying to help my department locate those MIAs. They are risking their lives right now being in Phnom Penh, and I have no doubt that during the next few days, while you're resting your tight, elegant, little ass in your elegant office at the Embassy, they will be taking even bigger risks.'

She had moved close enough to the CIA man that they were almost eyeball to eyeball. Very quietly, she asked: 'How many agents do you have in-country?'

His answer came immediately. 'Ten. Four Americans including me, and six Cambodians.'

Susanna backed away, turned to Creasy and said: 'I'm sure my department can get authorization to use those agents, including Mark here.'

Creasy looked at Guido and they simultaneously burst out laughing. Then Creasy said to the CIA man: 'No offence, Mark, but if you offered me a company of Rangers, I couldn't use them. The last thing we need is another Mogadishu.'

Susanna had diplomatically moved back to the coffee table. She brought cups for Creasy and Guido and said to Jennings: 'They work in different ways, Mark. It's not a question of fire-power. There's more to this situation than meets the eye and I'm afraid that the reasons for that are classified, even to you.'

Jennings' irritation was mirrored on his face. He was look-ing at Creasy. He said: 'So I'm just a messenger boy, Mr Creasy. I've been in the country for the past eleven months and you've been here for the last couple of days. Maybe you don't have much respect for the American armed forces, but that's no reason to insult people who are trying to help you.'

Creasy's voice was relaxed. He said: 'I appreciate your help, Mark . . . I hope you don't mind my familiarity in using your first name . . . I have a lot of respect for the American armed forces. I was a Marine before being dishonourably discharged. It's a ques-tion of overconfidence. With all the technology they've got these days, they rely too much on gimmicks. That's why they fucked up on the raid to try and get the hostages out of Tehran. It's why they fucked up in Mogadishu trying to capture a warlord. And it's why they would fuck up if they went gung-ho into that temple. Have you ever been in combat, Mark?'

'No.'

'Have you ever killed a man?'

'No.'

'How old are you?'

'Thirty-six yesterday.'

'Happy birthday, Mark! The guy I'm looking for was twenty-one years old when he was hit on the Vietnam-Cambodian bor-der. He'd been in the army for three years and had been fighting in

Vietnam for eleven months right on the front line. He was a good soldier, he was a patriot. He didn't have to be drafted, he enlisted. It's just possible that he's alive and has been a slave of these people for the past twenty-six years. Now I appreciate your help.' He gestured at the photographs on the table. 'And of course technology plays its part. I need your help to continue, and I had no intention of putting you down or denigrating the US armed forces. But for this job I need to rely on myself and my own people. I may need to obtain false passports and papers for them. I will certainly need weapons. I plan to move within the next seventy-two hours. Your role will be very important; even vital. I want you to liaise with Susanna here and act as base commander. It may bring you into danger, even though you are an in-house agent and under diplomatic immunity.' He leaned forward slightly, and his voice hardened. 'Even a diplomat hasn't got immunity from a bullet in the head. Are you armed?'

'No, sir.'

'When you get back to the Embassy, you'll arm yourself and remain in that condition until this mission is over. I assume you've been trained in small arms?'

'Yes, sir.'

'You'll also assume responsibility for the protection of Susanna.'

'Yes, sir.'

'Is that necessary?' Susanna asked.

'It is,' Creasy answered. 'We know that Connie Crum has her people here in this city. When I make my strike, they may try to get at you.' He turned back to the table and looked down at the photograph of the temple. Then he glanced up at Guido. 'I'm going to need a parachute,' he said.

Guido was nodding. He said: 'We're going to need two.'

'No,' Creasy answered. 'I go in alone. You bring up the cavalry when it's needed.'

CHAPTER FIFTY-FIVE

'You want something special?' the girl asked coyly.

'Like what?' Jens asked.

She giggled and said: 'I can make you happy in many ways, but it costs one hundred dollars extra.'

The Dane sighed and concentrated his mind on the small apartment in Copenhagen and his loving wife and daughter. For the last hour he had been lying on the huge double bed in his room at the Dusit Thani Hotel in Bangkok. And for the last hour a young, nubile girl in a brief white tunic had been massaging his body and relieving the tension of the flight from Hong Kong. The Owl was in the next room getting similar treatment.

'Thanks, but I'm a married man,' he answered.

The girl dug her thumbs into the muscles of his shoulders and said: 'So?'

'So I love my wife. And I don't fool around.'

'You're a very strange man,' she said, and smacked his bottom lightly to indicate that the massage was over.

When she had left, he went into the bathroom and took a very cold shower.

The Owl knocked on his door twenty minutes later. He seemed very relaxed.

'I like this town,' he stated.

'I'll bet you do,' Jens answered. 'Now we have work to do. I've contacted a Danish friend who works in this city and we meet him in half an hour. He's going to teach me how to bribe a senior Thai policeman.'

The Owl looked dubious. Jens explained: 'My friend is not exactly my friend. He's the friend of a friend. In foreign places we Danes stick together and help each other out. The guy here is called Søren Musholm and he's the manager of a large Danish trading company. He's been in Bangkok for the last twelve years and he knows how things work. The police here have files on any foreigner who lives or works in this country, and so for sure they have a file on Connie Crum. The only way I'm going to get to see that file is by paying a hefty bribe . . . Let's go!'

The meeting took place in a murky bar on Pat Pong Road. The Owl understood nothing of what was going on because naturally, the Danes spoke Danish as if they hadn't had a chance to speak the language for the past ten years. Of course they also drank Schnapps with hearty toasts of 'Skål!' Then Søren Musholm switched to English for the benefit of The Owl and explained the bribery procedure.

Passing Jens a business card he said: 'You call this man and make an appointment in his office. Once there, you tell him that you're a private detective and that you're checking up on the corespondent in a divorce case.'

'Sounds familiar,' Jens remarked.

'I'm sure you're very good at it. You give him the woman's name and ask him if he has a file on her. Since he's the head of the department of overseas residents, he will immediately check on his computer, and tell you that of course he has a file, but of course he cannot show it to you. You then contrive to drop your wallet on the floor and say: "Oh dear! I dropped my wallet with two thousand dollars in it."'

'Two thousand!'

'Yes, that's the going rate. It's not like the old days, when five bucks would buy an audience with the king. This city is booming. There's a lot of money around. Police officers are notoriously underpaid. About eighty per cent of their income comes from dropped wallets. Don't try to do it for less. A couple of weeks ago, I went to see a minister to get a difficult import permit. I dropped my wallet and said: "Oh dear! I dropped my wallet with ten thousand dollars in it." The minister smiled and said: "No, Mr Musholm, you dropped your wallet with twenty thousand dollars in it!" I had to make a return visit with a fatter wallet! If you want to see that file, the going rate would be two thousand dollars. Of course you'll not mention my name, and you'll go alone. It's simple courtesy. There are no observers to such transactions.' He picked up the bottle, poured three more shots and asked: 'What the hell has gone wrong with our football team?!'

CHAPTER FIFTY-SIX

Creasy and Guido sat under a sunshade by the pool. They were wearing swimsuits, drinking beer and arguing.

Susanna had gone off to the embassy with Jennings to make sure that his fax to Interpol was legible. Guido was being forceful.

'Be logical,' he said. 'Connie Crum must know a hell of a lot about you and your capabilities. She knew you would follow the trail to Saigon. She knew that you would detect the follower. She knew you would pick him up and extract the information that had been planted in his head. She knew that you would locate the fax machine where he sent his messages and follow the receiver to his office. She knew that you would break in and find that file with the photographs. She knew that you would contact an expert and find out where that temple is. Let's assume that she also knows you were a paratrooper in the Legion. She might well know the story about how you once parachuted at night into a well-guarded Mafia Capo's compound on Sicily and killed him and his henchmen. She has structured your entire journey. In a strange way she has managed to look into your head, and that worries me.' He leaned forward and said intently: 'She did not have that minefield laid to keep you out of the temple. She had it laid to keep you in, because she expects you to drop in one night soon. She will be waiting for you.'

Creasy did not answer. He finished his beer and dived into the swimming pool. Home in Gozo, he always swam a hundred lengths every day and he had missed the exercise.

Guido waited patiently. He knew that while his friend was swimming, he was also thinking. He also knew that he would not let Creasy parachute into that temple compound; at least, not alone.

After half an hour, Creasy pulled himself out of the pool and padded back to the table. As he picked up his towel, he said: 'Maybe you're right. That woman bothers me. I guess I'll just pack my bag and go home.'

The Italian smiled. 'Don't joke with me. We have to find a strategy to get in and an escape route to get out. That's your department. But I'm telling you here and now that you're not going to parachute into that temple. Maxie and René will arrive in Bangkok tonight and wait there for a call. Jens and The Owl are already there.'

'We can't use Jens,' Creasy said. 'He's a mind man, not a soldier. But we can use The Owl. Anyone who can survive the backstreets of Marseille can look after himself in the battlefield. So our army will be five. Anyway, we can't make plans until we hear from Jens and until tomorrow afternoon, when Susanna should be receiving her mysterious message.'

'That one is quite a woman,' Guido said. 'She really stamped her personality on that Jennings guy. She's got him in a condition where he'd walk through fire for her.'

'She's a good one,' Creasy agreed. Then he turned at the sound of approaching footsteps and called out: 'Are your ears burning?'

Susanna sat down and the waiter materialized at her shoulder. 'I'll have a Coke and half of your normal fruit salad,' she said. Then she asked Creasy: 'What the hell are you talking about?'

'We were just talking about you,' Creasy answered. 'We decided that you're not entirely useless.'

She bowed in mock appreciation. 'I'm glad to hear it. As it happens, you're right. I bring interesting information.' She reached into her voluminous bag, pulled out a roll of fax paper and passed it over to Creasy. 'It came within an hour,' she said. 'My toyboy Jennings pulled out all the stops.'

After reading for two minutes, he looked up at Guido and said: 'Piet de Witt! He was among the four mercenaries known to have been recruited a year ago by a company in Bangkok which is thought to be a front for the Khmer Rouge.'

'De Witt . . . !' Guido muttered. 'A total bastard! And an expert on mine-clearing and laying. Who were the other three?'

Creasy looked at the papers and read out the names. 'Denderfield, Brad Shore and Gagnier.'

'Do you know them all?' Susanna asked.

'Yes. The first two are Brits who served with Mike Hoare in the Congo. And the other is a Frenchman who worked with Denard. All four of them are the pits of our trade. Piet de Witt is probably the worst. He's an Afrikaaner who did five years in the dirty tricks department of the South African army until even they could no longer stomach him. He was kicked out and then promptly hired by BOSS, which was the South African Security Service. He carried out several assassinations for them, both in South Africa and in Mozambique.' He laughed at the memory. 'Then he got caught fiddling his expenses, which went against the grain of the same bosses who had sanctioned the assassinations in the first place. They fired him and he ended up as a mercenary working in West Africa, and later moved to Europe. It's rumoured that he did some external jobs for the IRA. I once had a run-in with him. I almost beat him to death. I regret that I didn't. He's an Afrikaaner so he has to be our Dutchman. And in all probability he laid that minefield around the temple.'

'Do we know where he is now?' Guido asked.

Creasy shook his head. 'According to this Interpol report, he vanished from Bangkok eleven months ago. There were no records of him leaving the country. I guess that right now he's in Tuk Luy. But I can tell you one thing: if he is there, he doesn't know I'm coming.'

'How can you know that?' Susanna asked.

'Because after I gave him that beating, I told him that if I ever saw him again, I'd kill him. And he believes that. He knows it as certainly as the sun rises in the east.'

The waiter arrived with Susanna's drink and fruit salad. 'So what do we do?' she asked.

Creasy answered: 'We wait to hear from Jens and to see what kind of message you get tomorrow afternoon, if any.'

'If any? You think there might not be one?'

'It's very possible. I think we arrived ahead of schedule. I think that Connie Crum was not quite ready for me. But still, we have to wait; and while we wait we have to do some serious thinking about how we get to Tuk Luy and what we do when we get there.'

CHAPTER
FIFTY-SEVEN

'Do you know how to operate an IBM with WordPerfect software?'

'Of course,' Jens answered, and lifted the briefcase which contained his own IBM Notebook. 'I use the same software.'

The policeman stood up from behind the desk and said: 'Well, I have to go to the toilet, Mr Jensen. And then I'll probably take a coffee in the canteen. I'll be away for at least fifteen minutes. You will not be disturbed.' As he walked around his desk towards the door he said: 'The file name is CRUM/KHMER Number twenty-five. I take it that you have a spare disk in your briefcase? Just leave your wallet on the floor.' At the door he repeated: 'Fifteen minutes. I'm sure you can find your way out. If you need anything else, don't hesitate to call me. I'm always available.'

'I'll keep it in mind,' the Dane said.

It had gone exactly as predicted by Søren Musholm. The cheap, plastic wallet he had purchased on leaving the bar now lay at his feet. It contained twenty crisp hundred-dollar notes. He stood up and moved around the desk to the computer console. It was a new model with a large colour screen. Within seconds he had located the file. On the top right-hand corner it indicated that the file ran for 122 pages. He glanced at his watch and then for the next ten minutes read the first fifteen pages. He then opened his briefcase, took out a blank disk, inserted it into the slot and down-loaded the entire file. He left the office exactly four minutes later. At the door he turned and looked at the shiny black wallet by the chair. It had been worth every cent of the two thousand dollars.

Back at the hotel, a message was waiting for him at the reception. It was from The Owl, telling him to come to his room as soon as he arrived.

The Owl answered the door with his headphones on. He quickly switched off the Walkman and pushed the earphones down around his neck. 'How did it go?' he asked.

'Very well. I dropped the wallet and got to play with his computer.' He tapped his briefcase. 'I've got a hundred and twenty-two pages on disk which cover everything the Thai police knows about Connie Crum . . . She is one very dangerous lady, and I have to get the information to Creasy soonest.'

The Owl had moved to the minibar and taken out two bottles of Tiger beer. 'Sorry, no Carlsberg,' he said as he opened the bottles. 'Creasy phoned. Maxie and René are arriving this afternoon. I booked Maxie into the Erewan Hotel and René into the Sheraton. I think it's better that we remain dispersed. I've also left messages accordingly for them at the airport. Creasy also said that they had information on the target and it's very complicated. We are to stay in Bangkok until contacted. He also asked how you were getting on, and I told him you'd be in touch as soon as possible. He gave me the name and phone number of a man at the American embassy in Phnom Penh who can relay messages securely.'

'That's good,' Jens answered. 'Try to get the guy on the phone.'

Half a beer and two minutes later Jens was talking to Mark Jennings. 'Do you have a computer in your office? Good . . . what is it? Good . . . do you have WordPerfect on it? Good . . . Give me the number and an access code and I'll send you a file through my modem. Please call me back to confirm safe receipt and then print two copies and deliver them personally to Creasy as soon as possible.' He gave Jennings the phone number and the room number, then hung up and went to work.

The Owl looked on with admiration. He himself was useless with computers and their paraphernalia. It took only a couple of minutes for the Dane to set up his Notebook, connect the modem to the phone, insert the disk and tap in the number and access code.

'It's a crazy world,' The Owl said. 'I remember the days when it was almost impossible to get a phone call through from one end of Marseille to another.'

'I'm not surprised,' the Dane answered with a grin. 'The only things the French know are how to make Béarnaise sauce and ride a bicycle.'

'*Mon cul!*' The Owl answered fervently, and then raised his glass to take away any offence.

CHAPTER FIFTY-EIGHT

Creasy and Guido read the two copies of the file that Mark Jennings had brought to the hotel. After finishing each page, Creasy passed his on to Susanna and Guido passed his on to Jennings.

'I didn't even wait to read it,' Jennings said. 'I just printed it out and rushed over.'

Creasy finished first. He stood up and walked out of the French windows into the garden. Guido joined him ten minutes later.

'She's certainly her father's daughter,' Creasy said grimly. 'Evil through and through. The thing is that she's also highly intelligent. You certainly don't get a first-class degree from the Sorbonne University for being stupid.'

Guido was nodding in agreement. He said: 'Evil, clever and beautiful. It makes a formidable combination . . . But I'm surprised that the Thai police have such a complete file on her.'

'Don't be surprised. Ever since the Khmer Rouge first appeared on the scene, there's been close co-operation between them and some sectors of Thai business. The Thai police certainly have their informers among the Khmer Rouge. A lot of money has been made from timber and gemstones in one direction and arms in the other direction. Some of that money will have gone to Thai generals and politicians. That file shows that Connie Crum is in command of the Khmer Rouge in the Cardamom Mountains.

It's estimated that she's got at least two thousand troops under her command. It also indicates that for the past two years she's been clearing mines from that area and that most of her troops form a perimeter in the foothills leaving the mountains themselves largely unoccupied, except for local peasants in isolated villages. I don't know why she's done that.'

Susanna and Jennings joined them. She asked: 'Are you still going ahead after reading that?'

'Yes,' Creasy answered. 'The only question is how.'

Jennings interjected: In view of the contents of that file, I think the Cambodian government can be persuaded to make an airborne attack into the mountains. They could land inside the perimeter of her forces.'

'They don't have the training for it,' Creasy answered. 'And they don't have the resources. There isn't a single airborne battalion in the country. The most they could do would be to air-lift a few hundred troops by helicopter . . . and they wouldn't be enough.'

The American shrugged and asked: 'And you and your few friends would be enough?'

'We would do it differently,' Creasy explained, 'it would be an in-and-out operation conducted at night. We all know each other very well and have fought together many times. The Khmer Rouge are peasant soldiers without much sophistication or training.'

He turned back to the bungalow and the others followed him. Inside, he opened a map on the table and pointed to the area.

'It's only thirty miles from the Thai border south of Bangkok.' He turned to Jennings. 'I've had a change of mind and a change of plan. Connie Crum has read my mind and she assumes that I'll parachute onto that temple compound during the night some time in the next few days. We know from that report that she has a strong presence in Bangkok with her own companies and more than a hundred employees. I have to make her believe that I'm going to do exactly what she thinks. And I need your help on that.'

The American was eager. 'What do you need?'

'First, information. There must be at least one or two private flying clubs in the Bangkok area. I need to know what equipment they have and whether they charter out their aircraft. Second, I want to know if there's a shop in Bangkok that sells parachutes of the sporting kind. You know, they're like a wing and used by parachute clubs.'

Jennings said: 'Well, if there's no shop, I can certainly arrange to have some flown in.'

Creasy shook his head, 'It's better if there's a shop. Guido and I will be leaving for Bangkok tomorrow. The rest of my team will be there. It's almost certain Connie Crum's organization will have Guido and myself followed. They'll probably have our hotel phones bugged. We need to be seen to charter an aircraft for a certain night and to buy parachutes. What they must not know is that in the meantime, we acquire two Land Rovers or their Japanese equivalent and various armaments. Connie Crum has to confirm we're coming in from the air.' He pointed at the map. 'She and her people will be looking up into the dark sky while we cross the Thai border.'

'What about Susanna's message?' asked Guido.

Creasy shrugged.

'There'll be no message. That was just Connie Crum stalling.'

CHAPTER FIFTY-NINE

'We're going to make a deal,' Connie said.

'What kind of deal?' de Witt answered.

He was sitting on the stone floor with his left wrist shackled to an iron ring set in the wall. She was sitting at the table, dressed in jeans and a cream silk blouse and drinking a glass of chilled white wine. Behind her, two sentinels cut from stone, were her black-clad, female guards with their Tokarev pistols at their hips.

She took a delicate sip and said: 'I'm going to give you your life and you're going to give me some advice.'

His laugh contained no humour.' 'That's some kind of a deal. I give you the advice and then you kill me anyway.'

She shook her head. 'No. I'm even going to release you in a few minutes. You can take a shower and go and see your girl-friend. And then, in a few days, I'll arrange to have you sent over to Thailand together with your sapphires.'

He thought about that for a few moments and then realized he had no choice anyway. He asked: 'What advice do you need?'

'I need advice about the man you hate. The man called Creasy.'

His head jerked up. 'Creasy?'

'Yes. He'll be visiting me here within the next two or three days.'

She laughed at the sudden look of fear on his face and said: 'Don't worry, Dutchman. He doesn't know you're here. He'll arrive by air, probably with his friend, Guido Arrellio.'

The Dutchman got control of his mind. 'By air? But there's no airstrip here.'

'He doesn't need one. He'll come at night by parachute and he'll drop right into the centre of your minefield, right next to the temple. He'll never leave that place. I'll be waiting with my men.'

'Why would Creasy come here?' he asked.

'Because he's looking for an American called Jake Bentsen who was his friend many years ago. But Bentsen died three years ago. Creasy doesn't know that. He thinks he might be in that temple.' She smiled as if at a private joke. 'Creasy stands by his friends with the same fervour as he kills his enemies . . . You are not his friend, are you, Piet?'

The Dutchman shook his head. 'No; and if he finds me, he'll kill me.'

She reached out and stroked an elegant hand down his arm. 'He will not kill you, Piet. He's my enemy and I'll kill him.'

In a puzzled voice, the Dutchman asked: 'Why is he your enemy?'

'Because he killed my father. I've waited seventeen years for this moment. I have planned for it and spent a great deal of money. Every morning as soon as I wake up and every night before I go to sleep, I've waited for the moment. I was seventeen years old when I saw him kill my father. It's in my eyes now: the silenced bullet into his head; and then the flames. I watched it through the window and then I ran away. Creasy walked away as though he had just destroyed a cat or a dog. I made a promise to myself that night: one day, I would kill him like he killed my father. That promise is about to be fulfilled. Everything is ready. He comes in confusion, not knowing what to expect. But I know his mind exactly. He was a para and so was his friend Guido. They like to use parachutes. It's his favourite way of getting into a difficult situation. And for sure he'll get in, but he'll never get out!'

'So what advice do you want from me?' the Dutchman asked.

'You're a mercenary,' she answered. 'You've worked with him in the past. What weapons will he bring?'

The Dutchman thought for only a moment, then answered: 'He'll come armed to the teeth. He'll have an Uzi machine-gun, it's his favourite. He'll have grenades, plenty of them, certainly fragmentation and possibly phosphorous. He'll have a pistol and a knife. But he'll have something else which is more dangerous.'

'What is that?'

The Dutchman's eyes almost glazed in thought and memory.

'He'll have a ferocity like you've never seen. When he fights, he has no thoughts. Everything is instinct. I've never seen anything like it. I once trapped a civet cat in South Africa when I was a boy. It had been killing my father's chickens on the farm. I set what we call a VIP trap. It's where you bend a branch of a tree down or a sapling, peg it to the ground with a length of wire and a noose at the end. When the cat steps on a twig, which is like a trigger, the noose tightens around its leg and the branch is released. I caught that civet cat and it was dancing around. I was fourteen years old at the time and I had a shotgun. Pound for pound, the civet cat is the most vicious animal in Africa. I tell you, I've never seen anything like it. It was tied by its leg, but it took me six rounds before I could hit it. And then another four before I could finish it off. I never forgot its eyes: bright yellow and so full of hate. And even though it was tied down, I felt the fear to my balls. I never saw anything like that hatred again or felt that fear until one night many years later when I had a fight with Creasy. The problem was that I didn't have a shotgun and his leg was not tied down. I don't care how many men you've got or how much firepower. But *Gott verdam*, you'd better be careful!'

She was smiling. Her whole body was smiling. Her mind was far away, but her eyes were looking at the Dutchman. He felt an involuntary shiver. He was looking at a civet cat. A cat that did not release its prey.

CHAPTER SIXTY

Mark Jennings was like a stray puppy who had found a home: all energy and smiles.

The extent of his devotion to Susanna was almost embarrassing. He hung on her every word and jumped to her every suggestion. During one of the brief moments when he was absent making a phone call, Creasy remarked to her: 'It's like you have him on a mental lead.'

'I'm not sure I like it,' she answered ruefully.

'Don't let it bother you,' Creasy answered, it's not every woman who has a CIA agent in the palm of her hand. With the resources at his disposal, he could probably arrange to rob the local National Bank and shower you with riches.'

'I don't need riches. At any moment soon he's going to make a physical pass at me.'

Creasy shrugged. 'It's no problem, Susanna. Just threaten him with sexual harassment. Every full-blooded American male is terrified of those two words. They are the greatest invention that the women's liberation movement ever came up with.' His voice turned mockingly stern. 'But don't do that until this mission is over. Jennings is proving very useful and also inventive. His idea of trying to recruit a turned Khmer Rouge soldier from that region as a guide is a very good one. There have been quite a few hundred who have deserted in recent weeks to the Cambodian government. Jennings will select three or four and then you'll talk to them one by one and pick out the best.'

They were sitting on the patio of the bungalow. Guido had gone off to the business centre to send a fax to his Pensione in Naples, just to make sure that it had not burned down or been turned into a whorehouse by his assistant Pietro.

Jennings came back from the phone, pulled out his chair, sat down and said to Susanna: 'It's all set up. My liaison guy at Cambodian Army HQ has selected five ex-Khmer soldiers who defected over the last three weeks. They're all from that region. I've arranged for you to interview them in half an hour from now at their Intelligence Headquarters. I'll take you there myself. It's better that you don't mention the job in front of Cambodian Army officers.' He turned to Creasy. 'I can arrange transport to Bangkok on a US Army or UN aircraft. Nobody will know you've left Phnom Penh or even arrived in Bangkok.'

Creasy shook his head. 'Thanks, Mark. But Guido and I will fly on a civilian aircraft. I want Connie Crum to know that we've left Phnom Penh and I want her to follow us when we get to Bangkok . . . at least, at the early stages. But it would be good if you could smuggle Susanna and the ex-Khmer Rouge guy into Bangkok unnoticed.'

'And myself!' the American said firmly.

'Yourself?'

'Of course. From that file we know that Connie Crum has a big organization in Bangkok. If Susanna is going to be in that city, she needs protection while you guys cross into Cambodia.' He tapped a spot under his left armpit. 'I've got my Colt 1911 right here, and it's going to stay there until Susanna is safely out of Indo-China.'

Creasy glanced at Susanna, who was trying hard not to smile. 'OK, it's agreed,' Creasy said. 'We'll all feel better knowing that you're around. You can also handle the collection of the weapons we need and the two four-wheel-drive vehicles.'

'That's in the pipeline,' Jennings answered. 'They'll be ready by noon tomorrow.' He looked at his watch and said to Susanna: 'We have to leave now. Those guys will be waiting.'

They all stood up and Creasy said to Susanna: 'Try to find one who's got a really serious grudge against the Khmer Rouge. Something that will give him more motivation than mere money.'

'I'll do my best,' she said. 'And incidentally, how much money do I offer him?'

'Five hundred dollars.' 'That's all?'

'Yes, that's all. If you offer him more, he'll think it's a suicide mission.' He turned towards the door, saying: 'And for him it will be. If he gets out . . . if we all get out, he'll get a bonus.'

CHAPTER SIXTY-ONE

He was tall for a Cambodian, with clean-cut features and intelligent eyes. Susanna felt an empathy with the man. She had not felt it with the previous four. They had been mere pawns in the ever-shifting Cambodian scene. This man was of a higher calibre. He was in his mid-forties and he had a stillness about him, a watchfulness. As he sat down, he greeted her formally and after listening to her opening sentences, complimented her on her Khmer language. She looked down at the file in front of him. His name was Nol Pol, and he had turned himself over to the Cambodian army only a week before. Mark Jennings sat to her left, slightly behind her. He had been studying the local language, but only for a short time. He could take no part in the discussions.

'Why did you defect?' she asked the Cambodian.

'It was a family matter.'

'In what way?'

Nol Pol sighed and asked: 'Do you know the history of Cambodia over the last twenty or thirty years?'

'I'm not an expert,' she answered, 'but I'm familiar with it.'

'Then you know that when the Khmer Rouge was formed, its ideals were of the purest communism. I joined them out of idealism against the wishes of my family, especially my elder brother. Many families were split at that time. For many years I managed to keep my idealism, even through the killings. The ideals started to fade after the Khmer Rouge turned against the results of the election and continued to fight. The ideals died completely when I recognized my elder brother as a prisoner of the Khmer Rouge. I had no chance to speak to him. It was too late. I could only watch as a woman ordered our soldiers to force the prisoners, my brother included, into a minefield to clear it with their own lives.'

Susanna felt goose-bumps on her skin. She glanced at Jennings, whose face showed total lack of comprehension. The Cambodian continued talking, his voice very tight as he struggled to control it.

'There must have been a hundred prisoners. I did not realize what was happening until the explosions started and their bodies were thrown into the air . . . I saw my brother die.'

'You did not try to help?' Susanna asked.

He shook his head. 'I could do nothing. If they had known I had a brother in the Cambodian army, they would have sent me also into that minefield.'

'Who was the woman that gave the order?'

'She's the local commander.'

'What's her name?'

'Her name is So Hoan in our language. Her nickname is Talian, which means a very dangerous snake. Foreigners call it a cobra . . . But she has another name. She's only half Khmer, the other half is Western.'

'What is the other name?'

'Connie Crum.'

With those two words she felt Jennings beside her come alert. She raised her hand to keep him silent and said to the Cambodian: 'So she ordered your brother's death?'

'Yes; and many others. For her, making death is as easy as chopping leaves from a tree. I have seen much evil these past years, but none more than Talian.'

Susanna looked again at the file and then said: 'You're from the town of Pursat?'

'Yes.'

'And you know the Cardamom region well?'

'Of course.'

'Do you know a town called Tuk Luy?'

'Of course. I was stationed there for three years.'

Susanna drew a deep breath and asked the all-important question. 'If you had a chance to see So Hoan killed or captured, would you take it?'

The Cambodian leaned forward and answered immediately: 'I would give my life to see it!'

Susanna turned to Jennings and said: 'I think this man's C.V. fits the job profile.'

CHAPTER SIXTY-TWO

'I'm going in with you,' Susanna said.

Creasy sighed, knowing that he was in for another argument. He said: 'That's out of the question.'

'Because I'm a woman . . . and pregnant?'

They were lying in bed in Creasy's room. They had just been making love. It was only the third time, but it seemed to be reaching an ever-increasing level of intensity. Susanna pushed herself up and propped the pillows behind her. He looked up at her and said: 'Maybe that's ten per cent of the reason. But ninety per cent is that you're not trained for it. You would be a liability. I'm going to have the same argument with Jens in Bangkok tomorrow and he's going to get the same reason. You have to understand that I fought with all the others many times. The very fact that we've survived means that we know what we're doing. We have an almost telepathic understanding. I hardly have to give an order. They know how I work. If you came along, one of them would have to look after you, and I can't spare any of them, it's that simple. So forget it.'

'Maybe Mark could come along and look after me.'

Creasy chuckled. It seemed to come deep from his belly. It was a sound so rare that she treasured it. He said: 'Then I'll have to detail someone to look after Mark . . . I don't have an army, just four very experienced firefighters.' He also pushed himself up and put an arm around her. 'You've been a major part of this whole thing. We wouldn't be here now without your knowledge of the language, without your connections. You'll continue to help in Bangkok. But Susanna, after we cross that border it's a question of believing in the motto: "They also serve who stand and wait".

The waiting will be hard. It'll be hard for you and it'll be hard for Jens. It's always like that. But it won't take long. We have to get in there and do the job and get out by dawn. You and Jens and your bodyguard Mark will be waiting at the border. I repeat that you've been a major part in the whole operation, especially in finding that guy Nol Pol. It could make all the difference. By the way, did he accept the offer of the money?'

'Yes. His parents and his elder sister are still alive, living in Battambang. The money will keep them for at least a year. Times are tough in this country.'

Creasy nodded: 'And they're going to stay tough for a long time. If he comes out alive, I'll make sure they're comfortable for a long time.'

'What about the language? How will you communicate with them?'

'It's not a problem. You said he speaks a little French.'

'Yes, but not perfectly.'

'It'll be enough,' Creasy said. 'Guido and I speak French from the Foreign Legion. René speaks it as his first language.' He pulled her close and brushed her lips with his. 'We didn't do anything back there, did we?'

'Back when?'

'Back about half an hour ago.'

'Nothing that I can remember.'

'Me neither.' He pulled her back down onto the bed.

CHAPTER
SIXTY-THREE

It was a city that Creasy had never liked.

'It's a whore's place,' he said to Guido. 'Every fat, ugly German or Englishman or Frenchman who hasn't got the charm or the time to find a girlfriend in his own country flies in here and pays for women who always look like teenagers. They suddenly become Cary Grant about an hour after they step out of the jumbo jet.'

'It's always been like that,' Guido answered.

'No it hasn't. Two events created this whorehouse. The Vietnam War and the tens of thousands of GIs who came in here on their five days of R-and-R with their pockets full of money, and then the boom in tourism and the advent of charter flights. If a German or an Englishman wants to go to a high class whorehouse in Hamburg or London, the cost of the night with a couple of girls is more than the cost of a two-week package holiday in Thailand. Half of Europe's paedophiles save their weekly wages to spend their holidays here.'

The Italian glanced at his friend. 'Are you suddenly getting moralistic?'

Creasy grunted. 'I've always been moralistic. I don't blame the men. Too often it's the only chance they have to get into bed with a woman. I don't blame the women either. They're just the victims. I blame the fat cats and the government. Most of the massage parlours and whorehouses are owned by army generals and their compliant politicians. It's been estimated that more than a third of their foreign exchange comes from sex tourism.'

The taxi was jammed up behind a row of cars and trucks which moved at a snail's pace. Creasy gestured out of the window. 'It wouldn't be so bad if they used some of the billions of dollars they earn from that trade to build a metro or supply decent drinking water to the millions who live here.'

The Italian shrugged noncommitally. He said: 'You've seen Naples. We have slums there as bad as they've got here. The only difference is that it's not army generals making the money, it's the Mafia.'

'It's about the same thing,' Creasy answered, and then shrugged off his mood. 'It was fortunate that Susanna questioned those defected Khmer Rouge. This guy Nol Pol is a real find. If we'd hired some other guy, he could have led us right into a trap for a little more money than we are paying. This guy is motivated and Susanna was clever enough to pick it up.'

Guido did not answer immediately. He was looking out at the crowded streets. Then he turned and asked seriously: 'Are you falling in love with her a little bit?'

Creasy thought about that while they edged forward another few metres. Then he said: 'Just a little bit. She is kind of special.'

'Is she good in bed?'

'That's a strange thing,' Creasy answered. And then he uttered the phrase that he and his type always answered if asked if they ever killed anybody: 'I can't remember.'

The Italian laughed softly. 'Then she must be. I agree with you, she's a fine woman. And I think she's good for you.'

Again there was a silence. Then Creasy said: 'Maybe. I'm not sure about these things any more. Everyone I get close to ends up getting dead. Maybe Susanna is better off with a guy like Jennings, or that professor back in Washington.'

Guido chuckled. 'I don't know about Jennings. After all, he's CIA. Not exactly a safe profession.'

Creasy snorted in disagreement. 'For CIA in-house agents, life is safer than being a bank manager. It's only the poor non-American agents out in the field who get chopped down because some guy back at Langley takes half a million bucks to buy a new house. Jennings is crazy about her.'

'That's his problem,' the Italian said. 'He shows it too much. Women like the strong silent types.'

The taxi had finally reached the splendid entrance to the Ducit Thani Hotel. Creasy punched Guido on the shoulder and said: 'Spoken like an Italian.'

CHAPTER SIXTY-FOUR

They had become friends.

Creasy realised it as she was getting dressed. Her body was beautiful, and also her face, and he realized that even after the recent lovemaking he looked on her as a friend more than a lover. He loved her mind more than her body.

'Do you feel all right?' he asked.

She finished buttoning the silk blouse she had bought that afternoon and looked at him curiously. 'It's not like you,' she said, 'although you are born American, you don't act like an American.'

'What do you mean?'

She shrugged. 'A lot of American men need assurances after they've made love. They ask silly questions like "how was it for you, honey?" It's the last thing a woman wants to hear.'

'I didn't mean it like that. We didn't do anything in the last hour except somehow communicate. And the communication was good.'

She smiled. 'Of course we did nothing . . . And yes, it was good. And what did you mean?'

Creasy swung his feet to the floor, picked up the sarong he habitually wore in bed and tied it around his waist. He said, 'We haven't had a chance to talk since Phnom Penh. The minute you walked into my room we somehow got involved in things other than conversation. I asked how you felt because of your condition.'

She laughed softly. 'It's such a quaint old-fashioned expression, "my condition" . . . You mean how am I handling my early pregnancy?'

Creasy had moved to the minibar in the corner of the room and taken out a bottle of mineral water. As he poured the water into two glasses he said: 'I may be old-fashioned and proud of it, but I'm not quaint. How are you feeling?'

The tone of his voice was serious and she answered in the same way.

'Physically, I'm feeling fine except for a little nausea early in the mornings, which I'm told will get worse before it gets better. Mentally, I'm a little schizophrenic.'

Creasy carried over her glass and asked: 'What do you mean?'

She took a gulp of the water and answered: 'I feel the reflection of a great deal of affection, both from you in a physical way, and of course from Jennings. It's a little strange. In all my life I never had a young man like that literally at my feet; but I also feel the affection from Jens and The Owl and from Guido. I even felt it from Maxie and René during the short time that I was with them in Saigon.'

'It's part of being a team,' Creasy said. 'We are all very much individuals, and it's only when we're on a mission like this that the affection becomes apparent. It's a matter of sharing the danger which is always present, even now. You are part of that team, and Jennings has become part of it.' He tapped her on the chin and spoke as though he were a lecturer. 'It's called camaraderie. Each member of the team becomes part of you. I first felt it in the Legion, and I guess in a way it's why I'm here. You see, Jake Bentsen was once a comrade.'

Susanna was intrigued. Step by step, she was learning about Creasy's thoughts and motivations. It was like peeling off the layers of an onion.

'What about the others?' she asked. 'Guido and Maxie and René, for example . . . What are their motivations?'

Creasy had gone to the wardrobe. As he laid his slacks and underwear and shirt onto the bed he said thoughtfully: 'They are all mental orphans, and above all they seek the camaraderie I mentioned. Maxie is happily married and has his own bistro, which is successful. But after a few months of serving his customers he pines for the camaraderie of action. When he got married he promised his wife that he was retired from the mercenary world. But she is a very wise woman and she knows what he needs. She released him from that promise, which is why he's here now. René has no wife, just a series of short-term girlfriends. He's a lonely man except at times like this. Guido is simply Guido; my best friend. My life is his life and vice versa. If I have a problem or get into a dangerous situation, he has the same problem and the same situation and that's the way it is.'

He started to get dressed and she looked at the scars that she had so recently stroked. 'What will you go home to?' she asked.

He notched the buckle of his belt and answered quietly: 'A beautiful old farmhouse on a hill on the beautiful island of Gozo. It looks out over the Mediterranean to the islands of Comino and Malta. It's an idyllic life. I buy my food from a small shop in the nearby village. I drink at an old bar called Gleneagles, which looks out over the small harbour. The locals are my friends. I go to the village fiesta and drink too much beer and wine. I sit in the sun and play cards. I go fishing with the fishermen, and afterwards we barbecue the fish on the beach and dance to a mobile disco under the moon. I have an adopted daughter called Juliet who's studying medicine in America. She visits me on her holidays; and I'm proud of her. Like I said, it's an idyllic life.'

'And sometimes you get bored in Paradise?'

'Yes.'

'Just like the others?'

'Yes. Sometimes I need the camaraderie which only comes from risk and danger. It's our drug. Others drink liquor or shoot up with heroin or sniff coke. We go for the danger.'

He had finished dressing. He turned and gave her one of his rare smiles. 'And one day, like all drugs, it will kill us. But not tomorrow.'

'How do you know?'

'It's like a motto. You never die tomorrow.'

He walked over, kissed her softly on the lips and said, 'Enough of that. What about this schizophrenia you speak of?'

She held him close for a moment and then answered, 'In spite of all the affection I feel, I'm also a little frightened. It's not the danger I may or may not be in; it's the fact that a baby is growing inside me. I don't feel it yet, but it's very much in my mind. Of course it's impossible for a man to understand, and it's impossible for a woman to explain. But in spite of your so-called camaraderie I feel a little lonely.'

She gently pushed him away and said, 'And that's enough of that. I came from our Embassy here. Jennings has arranged everything you need. He's acquired two Mitsubishi Shoguns here locally for transport. I talked to my boss in Washington. Our agency will cover all the costs, including your hotel bills and other local expenses. The arms and other equipment will mostly be flown in tonight from a US base in Japan.'

Abruptly, Creasy was all business. 'Did he manage to get the Uzis?'

'No.' She took a slip of paper from her pocket. 'They are supplying five Colt XM177E2 submachine-guns. Apparently they can also launch grenades.'

Creasy nodded in satisfaction. 'It's a good weapon. Did Jennings get the light-enhancing glasses?'

'Yes, he got everything on your list apart from substituting the Colts for the Uzis . . . What about the other arrangements?'

'They're in hand,' Creasy answered. 'Guido has chartered a Cessna for tomorrow night from the Pattonong Flying Club. Together with a pilot. Right now he's buying two parachutes from a sports shop. He will also have a tailor run up a Khmer Rouge type uniform for our guide. If we get stopped early on inside Cambodia, he'll explain that we're mercenaries hired by Connie Crum on a short-term contract to clear mines, just like Piet de Witt. At midnight tomorrow we'll be leaving the village of Trat which is just a few miles from the Cambodian border. For the next hour or two Connie Crum will be getting a stiff neck looking up into the night sky. I'll arrange for the plane to fly within a mile of that temple to synchronize with our arrival.'

CHAPTER SIXTY-FIVE

The satellite phone buzzed just after six p.m. Connie Crum picked up the receiver and had a two-minute conversation, then she turned triumphantly to Van Wan Luk and said: 'It's like a perfect game of chess. All the pieces have been moved, my opponent is now going to make his last move into checkmate.'

'He's in Bangkok?'

'Yes, he's at the Dusit Thani Hotel. He has been there all day, but his friend Arrelio has been moving around. He has chartered a light aircraft from tomorrow at midnight and also purchased two parachutes of a modern design.' She looked up at the sky. 'The weather forecast is good. It will be a clear night with half a moon. We'll be waiting for them.'

They were standing beside the temple, which was circled by an eight-foot stone wall. The temple itself was richly decorated with ancient stone carvings. They were not all original to the temple. Some of them had been brought from the famous temple of Angkor Wat. She walked into the temple itself and Van followed.

Inside it was starkly bare except for a blank, marble sarcophagus rising five feet from the stone floor and measuring eight feet square. On top of it was a pyre of wood. It was the first time that Van Luk Wan had ever been to the temple. He stood at the entrance looking at the black square of marble. Behind it, standing like sentinels, were Connie Crum's two black-clad, female bodyguards, cradling AK47 rifles in their arms.

Connie Crum stood beside it and said reverently: 'My father's ashes are contained here. I had them brought from Hong Kong last year. It's his last resting place.'

The Vietnamese did not know what to say or do. He owed his life to Bill Crum. After standing immobile for several seconds, he slowly bowed low towards the marble sarcophagus. Then he lifted his head and looked at the woman. Her face was serene. She gestured at the pyre of wood, which covered the entire surface to a depth of two feet.

'Creasy will die there,' she said. 'Like my father, he'll burn to death and become ashes. He'll burn while he is alive. It will be slow; and he'll know why he is burning. Afterwards I'll have the Dutchman lay mines on the only track into the temple. Then I'll kill the Dutchman. My father's soul will rest in peace and tranquillity.'

Van was looking at the wood on top of the marble. He could picture Creasy lying there tied down. In his mind he could see Connie bringing a torch to the wood and Creasy's body jerking on top of the flames. He felt the adrenalin pumping through his veins.

He asked: 'How many soldiers will you have here?'

Connie gestured at her two bodyguards. 'Just these two, as always, and then you and me.'

His head jerked around to look at her and his voice crackled with astonishment. 'Just four of us? You know what those two men are like . . . You need a small army in here.'

She laughed at him and at the fear that had crept into his eyes. 'We'll have one other "soldier",' she said. 'A very effective soldier. One that even Creasy and his friend Arrellio will not know about and cannot fight. Come with me.'

She led him back out into the compound. First she went to the massive iron gate and pointed. 'Notice that the gate is built in such a way that when closed, it's completely sealed.' She pointed to the walls on each side of the gate. 'Notice that the walls have been very carefully made and plastered.'

She walked back to the temple, with Van following like a little dog. She pointed to several metal holes that were recessed into the stone carvings. He had not noticed them before. She walked back to the entrance to the temple. Beside it was a metal box. She took a key from her pocket and opened it. Inside were two handles, one red and the other green. She tapped the red handle.

'When I turn that, it will release through a series of pipes a nerve gas called Amiton from cylinders beneath the temple. That gas was first developed in America in 1952, and is lethal unless an antidote is given within minutes. It's also heavier than air so it will silt from the ground up to the level of the walls. When Creasy and his friend drop in, they'll lose consciousness within seconds.' She walked into the temple and pointed at a table to one side. On it there were several small cylinders attached by rubber pipes to rubber masks shaped to fit over a nose and mouth. 'That's the antidote. When Creasy and his friend drop into this compound, they'll be unconscious within seconds. We disarm them and tie them up and then give them the antidote. They'll come round in about half an hour. Then I'll tell Creasy his life history and why he's going to burn.' She was smiling as she spoke.

'What about us?' Van asked in trepidation.

She tapped him lightly on the shoulder. 'Don't worry. The four of us will be wearing protective clothing and gas masks.' She pointed to a pile of thick, bright yellow plastic overalls. 'We'll not be at risk.' She drew a deep breath of satisfaction. 'The Dutchman described Creasy and his friend Arrellio as maybe the two most dangerous men on earth . . . but they never had a fight with a "soldier" called Amiton!'

CHAPTER SIXTY-SIX

Mark Jennings watched the two men at work. They were experts in an expert field, and they used the most sophisticated electronic equipment. They took fifteen minutes moving around the small conference room, checking the walls and the ceiling and then the floor and the furniture, always closely monitoring the flashing lights on their gauges. Finally one of them dismantled the phone and, after checking every component, reassembled it and turned to Jennings saying: 'The place is clean, sir. Not a bug in sight or sound.'

Jennings nodded in satisfaction. 'Good. Would you please call the others and arrange to get some coffee in here. After that I want you to stay outside by the door and make sure that nobody comes in. Tomorrow night I have another job for you which will end about two a.m. Nothing dangerous, just flying around for a couple of hours in a light aircraft. After that you can head Stateside.'

The two men packed away their equipment and left silently on their rubber-soled shoes. Jennings took his oversize brief-case from the table, opened it and took out various papers, photographs and maps. He was enjoying himself. It was his first important mission since arriving in South East Asia. He had half expected this small conference room at the Dusit Thani Hotel to have been bugged. Not because of the impending meeting, but because of some past business meeting. In the modern age, most of the spying was done for businessmen. Even the CIA was not aloof from that. They had even bugged the office of the chairman of Airbus in Toulouse on behalf of the Boeing Corporation.

Creasy and Guido were the first to arrive. They greeted Jennings warmly, but the American knew that the moment Creasy walked into the room he was in control. Not by anything he said or by his actions, just by his presence.

Susanna came next, together with the ex-Khmer soldier Nol Pol, who was dressed in a new suit with a white shirt and a brown tie. She introduced him to Creasy and Guido and then listened while Creasy spoke a few words to him in French. Five minutes before, she had given the Cambodian his $500 fee. She was surprised when he now reached into the pocket of his suit and handed it back to her. In Cambodian, she asked him why.

He replied: 'This man tells me that tomorrow night I might be killed. If I am, he promises that you'll make sure that this money will get to my family in Battambang. I believe him, and I believe you.'

As she took the money, Creasy said: 'His French is better than I hoped.'

Jens and The Owl came next, together with one of the security men carrying a tray with coffee and cups. He was followed by Maxie and René. Before exchanging any kind of greeting, Creasy asked them: 'Are you sure you weren't followed?'

'Negative,' Maxie answered. 'We have not been watched since we arrived at the airport.'

Creasy was reassured. Maxie was the best tracker he had ever known and had the instincts to know when he himself was tracked.

Jennings looked on curiously as the mercenaries greeted each other with the customary kiss next to the mouth. He was startled to realize that these men were all middle-aged. They had come from an almost forgotten period, but they had not forgotten their craft. One glance into their eyes was enough to tell him that.

They arranged themselves around the oblong table. The Dane put his computer in front of him and opened it. Jennings slid a piece of paper in front of Creasy, who studied it and then nodded in satisfaction.

'I'm glad you got an RPG-7 . . . You've done a good job, Mark. Thanks!'

Susanna asked: 'What's an RPG-7?'

Guido provided the answer, 'It's a Russian made anti-tank weapon. The best there is.'

She thought for a moment, then asked: 'Do you expect to meet tanks down there?'

Guido shook his head. 'None showed up on the aerial survey, but that weapon has other uses. It can blow away heavy metal gates and doors, and of course other vehicles apart from tanks.' He glanced at Creasy. 'How many rockets?'

'Four. They'll be enough.' He looked up at Jennings. 'To save time, I'd be glad if you would brief Maxie and René on the aerial photographs.'

Jennings nodded importantly. As he laid out the photographs in front of him, the two mercenaries moved round to look over his shoulder.

Creasy turned to Jens and tapped the list of equipment in front of him. He said: 'The distance from Trat to Tuk Luy is about forty-eight miles, so with this VHF equipment we'll be in good radio communication with you. After we secure their base, Guido and I will go on to the temple. We'll keep in touch, but only when absolutely necessary. I doubt those guys have listening equipment, but these days you never know. That light plane should only take off from Bangkok when I give the word.' He turned and interrupted Jennings' briefing. 'Mark, you've lined up two guys to go on that aircraft to simulate Guido and myself?'

'Yes, two of our agents. The guys are outside the door. It just happens they're roughly the same build as you and Guido. They'll be fully briefed. Leave that to me.'

Creasy looked at him for a moment, then nodded. 'OK, that's your department. Meanwhile, the two jeeps and the rest of the equipment will be waiting at Trat?'

'Yes, they'll precede us by a few hours. I've secured a safe house with a compound down there.'

'Good. Then we need to arrange a safe assembly point in Bangkok and transport to Trat.'

Jennings could not keep the smirk turn out of his voice. 'That's been done. Don't forget, Creasy, we do have quite an organization as back-up.'

Creasy glanced at Guido. 'So they should,' he said, 'with a budget bigger than most small countries . . . OK, let's go over the details.'

They worked for the next two hours. Susanna was astonished at the attention to detail, and her conception of a bunch of hired gunmen dissolved into admiration as she listened to each of them make their contributions and suggestions. Although they deferred to Creasy as a leader, they were all very individual and forceful in the debate. At one point René suggested that three of them should make the assault on the temple. Maxie shook his head and pointed out that Creasy and Guido had always worked in partnership, and that having a third man along would be more of a distraction than a help. He said with a grin: if it takes three people to do it, then Creasy and Guido can do it alone.'

The Cambodian Nol Pol had been deftly brought into the discussion, and was treated by all of them as an equal. They pored over the large-scale maps and aerial photographs, and the Cambodian pointed out the best routes.

Finally, when the meeting broke up, Nol Pol spoke a few words in French to Creasy before being guided away by one of Jennings' security men.

'What did he say?' Susanna asked.

Creasy shrugged, and answered: 'He asked that if possible I bring him from that temple the head of Connie Crum . . . You picked the right man, Susanna.'

CHAPTER
SIXTY-SEVEN

When Susanna got back to her room the message light on her phone was flashing. She called the reception and was told that a Mr Elliot Friedman had phoned and asked her to call him on a personal matter. The message was timed half an hour previously. She looked at her watch and calculated that it was now seven thirty a.m. in Washington. Elliot must have been up early. She phoned him at home.

He immediately said: 'Don't discuss your project. I'm getting fully briefed via our friends over at Langley. Just wish the guys good luck from me.'

'So why are you calling?' Susanna asked.

She could hear the sigh come down the line. 'I've got a problem with a certain Professor Jason Woodward.'

Susanna had been standing by the bed. Abruptly she sat down on it. 'What's the problem, Elliot?'

'He's pestering me all the time. He's desperate to get in touch with you. What the hell have you done to that guy? I thought it was a kind of low-key relationship. But he calls me half a dozen times a day at the office, and even at home. Yesterday he barged into my office demanding to know where you are and what you're doing. What do I tell the guy?'

'Tell him the truth,' she said. 'I'm in South East Asia on a mission connected with MIA. The mission will be over within seventy-two hours, after which I'll call him.'

'And I promise him that?'

'Yes, Elliot. Promise him that I'll call him within seventy-two hours.'

'OK. Good luck to you and the guys. Take care of yourself, honey.'

'Thanks, Elliot. Goodbye.'

She cradled the phone and sat on the bed thinking for several minutes, wondering what was in Jason's head. She thought that maybe it was a question of anxiety that she had decided to keep the baby. On an impulse she picked up the phone and started to dial his home number. But as soon as she had tapped in the first digits, she changed her mind. He could wait. Tomorrow night it was possible that men could be dying, men who had become precious to her. Right now those thoughts were more important than anything else. She stood up and walked to the bathroom. But before she was halfway there, the phone rang. She went back and picked it up. It was Creasy.

'Have dinner with me tonight,' he said in his gruff voice.

'Is that an order or a request?' she asked.

'It's an order. We need to discuss the whole operation for tomorrow night.'

'I thought we just spent two hours doing that.'

'Yes, we only have to discuss it for thirty seconds.'

'Then what?'

'Then we can talk about what's not going to happen after dinner.'

'OK. Where and when?'

'Let's meet at eight o'clock in the bar.'

'It's a deal.'

She put the phone down and again headed for the bathroom. As she reached the door, the phone rang again. She went back. It was Mark Jennings. His voice was tentative.

'I was wondering whether, if you have nothing planned for tonight, you might have dinner with me?'

She stood by her bed with the phone at her ear and suddenly felt an overwhelming sense of being wanted. She let him down gently.

'Mark, I'd love to have dinner with you, but I can't. Creasy just called and we need to have a discussion about the operation tomorrow.'

'I thought everything was worked out now?'

She thought quickly and answered: 'Everything is worked out. But there are other details. If anything happens to the other men, Creasy wants me to arrange matters for their families. He needs to explain what I have to do. You can understand that, Mark. Six men are going deep into Khmer Rouge territory. You know the danger. Some of them may not come back. Creasy wants to be sure that their personal arrangements are taken care of.'

There was a silence and then he said reflectively: 'Yes, he would. He's that kind of guy.'

'Let's take a rain-check on that dinner.' 'Is that a promise?'

'It's a promise! See you in the morning.'

This time, she made it to the bathroom.

CHAPTER SIXTY-EIGHT

They left Bangkok at dawn, travelling south in a minibus. After three hours they stopped on the outskirts of the town of Sattahip and ate the sandwiches and drank the coffee supplied by the hotel. The six men who would be crossing into Cambodia somehow grouped together by the roadside. Susanna, Jennings and the Embassy driver stayed inside the minibus.

'They seem relaxed,' Jennings remarked. 'You'd think they'd be as tense as hell. Even that guy Nol Pol looks relaxed. And he knows better than any of them what he's going into. If they catch him over there, it'll be a slow death.'

Susanna looked at the Cambodian. He was talking to Guido and occasionally smiling at something the Italian was saying.

'How do they communicate?' Jennings asked.

'In French. Guido was in the Foreign Legion.'

The men were in a loose circle, holding their mugs of coffee.

'It's like a form of osmosis,' Susanna remarked. 'In a way, they have sucked him into their team. He feels like an equal. That's how they do it. Creasy is the leader, but any occasional observer would never know that. They're all equals. They'll all rely on each other. They're relaxed because they're doing what they enjoy. In a way, they never grew up. They're a sophisticated form of a street gang, a bunch of kids about to do something naughty.'

Jennings laughed softly. 'Something naughty! Susanna, you have a gift for understatement.'

The men finished their coffee and climbed back into the minibus. The driver headed due east along the coast road. The Gulf of Thailand stretched away in a blue swatch to their right.

———

The house was secluded; set in a walled compound within a grove of banana trees. The two Shoguns were parked at the rear. They were painted black. As the minibus pulled up beside them, an elderly Thai couple emerged from the back door and greeted them.

'Who are they?' Creasy asked Jennings.

'They're secure,' Jennings answered. 'I won't mention their names, but he was one of our covert agents for thirty years before he retired about five years ago. Let's go inside.'

They filed into a spacious room with a single fan rotating above a long table. As Susanna looked at the table, she felt a sudden wave of embarrassment. It was covered with weapons from end to end. Submachine-guns, pistols, spare magazines, knives, grenades, black uniforms, webbings and flak jackets. At the very end of the table was a black rocket-launcher and four cone-shaped rockets. She was embarrassed about her earlier words to Jennings. This was no street gang going out to do something naughty. This was warfare in its starkest light.

But the men did not seem to see it that way. They crowded around the table, handling the weapons and commenting to each other about them. Creasy picked up one of the submachine-guns and then asked Nol Pol a question in French. The Cambodian shook his head.

Creasy passed him the weapon and then said to Guido: 'He's only ever used an AK47. Please show him how to use it and strip it down.' He turned to René and Maxie. 'You're familiar with it?'

They both nodded. Maxie glanced at The Owl, who shook his head and said: 'I don't use things like that. I've got my MAB pistol and that's all I want.'

Creasy picked up the rocket-launcher and nodded in satisfaction. it's the model D,' he said as he unscrewed the tube, it makes it easier to carry.' He looked at René. 'You're the mechanic,' he said. 'Please check the engines of the jeeps while the rest of us strip down these weapons and check them out. Then we'll all try to get a few hours' sleep.' He looked at his watch and then at Jennings. 'It's better we eat about seven o' clock.'

'No problem,' the American said. He gestured at the Thai woman. 'She used to keep a safe house for us in Bangkok, and I'm told she's a fine cook.'

The small, round-faced woman obviously understood English and was pleased with the comment. She smiled broadly and said: 'You want steaks or Thai food?'

Creasy looked around at the group. Only Maxie chose a steak. 'Typical Rhodesian,' Creasy noted. 'Everything that doesn't have horns and four legs is uneatable.' He looked again at his watch. 'Nol Pol estimates four hours to Trat. So our ETD will be eight thirty.' From the table he picked up one of the VHF radios which was about the size of a large mobile phone. He gave it to Jennings and said: 'Mark, please go with the minibus about five miles away from here and test transmission. Your code name will be "M". The code for this house will be "B" for base. Keep the transmission short.' He moved down the table and picked up a single, green uniform with a flat, peaked hat and passed it to the Cambodian, saying in French: 'So now you've rejoined the Khmer Rouge, at least for one night.'

The Cambodian held the uniform in his hands, looking down at it. His face had turned sombre.

CHAPTER SIXTY-NINE

They kitted up after dinner, first changing into black uniforms - apart from Nol Pol, who put on the dull green trousers and tunic of the Khmer Rouge. Susanna, Jennings and Jens watched as they went through the ritual facing each other in pairs, one checking the other's equipment. Again the thought of a ragtag bunch of mercenaries was dispelled forcibly from Susanna's mind. These men were serious soldiers; even The Owl, who looked a little incongruous in his black uniform and thick spectacles. She asked if he would be taking his Walkman with him and he replied with slight astonishment: 'Naturally.'

She glanced at Jens, wondering about his thoughts. Would he feel left out of what was the culmination of a team effort? His normally animated face was now serious as he watched his friends prepare. Then she witnessed the depth of Creasy's leadership. He turned to the Dane, pointed at the VHF radio in front of him and said: 'Now you're in charge, Jens. You have to co-ordinate everything we do. After we take that base and Guido and I assault the temple, there may be some confusion. There always is in a firefight. We know that the radios work well. I'll have one with me and Maxie will have one at their base. But you must monitor all our calls in case there is any kind of interference. In effect, this house is now our operational base. You know our plan. As soon as we secure the base, we'll let you know. Then you'll ask Mark to activate his agents in Bangkok to take off on that chartered aircraft.

We need to know the moment that it's airborne and that it's heading on the bearing of one-twenty degrees. It should continue on that bearing until it's about a mile from the temple. It should then turn onto a bearing of one-nine-oh and circle the coast over the Gulf of Thailand before returning to Bangkok about an hour later.'

Jens tapped his computer. 'Don't worry, Creasy. It's all in here. What about code names?'

'You are "Base". I am "Green One", Guido is "Green Two", Maxie is "Red One", René is "Red Two", The Owl is "Red Three" and Nol Pol is "Blue One".'

The Dane fed the information into the computer.

Creasy looked at Susanna and said: 'We don't say long good-byes. We think that's unlucky. We'll see you in the morning.'

He picked up his SMG and led the men out into the compound. Over his shoulder, he said: 'Jens, we'll do a radio check after we've crossed the border.'

Susanna and Jens and Jennings stood by the door, watching as Nol Pol climbed into the driving seat of the lead jeep. Creasy sat beside him, with Guido in the back carrying the rocket-launcher. Maxie drove the second jeep with the other three. They drove out of the compound without a backward glance.

They trooped back into the house. Jennings said: 'I wish he'd have let me have a back-up force ready. If things go wrong, I could have had a bunch of hard guys to chopper in there.'

As they sat down at the table, Jens said to him: 'I'll explain why he didn't let you do it. It's like these modern explorers or solo round-the-world sailors. They might be in the middle of the roaring forties or halfway across the Arctic icecap. If they get into trouble, they pick up their radio and say "Help". Back at base, a plane takes off and in a couple of hours is dropping supplies or even people to help them out.' He gestured with his thumb. 'Those guys are like Scott or Amundsen. They don't want a nanny watching over them. It's why they do that kind of work. It's not just the money, especially in this case. It's the thrill of the danger. They're hooked on adrenalin.'

'Even The Owl?' Susanna asked.

'Yes, even him.'

She decided to satisfy her curiosity and asked: 'But not you, Jens?'

The Dane shook his head and then tapped it with his fore-finger. 'I'm more cerebral. I'm not saying they're stupid. In fact, they're all highly intelligent.' He thought for a moment and then went on: 'You might say it's a question of co-ordination. You can be sure that they would all have been good sportsmen. They have the co-ordination between eye and limb that enabled them to become experts with the weapons they just took out of here.' He smiled. 'I was always hopeless at sports. It was embarrassing at school. We played football and handball and I hardly knew which was which. When I was in the Danish police, I had to take a fire-arms course like everybody else. The instructor was being gener-ous when he told me that the target was safe when I held a gun.'

Jennings had been listening intently. He said: 'You're an hon-est man.'

Jens shrugged and answered: 'I'm also important. I don't feel bad about not going in with them. I do the investigating and the planning and when the action starts, I'll be co-ordinating. I've done it before with this team. It makes it easier for them, know-ing that I'm here. Someone has to do it and I'm happy doing it.' He looked at his watch. 'They'll be crossing the border in about an hour. That's the crucial time. If they get through undetected, there's very little Khmer Rouge presence until they ford the upper reaches of the Tamyong River. Then it's a grey area until they reach Tuk Luy. We know from the aerial survey that most of the Khmer Rouge soldiers there have moved south. We don't know how many remain. When they get to within a kilometre, Creasy will send in Maxie to recce. He's the best there is.'

CHAPTER SEVENTY

'We're in Cambodia,' Nol Pol said, braking the jeep to a stop.

Creasy was looking at the map. 'Are you sure?'

'Yes. The countryside is the same, but I can feel it. We're in the killing fields.' He pointed across Creasy to the left. 'Soon we should see the lights of the village of Cam Tray. They have no electricity, but they have kerosene lamps. Then in another ten minutes we should reach the Tamyong River. It's only a stream up here. After that, we're deep into Khmer Rouge territory.'

They were on a dirt track, which the Cambodian explained was usually only used by bullock carts. From the back seat Guido asked: 'Does the track continue like this?'

'No,' the Cambodian answered. 'It gets worse as we near the river. That will be a danger point. The Khmer Rouge have several camps along that river. After that we have a clear run through to Tuk Luy.'

Creasy said to the Cambodian: 'When we get near the river, turn off the headlights and wear the night sights. It's difficult, but possible.' He picked up the VHF radio, switched it on and said: 'Green One to Base. Do you read?'

Three seconds later, Jens' voice came back: 'Base to Green One, loud and clear.'

Creasy spoke again: 'Green One, to Red One. Do you copy?'

From the jeep fifty metres behind, Maxie spoke into his radio: 'I copy.'

Creasy said: 'We're in Cambodia. In about ten minutes from now, we'll switch off our headlights. Do the same and wear night sights.'

'Affirmative.'

Creasy nodded to the Cambodian, who engaged the first gear and edged the jeep forward.

It happened as they came down the track towards the river. Both Nol Pol and Creasy were wearing the Trilux night sights strapped to their heads. Simultaneously, they spotted the two figures standing on the track. They both held rifles. Creasy picked up the radio and quietly said: 'Two Khmer rouge ahead. We're stopping. Slow down and have Red Two and Red Three leave your vehicle and cover us from the flanks. Then drive on and stop behind us.'

Maxie's voice came back. 'Will do.'

The two men on the track had raised their rifles. They were AK47s. Nol Pol gently braked to a halt. One of the Khmer Rouge moved away to the side. The other approached the jeep, his gun held high. From the back seat, Guido whispered: 'I have him covered.'

Creasy lifted off his night sight, saying to the Cambodian: 'Take yours off. You know what to tell them.'

Nol Pol followed the instruction and then said: 'I've rehearsed it many times. These two are peasants and not regulars. They use them simply for patrolling.'

The Khmer Rouge reached the driver's window. The AK47 was pointed at Nol Pol's head. He looked at Creasy and at Guido in the back and then turned abruptly as the second jeep pulled up behind. He shouted something to the other Khmer Rouge, then pointed his rifle at the second jeep.

Creasy was startled by the tone of Nol Pol's voice. He shouted at the Khmer Rouge. When the soldier tried to say something, he shouted at him again. The soldier backed away about a metre, but his gun was still pointed at Nol Pol. Creasy realized that he was listening to an officer addressing a very junior soldier. Nol Pol lowered his voice slightly as he spoke several sentences. Creasy knew that he was explaining that Nol Pol was an officer in the Khmer Rouge and he was escorting five mercenaries who had been hired by Connie Crum, the Cobra, to clear mines in her region. They were moving without lights because there had been rumours of government troops in the area. Had the soldiers seen any government troops?

Slowly, the Khmer Rouge soldier lowered his AK47. He spoke to Nol Pol respectfully, with his sandalled feet loosely at attention. Then Nol Pol turned to Creasy with a slight smile. He said: 'He has heard of no government troops in the area, although they bombed a Khmer Rouge camp about ten miles away yesterday . . . Do you have any cigarettes?'

'I don't smoke. Do they want cigarettes?'

'They always want cigarettes, especially American cigarettes.'

From the back seat, Guido said: 'René smokes Marlboros.'

Creasy opened the door of the jeep and jumped down. He called out: 'René!'

From the bushes thirty metres away, René emerged with his submachine-gun held ready. The other Cambodian soldier swung his AK47 to cover him. Nol Pol shouted an order which was repeated by the other soldier. The AK47 was lowered.

'Do you have any cigarettes?' Creasy asked René.

'Naturally,' the Belgian answered. 'I've got a couple of packs.'

'You'll have to sacrifice them,' Creasy said. 'Give them a pack each. We're among friends.'

René lowered his SMG and reached into his tunic pocket, saying: 'I'll give them a pack and a half to share between them. I'm not going through withdrawal symptoms in the middle of a fight.'

The atmosphere became convivial. Both the Khmer soldiers rested their AK47s against their side of the jeep while René counted out the cigarettes. Then they had another conversation with Nol Pol, picked up their rifles and moved down the track. He started the engine, saying to Creasy: 'They'll show us the best place to ford the river.'

As the jeep moved forward, Creasy asked: 'Will they communicate with Tuk Luy?'

'No. They cannot. They have no radios. They come from the village we just passed. They assume that I'm a Khmer Rouge officer. Of course, in such a rural countryside, the word will eventually get around that we've been here. But by that time, we should be out.'

The two jeeps surged across the shallow river half an hour before midnight, with the two Khmer Rouge soldiers wading in front, puffing away at their Marlboros. Then, with waves of goodbye, they watched the jeeps move off into the darkness towards Tuk Luy.

Nol Pol said: 'It won't be so easy if we run into regular units. We're entering the area from which I defected. They might know me.'

'They won't open fire without warning,' Creasy said. 'They'll have a look first. If they recognize you, we'll gun them down. Guido will have you covered at all times.'

From behind, Guido slapped the barrel of his SMG and said: 'You're covered. And if we're stopped, René and The Owl will be on each flank before they see the second jeep.'

CHAPTER
SEVENTY-ONE

'What happens if he meets any Khmer Rouge soldiers?' Nol Pol asked.

'He won't,' Creasy answered. 'He's the best scout I know. He moves like a cat, and at night, cats don't bump into dogs or anything else that might be dangerous.'

They were parked on a ridge about a kilometre away from the faint lights in the distance. Maxie McDonald had just merged into the darkness in front of them. Creasy looked at the dial of his watch. 'It'll take half an hour,' he said. 'Let's have some coffee, Guido.'

They quietly climbed out of the jeep and the Italian produced a Thermos flask and three plastic mugs. He also produced a small medicine bottle and shook three pills out into his palm. Creasy took one and gestured at the Cambodian to do the same.

'It's Dexedrine,' he explained, it keeps you awake and alert. It's banned by the Olympic Athletics Committee, but I don't think anyone will turn up here to give us a test.'

Nol Pol washed down the pill with his coffee and asked: 'So now we just wait?'

'Yes, we wait for Maxie to call in. No one is going to surprise us.' Creasy gestured off to his left. 'René is out there on the left flank and The Owl on the right flank.' He took a sip of his coffee and asked: 'How long were you with the Khmer Rouge?'

For the next twenty minutes, prompted by the curious questions of Creasy and Guido, the Cambodian talked about the insanity of the Pol Pot regime. He described how anyone with an education was considered an enemy of the State, and the absurdity of the fact that Pol Pot and all his cadres were educated men themselves. He talked of the collective madness where even infants of educated people were considered tainted and to save wasting a bullet were clubbed to death.

'It's always the kids,' Creasy remarked.

The Cambodian nodded and said: 'It was Day One. I'll never forget listening to the cadre on that day when we took Phnom Penh. He addressed the soldiers in my unit and told us the Khmer people had no history. Our culture, our temples and our monks were nothing and would be destroyed. We were beginning the first day of the Khmer people. Everything that happened before Day One had to be eliminated. We would be a clean and new people. We cheered and the killing began. It was a mass blood lust. After a while, killing people became meaningless. It was part of our new culture.'

'It's not the first time it has happened,' Guido said sombrely. 'And it won't be the last.'

They were interrupted by Maxie's voice coming from the radio clipped to Creasy's webbing.

'Red One to Green One.'

Creasy pulled up the radio. 'Green One, go ahead.'

'I'm in the village. It's just a cluster of houses and huts. No sign of Khmer Rouge activity. The only lights are in the main house. I managed to get a look through a window. There's a Caucasian guy in there, shackled to the wall, with two guards wearing Khmer Rouge uniforms. They're sitting at a table drinking beer. I've done a complete perimeter check and there's no activity at all. Over.'

Creasy pushed the 'Send' button on the radio. 'Green One to Red One. Good situation. We're coming in. Meet us half way.

Green One to Red Two and Three. Start moving in two minutes, staying a hundred metres out on the flanks. After we take that house, close in, but stay outside and cover. Green One to Base. Do you copy?'

The Dane's voice came in with a slight crackle. 'We copy.'

Creasy said: 'We should acquire that house in the next fifteen minutes. Then I'll call you to have that aircraft take off.' He switched off the radio and clipped it back onto his webbing, picked up his SMG and said: 'Let's go!'

CHAPTER
SEVENTY-TWO

The Dutchman had decided that he was going to die in spite of Connie Crum's consoling words. He had been in danger many times in his life, but had never felt the premonition of death. He felt it now. He looked at the two Khmer Rouge soldiers sitting at the wooden table laughing and joking, and he felt the rage welling up inside him. He had been paid for the job, but he had done the job well. He always did his work well. It was a matter of principle, regardless of the paymaster. He looked at the shackle on his left wrist. It seemed to represent his entire life. He had never been really free. There was always someone to tell him what to do and how to do it. His one regret was Tan Sotho. He had become fond of her. It was not a word normally associated with people like him.

The rusty hinges of the door squeaked as it opened. The Dutchman looked up. Creasy was standing there. He had a revolver in his hand, unbalanced by a fat silencer.

The Khmer Rouge soldiers scrambled for their rifles. Creasy shot them both. As they fell to the floor he stood aside and another man came through with a submachine-gun held ready. De Witt recognized Guido Arrellio. He moved quickly to the two soldiers and checked that they were dead. Then he nodded to Creasy, who walked over to de Witt and looked down at him. He said: 'I told you the last time I saw you that if I ever saw your face again, I'd kill you.'

De Witt laughed harshly and said: 'It makes no odds. If you don't, she will.'

'She is Connie Crum? She's in the temple now?'

'Yes. She is waiting for you.' He laughed again. 'She expected you to come by parachute.'

'How many men does she have?'

'I don't know. Nobody knows.'

Guido had moved over to stand beside Creasy. He asked the Dutchman: 'How long have you been here?'

'Ten months.'

'Have you seen any Americans?'

'No. But there were some here until about three years ago. They were prisoners of war and they were used to clear mines. I was told that the last one got blown up three years ago.'

'Who told you?' Creasy asked.

'A woman, she's Vietnamese. She was trapped here. They make her work as a prostitute. She has a young son by one of the Americans.' He looked up into Creasy's eyes and said: 'Whatever you do to me and anybody else, I ask a last favour: that she is not hurt.'

Creasy glanced down at him and replied: 'I don't make war on women who don't make war on me . . . You laid the minefield round that temple?'

'Yes . . . It was a work of art.'

'How many accesses are there?'

'Just one, only a metre wide.'

'You have a map?'

'No. No-one has a map. The men I trained here laid that field with me. After it was finished, she had them all killed.'

'So how did she get into the temple?'

The Dutchman shrugged. 'I showed her the bearings. She took notes.'

Creasy turned to look at the two dead soldiers and then gestured at the shackle on de Witt's wrist. He asked: 'Do they have the key?'

'No, she has the only key.'

Creasy said to Guido: 'Call The Owl. He'll open that thing up.' As Guido walked to the door, Creasy asked de Witt: 'Where are that girl and her child now?'

'She lives in the house at the end of the track with her son. Her name is Tan Sotho.'

Guido returned with The Owl. Creasy pointed at the shackle. 'Can you open that?'

The Owl squatted down and looked at it, then pulled out his lock-pick. 'No problem,' he said. 'It'll take a couple of minutes.'

Creasy said to Guido: 'There's a woman called Tan Sotho who lives in the house at the end of the track. She has a young child. Please bring them both here.'

Guido went back to the door. Creasy asked de Witt: 'What do you know about the Khmer Rouge deployments in this area?'

The Dutchman looked up and said: 'Before I tell you anything else, answer this question. Are you going to kill me?'

Creasy shook his head. 'As far as I'm concerned you're vermin and you always were, but I'm not going to kill you. In about half an hour, you're going to lead me through that minefield. Then, if we get out, I'll take you back to Thailand and you go free.'

The Dutchman thought about that and then nodded. He said: 'I hate your guts, but you're known as a man who keeps his word. There were a lot of Khmer Rouge in this area until about two weeks ago when Connie Crum moved them out to the southeast. As far as I know, there's only one detachment remaining, which is in a village called Ak Lau about a mile due south from here with about twenty men.'

The Owl had done his work. He pulled open the shackle. De Witt stood up, stretched his frame and rubbed his wrist.

'Don't try anything,' Creasy said, 'or you'll surely die. I have other men outside, men like Maxie Macdonald and René Callard . . . Not exactly friends of yours.'

'You brought the cream,' de Witt said wryly.

The door opened and Guido ushered in the woman and the child. She looked at the two dead bodies and then at de Witt. Her fear was evident in her eyes.

'Do you speak English?' Creasy asked.

She nodded.

'Then understand that you have nothing to fear from us. We will leave soon for Thailand. If you wish, you can come with us, with your son.'

The boy had a round face and button eyes. He was holding on to his mother's leg. Creasy asked her: 'Do you know a man called Jake Bentsen?'

'Yes.'

'What happened to him?'

'He was killed clearing a minefield.'

'When?'

'About three years ago.'

Creasy was looking at the boy. 'Is that his son?' he asked.

She hesitated, and then said: 'I think so . . . I hope so. Jake was a good man, gentle and honest. He never hurt me like some of the others do.' She put her hand upon the boy's head. 'Jake died three months before Kori was born.'

Guido had pulled the two dead bodies into a corner and covered them with the stained cloth from the table. Creasy asked de Witt: 'When Connie Crum was here, where did she stay?'

'In the house next door.'

Creasy turned to The Owl and said: 'Go and check that house. Look into every room, look for documents and maps. If you locate a safe,' try to open it. But you only have ten minutes.' To Guido he said: 'Radio Jens. I want that plane to take off from Bangkok in five minutes.' He turned to Tan Sotho and gestured at the table and chairs. 'Please sit down. I want you to stay in this room with your son until we return.'

As she sat down with her son on her lap, Creasy asked: 'Do you know a man called Van Luk Wan?'

Before she answered, he saw the look of distaste on her face. 'Yes. He's a bastard and a sadist. I'm ashamed that he's a Vietnamese.'

De Witt said: 'He was with Connie Crum yesterday, and I guess he's still with her now.'

Creasy nodded in satisfaction. 'Good. This time I won't miss.'

Tan Sotho was watching his face. Abruptly, she said: 'You're Creasy?'

He glanced at Guido and then asked her: 'How would you know that?'

'Because Jake spoke about you. He was your friend.'

Creasy sighed. 'Yes, he was my friend. And I'm sorry I got here three years too late.'

CHAPTER
SEVENTY-THREE

The satellite phone buzzed and Connie Crum grabbed up the receiver. She put it to her ear and listened, then gave Van Luk Wan a wicked grin. She said: 'That chartered plane has just taken off from Bangkok. It filed a flight plan for Phnom Penh, and of course it will make a slight diversion over here.'

She spoke a few words into the phone, then hung up and looked at her watch. 'My people confirmed that there were two passengers, both Caucasians and carrying big canvas bags. I estimate that they'll be overhead in half an hour.' She stood up and carried a can of petrol from the table to the marble sarcophagus. She placed it reverently on a corner, saying: 'In twenty minutes we turn on the gas. And then I soak the wood and we burn Creasy black!'

CHAPTER SEVENTY-FOUR

The Owl returned ten minutes later, accompanied by René. Together they carried a large wooden box and in his left hand The Owl had a leather pouch. They hefted the box onto the table and René went back out. The Owl tossed the leather pouch to Creasy, saying: 'There was an old French-made safe, a MITEL. I did my apprenticeship on those things. That was inside.'

Creasy untied the drawstring of the pouch. Inside were hundreds of sapphires. He passed the pouch to Guido, saying: 'We got lucky, at least on the financial side.'

Guido held the pouch, but did not look inside. His eyes were focused on the wooden box and the lettering on its side, which was in French.

'Where did you find that?' he asked The Owl.

'In a storeroom at the back of the house.'

They all approached the table. The black lettering stated: *Costumes et masques protecteurs contenant calcium hypochlorite contre gas neurotique de type V. 8 unités.*

Creasy, Guido and The Owl immediately understood the implication, but de Witt had no French. Creasy translated for him. 'Protective clothing and gas masks containing calciumhypochloride against V-type nerve gas. Eight units. Where the hell would that bitch get nerve gas?' he asked.

Guido hefted the leather pouch in his hand. He said: 'This alone would buy half a chemical factory.'

The Owl had prised open the top of the wooden box. He said: 'There are four suits and masks here. It originally contained eight.' He started to lift out the bright yellow overalls and the masks.

De Witt said: 'No wonder she was confident. She knows all about you and Arrellio. She knows about your character and your history. I never met anyone in my life more cunning and more frightening than that woman.'

'If we had dropped into that compound, we would have been dead in seconds,' Guido mused.

Creasy looked at his watch.

'She'll be sitting up there now, together with Van Luk Wan, dressed in this gear and waiting for us to drop out of the sky. She's going to get a nasty surprise. We move in five minutes. De Witt will take us through the minefield. We need something to lay a trail for when we get out.'

Guido walked across the small room into the kitchen and came back holding up a large bag of sugar. Creasy nodded in approval. 'You bring up the rear,' he said. 'I'll have the RPG-7 and blow away the gate. Meanwhile, Maxie and René had better keep guard to the south. If there's any shooting, that Khmer Rouge contingent will come around.' He turned to The Owl. 'Bring up one of the jeeps. And when I call you on the radio, drive it to the edge of the minefield. De Witt will show you the place on the map.' He turned to the Dutchman and said: 'You had better think it through. Your only chance to get out of Cambodia is with us. You're certainly going to lead us through that minefield, because you'll have my gun at the back of your head. But for the sake of enlightened self-interest, that should not be necessary. You had better make your mind up which way to do it.'

De Witt was looking at the leather pouch. He said: 'Do I get my cut?'

Creasy looked at Guido, who gave him a wry smile and said: 'It was always that way with de Witt. Let him take his cut and he goes through the gate with us. At least the bastard knows how to use a weapon.'

Creasy nodded in agreement and gestured at the two AK47s propped against the table. He said to de Witt: 'Pick one out, strip it down and check it. Then we leave for your minefield.'

CHAPTER
SEVENTY-FIVE

They put on their protective clothing at the edge of the minefield, and then pulled the gasmasks over their heads. Creasy's voice was muffled, but audible as he gave the instructions.

'Naturally you lead, de Witt. I follow you with the RPG-7. Guido brings up the rear, laying a trail with the sugar and carrying a spare rocket in case I miss with the first one and in case the temple itself is secured by a door. How far from the gate does the track straighten out?'

'Exactly fifteen metres,' de Witt replied.

'OK, I'll launch the rocket from there. Let's go!'

The Dutchman carefully took his bearings and then moved forward as though walking over ice.

Twice they stopped while he took more bearings, using trees and shrubs. There was a half light from a half moon, but still he used the Trilux night sight. He moved slowly, but comfortably. It was his minefield and he knew his way through it. Creasy followed two metres behind, putting his feet in exactly the same places as de Witt had trodden. Guido followed the same distance behind, also putting his feet in the same places and spilling the white sugar.

Inside the compound Connie Crum, her two bodyguards and Van Luk Wan were dressed in the same protective clothing and masks. She had turned on the gas several minutes before. When it was over she would turn a green handle and release the calcium-hypochloride to make the compound safe. They were standing in a line with their backs to the compound wall and their guns held ready, looking up into the sky. Very faintly, Connie Crum heard the drone of an aircraft.

Her two bodyguards moved out and positioned themselves on either side of the temple with their AK47s raised in expectation.

De Witt made one final turn and then stopped. He turned around and pointed to the compound wall looming above them, with a thick metal door in its centre. He pointed to the trunk of a tree at his left and the bush on his right, indicating where the minefield enclosed them. Then he took one step sideways. Creasy moved past him and laid his submachine-gun on the ground. The tube of the RPG 7 was strapped to his back with the cone-shaped missile in place. Guido moved up, unstrapped the rocket-launcher and passed it around Creasy's body, then crouched down beside him on his right. The Dutchman also crouched down, to his left. The path was strewn with small stones and angled sharply upwards. Carefully, Creasy lifted the tube on to his shoulder and sighted on the metal door.

Beyond it, Connie Crum was puzzled. The drone of the aircraft was receding. It had not flown over the compound.

Van Luk Wan said: 'They could have dropped a mile away. Those modern parachutes are more like wings. The wind is in the right direction.' His voice was nervous as he strained his eyes looking up into the sky.

Creasy pulled the trigger. Flame gouted from the back of the tube and, a second later, the missile detached. At first it seemed to move in slow motion, but then it gathered speed and smashed into the door with a hissing explosion. Guido was already up and running, with de Witt close behind.

Creasy was going backwards. The recoil had moved him back a couple of feet, as he had expected, but then his feet had caught a bunch of loose stones and the weight of the launcher had tipped him backwards with gathering momentum. He managed to slam it down on to the path, but in the cumbersome protective clothing, he could not stop himself from rolling. When he finally came to rest, he looked up. The tree trunk that de Witt had pointed out was to his right. It was about seven metres away. He was lying in the minefield.

Guido heard Creasy crash down behind him. He did not look back; his instinct was in control. The gate was blown wide open, the Dutchman was next to him. Guido shouted to him, 'Go left!'

Part of his brain was listening for an explosion behind him - the explosion that would tell him Creasy was gone for ever. The rest of it focused on the expanding view of the compound: the temple at its centre; the two bulky, yellow-clad figures one at each corner. He ducked through the entrance, moving to his right, crouching with the wall at his back. There was no explosion.

Guido's thought processes were in neutral: his body, and all its nerve endings, knew exactly what to do. His SMG was aimed slightly to the left of the yellow-clad figure his side of the temple. As he squeezed the trigger, and clamped down on the recoil, he traversed the muzzle to the right, sending an arc of bullets across the target. He saw the muzzle flashes of return fire and crouched lower as bullets smashed into the wall above his head and the target was punched backwards, emitting a high-pitched scream.

Guido turned to his left. De Witt was lying crumpled against the wall, his posture proclaiming death. Across the compound, to the left of the temple, another yellow-clad figure sprawled on the ground.

At least he got one of them, he thought, his eyes sweeping the compound, looking for the other hostiles he knew were there. Instinct and logic meshed: the two dead would be guards. Connie Crum and Van Luk Wan would be the second phase.

His thoughts strayed to Creasy. Still no explosion, so he was alive. But if he had come to rest on the pathway he would have arrived by now: he must have slipped into the minefield and somehow avoided contact. He would not come rushing out, Lady Luck would not be so generous. Creasy would probe his way out as cautiously as a boy opens a girl's buttons on his first date. Guido would have to give him time, so he could not rush the temple. He eased himself to his right, giving himself a better angle of fire to the temple entrance.

Connie Crum and Van were behind the temple. She was struggling for composure while emitting a stream of curses.

The moment the gates blasted open was the lowest point in her life since the day she had looked at her father's charred body. In an instant she realized that Creasy had tricked her. They had been gazing up at the sky, searching for parachutes - and then the white flash of light, the rolling explosion, and the gates buckling off their hinges to frame two yellow figures.

The entire scenario flashed through her mind in seconds. The aircraft was a decoy; Creasy had come overland. He had forced or persuaded de Witt to guide him through the minefield; they had found the spare anti-gas suits. She felt a rare start of fear, quickly overlaid with hatred. She would not be stopped now.

Connie peeked around the corner of the temple wall and saw the dead figure of one of her guards. She presumed the other was also dead. There was a prone figure by the gate, and she caught a glimpse of someone else by the wall. She pulled back and assessed the situation.

Something bothered her. She knew Creasy's methods: he would not hesitate. Maybe the dead one was the Italian, and Creasy was biding his time, waiting for her to make her move. He would not have to wait long.

She turned to Van and whispered, 'I think it's Creasy against the left-hand wall. Make your way to the other side of the temple, and then move forward firing when I shout "Go!" I'll attack from this side.'

The Vietnamese stood as solid as if petrified. She pushed him, hissing: 'We kill him or he kills us.' Slowly, Van moved to her right, clutching his SMG like a child clutching its mother's breast.

Creasy knew the density of the minefield, and knew what luck it was that his tumbling roll had not set off a mine. He also knew that luck and his own skill would have to get him back onto the path; there was nobody to help him. And one false move would send his torn body straight to hell.

He lay still, listening to the bursts of fire above him. Heard the one shrill, female scream, then silence. Then, very slowly, he pulled out the knife which was strapped to his right leg and began to probe gently at the soft earth in front of him.

As he worked, he mentally kicked himself very hard. He should have adjusted to the slope and the surface before he fired. His mistake could cost Guido his life.

Then he kicked away the remorse. There was not time for it. If Guido was alive, the only way he would stay alive was for Creasy to get himself out of this fucking minefield.

He drew in a deep breath, and began probing again.

Guido calculated that, at most, Creasy could only have slid four to five metres into the minefield. But it would still take him many minutes to get out. He glanced at the dead Dutchman, and then at the temple entrance. He decided that Connie Crum was too smart to let herself be trapped in the building, so he concentrated on the rear corners.

The concentration paid off. He saw the yellow figure erupt from the left, and was already squeezing the trigger of his SMG before the target could line up his weapon. The target spun to the ground, and Guido gave it another half burst to make sure.

Guido could change a magazine in less than three seconds. It was during those three seconds that another figure dashed out, this time from the right. He saw the white muzzle flashes, and felt the splinters from the wall beside him. His magazine clicked in - and it was too late. The enemy was traversing. The bullet smashed into his right shoulder, spinning him around. His SMG clattered to the ground.

Creasy paused at the renewed burst of fire. He recognized Guido's characteristic half-second bursts; then silence.

He looked at the tree de Witt had pointed out as delineating the path. It was still about three metres away. One part of his brain wanted him to make a dash for it. The other, more disciplined, part steadied him down. He probed again, felt the hard object and inched around it.

Guido lay on his side, watching the figure approach him cautiously. From the feline movements, he knew it was Connie Crum. He was helpless. The palm of his left hand was pressed to the hole in his suit, to staunch the blood and in case the gas could penetrate the skin. His pistol was at his right side, under his body.

The woman took in the situation. Distorted by both their masks, he heard the cruel laugh. She edged away to his right, always keeping her AK47 lined up on his chest. At the compound gate she glanced down the empty path, and laughed again; then she moved back towards Guido and stood over him.

The AK47 was now pointed at his head. Guido knew he had to buy time. He sent a mental message down the path: 'Don't be too long, old buddy.'

He heard the woman's voice through the mask and felt the hatred in it.

'Are you Creasy?'

Of course - in the protective suit, he was unrecognizable. Guido looked down the barrel of the gun and heard his own voice imitating Creasy's slight American accent, 'Yes, I'm Creasy.'

Sheer triumph emanated from the yellow-clad figure. She said: 'I'm Connie . . . Bill Crum's daughter. I've waited a long time. I saw you kill my father in the temple in Hong Kong.' She gestured. 'His ashes are in a tomb in that temple. You're going to burn on top of that tomb!'

Creasy's knifepoint encountered something hard. He gently pulled it back and probed to his right into the soft soil, then inched forward behind it. Seconds were passing like hours, but he had also heard the faint, deep voice of Guido. He knew the woman would not kill him immediately. That was not in her character. The death would be slow.

He still could not see the path with the white trail of sugar, but he could faintly hear the woman's voice from above and could hear the gloating triumph in it. That part of his brain which controlled his emotions urged him again to leap for the path, but the part that controlled his instincts was stronger. He would be no use to Guido if he blew himself up. He kept his elbows and knees and feet very close together, and his body moved and rippled along the ground like a snake.

It took him another ten minutes to reach the sugar. Then he stood up, put the knife back into its sheath, and crept up the hill to the submachine-gun.

'Get up!' Connie Crum said. 'Or I'll shoot you where you are!' She had backed off about two metres, with the barrel of the AK47 never wavering.

Guido put his left hand on the ground and pushed himself to his feet with a grunt of pain, immediately putting his gloved left hand over the hole in his protective clothing. She laughed.

'You're going to die anyway, Creasy! I'm going to watch you burn, just as my father burned.'

Guido did not move. He had to play for time still.

'I fooled you,' he said. 'You thought you outguessed me, but I'm smarter than you. You've studied my history and you thought you could read my mind. You were standing there like an idiot looking up at the sky, waiting for a parachute that never came. You're not as clever as you think.'

He saw the barrel of her AK47 drop, and saw the flame shoot from the muzzle. The bullets tore up the ground within inches of his right foot. But then, as she expertly changed the magazine in a blur of speed, her voice carried more venom than the bullets.

'The next time you open your mouth, Creasy, I put a single bullet into your stomach. You will die slowly.' She moved half a yard closer. 'Now move.'

Very slowly, Guido shuffled forward, towards the entrance of the temple. Connie Crum waited until he was alongside the inert body of de Witt, then she flicked her SMG on to single fire and fired a bullet into the back of the Dutchman's head. She laughed and said: 'That's just to make sure your friend Guido is stone dead. I assume de Witt told you the way. I should have killed the bastard the minute the last mine was laid.' She gestured with the gun. 'Now move, Creasy, or take the bullet right here.'

Again, Guido turned slowly and shuffled towards the entrance.

'Faster!' she demanded.

'I'm wounded, damn it,' Guido said, trying to remember to keep Creasy's accent.

'So was my father,' Connie Crum hissed. 'He was crippled in both legs with arthritis and he was dying of cancer. He couldn't move out of that chair without help, and you just shot him as though you were aiming at a rat.'

Guido had reached the entrance of the temple. Over his shoulder he said, 'So I did him a favour. Anyway, he was a murdering, lying, corrupt son of a bitch who had no place on this earth. Just like his vile daughter.'

He was looking at the black sarcophagus and the branches covering its top. He sent a silent prayer to any god that might be listening, that Creasy would soon probe his way out of that minefield.

Her laugh could have been a pleasant sound in other circumstances. She said, 'Take a good look, Creasy. This is where you die. First you're going to climb onto those branches. Then I'm going to shoot you in both kneecaps and both elbows.' She gestured to a black Zippo lighter on the table to her right. 'Then I light your funeral pyre and then I watch you burn. This is the moment I have worked for since the day I watched you shoot and burn my father. You will burn just as he burned. I will savour every second, Creasy.'

From the darkness behind her, a voice said: 'You've got the wrong man, Connie. This is Creasy. And I don't like pyromaniacs!'

She turned twisting, swinging the AK47. Guido dropped flat to the ground as he heard Creasy's SMG bark into life. A second later she was lying across his body, gasping out her final breath.

Creasy's masked face loomed over him. 'Are you hit bad, Guido?'

'Nothing fatal. But I took one in my right shoulder.'

'Don't move. Wait while I look around. It seemed like de Witt finally got his ticket.' The face backed away.

Guido lay under the body and waited. A few minutes later the weight was lifted from him.

Creasy said: 'There were four of them, including Van Luk Wan.' He gestured towards the sarcophagus. 'She had a nice little reception waiting for us. A nice little ceremony.' He reached down, put a hand behind Guido's neck and helped him to his feet.

'Can you walk?' Creasy asked.

'Yes, it's just the fucking shoulder!'

'Keep your hand over the hole,' Creasy said. 'I don't know what nerve gas she used, but it could be the type that penetrates through the skin.' He was looking down at Connie Crum's body. Then he glanced over to the table and the Zippo lighter. He walked over, picked up the lighter, and lit the paper under the wood.

It must have been soaked in petrol because immediately the flames shot up. Creasy laid his SMG on the floor, picked up Connie Crum's body, tossed it onto the flames and said to Guido: 'Pity to waste all the preparations. Let there be ashes to ashes.'

CHAPTER
SEVENTY-SIX

'I had no choice,' Elliot Friedman said down the phone. 'That guy has some influence. For one thing, he's a consultant to the State Department. I had a lot of pressure - the guy even stood in my office threatening me with physical violence.'

'He knows I'm at the Dusit Thani Hotel?'

'Yes. He left Washington yesterday. I guess he'll be there any time soon. Now, what about the remains?'

'We've got them,' Susanna answered. 'The woman, Tan Sotho, showed Creasy the graves and the guys dug them up. It's up to Forensics to identify them, but one is certainly Jake Bentsen. Did you get the paperwork fixed for the visas?'

'Yes. An Air Force transport will fly you, the girl and the kid, and the remains back from Bangkok tomorrow. What about the guy, Arrellio?'

'He'll be OK. They got the bullet out this morning. He's a tough one!'

'You did a good job,' Friedman said. 'I'll be at Andrews Air Force Base to meet you. You'd better be wearing a uniform, because there'll be a ceremony to greet the remains.'

She hung up and turned to Creasy, who was sitting in a chair on the other side of the bed.

'What was all that about?' he asked.

'That was about Professor Jason Woodward.' She tapped her stomach. 'The father of this embryo inside me. He's on his way here.'

Creasy walked to the minibar and took out a beer. He said: 'It seems to me that the guy might love you.'

'Yes, he might. He's not the kind of man to do impulsive things.'

Creasy drank the beer from the bottle. He drank it all, then gave her a level look and said: 'If he loves you, and if he's any kind of man, he has changed his mind about that baby.'

'Maybe.'

He put the bottle down, walked around the bed and took her hands in his.

'It's decision time, Susanna. And we don't need any drama. You talk to the guy, you make up your mind. We kept pretending that we never made love. We both know the reason for that. It was like a series of dreams. Dreams that will be remembered - but still, just dreams. People can be in love in a dream just as seriously as they can be in love in real life.'

The tap on the door was like the last chord of a symphony. Creasy went and opened it and for a long moment looked at the man standing there. Then he turned and said to Susanna: 'He doesn't look all bad to me.'

EPILOGUE

It was early evening when the doorbell rang.

Marina Bentsen looked up from her magazine at her husband. It had been two days since the phone call from Colonel Elliot Friedman, informing them that their son's remains had been recovered and giving them the date and time of the military funeral which would take place at Arlington. She had bought a new dress for the occasion.

Her husband went to the door and returned with Creasy and a woman. Creasy introduced her as Susanna Moore. He said: 'I'm sorry about Jake's death. But I do know that it was very sudden. He would have suffered no pain.'

The old woman approached him, put her hands on his shoulders and kissed him on his cheeks. She said: 'We are at peace, Mr Creasy. And we thank you. At least we know he is back here in America. He will lie at rest together with his comrades. Will you come to the funeral?'

Creasy shook his head. 'I'm not good at funerals, Mrs Bentsen. But like you, I'm also at peace about Jake.' He glanced at Susanna and then at the old man. He said: 'There is one last detail. Before he died, Jake fell in love with a Vietnamese woman who, like him, was a prisoner of the Khmer Rouge. Three years ago she had a son by Jake. He's called Kori.'

The old woman looked at her husband and then asked Creasy: 'Are they still in Cambodia?'

Susanna answered for him.

'No, I brought them back to America. The thing is, Mrs Bentsen, my department can arrange accommodation for them. The mother is only twenty-four years old. She will get a grant for education and so on, and be well looked after.'

The old woman was still looking at Creasy. She asked: 'Where are they now?'

'Not a million miles away, Mrs Bentsen. In fact, they're outside sitting in our rented car.'

Marina Bentsen did not hesitate. She walked straight to the door.

The arrangements took no longer than five minutes. Mr Bentsen signed the papers that Susanna gave him without reading them. Mrs Bentsen took the boy and Tan Sotho upstairs to show them Jake's old bedroom. In those five minutes, the old couple seemed to shed twenty years in age.

As Susanna drove Creasy back to the airport, he pulled a small ebony box from his jacket pocket and put it on her lap, saying: 'You wouldn't accept your share of the gemstones The Owl located back in Tuk Luy. But you'll accept that. Consider it a wedding present.'

With her left hand, she reached down and slid open the wooden box. Inside was an intricate silver bracelet studded with sapphires. She closed the box and said: 'Will you come to the wedding? It's in two weeks, in Washington.' He shook his head.

'I don't like funerals and I don't like weddings. Especially when they involve past dreams.'

She had pulled up in front of the terminal building. He got out and retrieved his bag from the back seat and then made a gesture resembling a salute . . . A gesture of farewell. Before he could turn away, she asked him a last question: 'Creasy, do you think that boy is really Jake Bentsen's son?'

He shrugged and answered: 'There's a one in three chance, and that's good enough for me!'

NOV 2 6 2018

Made in the USA
Columbia, SC
20 November 2018